CU00923201

# THE CONNECTION

## SPRINGBROOK HILLS - BOOK 4

## MORGAN ELIZABETH

*To Alex, who makes sure I never feel alone and always takes the load from my shoulders.*

*Also, to R, O, and E who gave me the best job on earth: I love being your mom.*

# NOTES FROM THE AUTHOR

Dear Reader,

Thank you for choosing to put this on your mountainous TBR and even more, thank you for picking it up. Writing the Springbrook Hills series has been an absolute dream, made possible by readers who have fallen for these characters as much as I have.

**The Connection** contains mentions of aging parents, parental illness, childhood cancer, and child death. Please always put yourself first when reading—it's meant to be our happy place.

Love always,
Morgan

# PLAYLIST

Vindicated - Dashboard Confessional
    Marjorie - Taylor Swift
    Bluebird - Miranda Lambert
    Honestly - Cartel
    By and By - Camp
    Lover - Taylor Swift
    Make it Sweet - Old Dominion
    Paper Rings -Taylor Swift

# ONE

-Kate-

You LEARN a lot of things when you're pregnant and when you have a baby. A lot of these things center around babies and feeding them and caring for them and growing them. You're told you'll spend an inordinate amount of money on diapers, and an even more exorbitant amount of time begging your kids to eat.

But what they fail to mention is just how long you'll spend in a drop-off line, screaming at the car in front of you that clearly can't read the eleven hundred signs posted about how drop-off is supposed to go.

"Go!" I shout at the minivan in front of me, a long line of Mickey-Mouse-ear-donning stick figures representing their family, down to the two dogs and a cat. "Go, go, go!" Cal giggles in the back seat, very much used to this process. I glare at him in the rearview mirror.

"Can I unbuckle?" he asks and I nod, passing the sign that says 'student drop off' with an arrow pointing to the right. Every morning it's the same. Regardless of the signs plastered on every beam shouting, "DO NOT PARK!" it never fails that whoever I'm driving behind does just that, not even bothering to pull all the way up before slamming it into park and—

"Are you fucking kidding me?!" I say, my hand out towards the car in front of me as the driver's door opens and the woman driving hops out, leisurely walking around to open the door closest to the sidewalk. Once there, she helps three kids get out before opening *another* door to grab lunch boxes and camp bags, carefully placing them on each kid.

"That's a quarter, Mom," my son, Callum says.

"It's warranted here. When someone's being stupid, you can use a bad word."

"Can I use a bad word? If someone is being stupid?" I almost mumble yes, my mind already thinking how I can avoid being late to the Mason's house to clean. There's construction on Main, which means I really should have left ten minutes earlier as it was. Thankfully, I catch myself.

"Don't test me, Callum." Finally, the woman is kissing each duckling on the head and shooing them off, cars behind me honking as if it's *my fault* she stopped at the entrance to escort her kids up the walk. *Lord, give me the strength.*

As she walks around the car, she gives me a smile and an apologetic wave. It's unbearably clear she doesn't mean it because I've seen her specifically do this multiple times.

"Okay, ready kid?" I say as the car finally moves and I head down to the end of the drop-off line, unlocking the doors and rolling down my passenger window, as is my routine.

"Yup!" I look in the rearview to see his smiling face. One of his front teeth is missing, giving him the cutest, gappy smile.

"Alright, go!" I say, pressing the brakes and watching him jump out of my car, backpack already on. I've trained him well.

"Bye, Mom! I love you!" he shouts, slamming the door with a force a seven-year-old shouldn't have. Every day I half expect him to catch a finger, mentally bracing myself for the ER visit.

And the bill that would accompany it.

"Bye, kid, love you too!" I say, putting on my blinker to merge.

"You're the best mom in the whole world!"

"Go to camp, Cal!" I shout back, an eye on my mirror, watching the black truck I'm going to force to let me in so I can get on my way.

"Best mom in the whole *solar system!*" His voice cracks when he yells it, waving at my car. My heart breaks along with it, hating how big he's getting.

"Love you, Cal. Have a great day." And then I'm merging into traffic and on to my first job of the day.

———

The rest day of my day goes the same as nearly every other day. It's Tuesday, so after I clean the Mason's house, I take my laundry over to my elderly parents' house where I do double duty of completing my check in on them and avoiding the cost of the laundromat. Bonus, I also can avoid the guilt trip from my mother who loves to tell me she never sees her only child enough.

After the laundry is done, I run my weekly errands. First, the bank to drop off tips. Then, grocery shopping to stock up on kid junk food and easy dinners as well as a single bag of spinach I'll throw out in two weeks. It's not cost-effective, but seeing it in there makes it at least *seem* like I'm working on the vegetable thing.

At two, I walk downstairs from the apartment I live in to the bar I work in, Luna's Full Moon Cafe. At some point, Hannah will come and bring Cal home, watching him until I get off.

Until then, I'm on shift and it's ladies' night, which means locals. Unfortunately, locals almost always mean awkward small talk I have no desire to have.

You see, when you grow up in a small town, you learn quickly there are two groups of people.

As soon as the first group is old enough to understand, they pledge they'll leave said small town and never come back.

The other group is who I affectionately (and not so affectionately sometimes, depending on the person) call 'lifers'—someone born and raised in the town; someone who loves it here and never wants to leave. This person wants to get married, have kids, raise those kids, and eventually die in their small hometown.

Unfortunately, I'm in a unique third group you don't learn about until you're an adult and realize not everything is white and black.

This is the group that got out of the small town for a few blessed years before getting dragged back in.

As soon as I graduated from Springbrook Hills High, I moved across the country, fleeing my tiny town, its well-meaning but nosy citizens, my aging parents, and everything I ever knew.

Growing up here, I thought it was cruel torture, suffocating and uninteresting. Everyone knows you, following your every move, knowing who you've dated, who you were friends with, who you stopped being friends with because they kissed the guy you liked in 7th grade. Everyone remembers the time you barfed down the stairs in middle school and the time you got caught drinking the liquor you stole from your parents' cabinet under the bleachers.

And the worst part is, those quirks, those silly secrets normal people share as funny first date ice breakers, they become chains you can't escape. They become a part of your personality to the people around you, whether or not you like it. There's no escaping it except to leave.

So I did just that.

And then when I was 26, I had to come back.

The thing about coming back to your small hometown after pledging to leave, though, is just like how everyone remembers the time you messed up your line in the 6th grade play: everyone remembers how much you hated it here. How much you were dying to leave.

And the lifers, the ones who love it here and never wanted to leave? They hold it against you, rubbing salt in your wound.

"Kate Hernandez? Is that you?" Becca Mayfield says.

She says it the way that grabs your attention, not because she's asking you a question, but because she's asking you a question she already knows the answer to. She's setting up her volley for some kind of bitter spike.

Looking at her, I recognize her instantly. She was the homecoming queen the year I graduated.

A lifer, for sure.

She was also on the yearbook committee and undoubtedly saw me nominated, "Most Likely to Never Come Back." Great.

Honestly, that one was kind of just tempting fate, ya know?

I put on my customer service smile before facing Becca. "Hey, Becca. Nice to see you. How are you?" I ask halfheartedly, shaking a martini before pouring it into a frosted glass. Ladies' night at Luna's Full Moon Cafe is typically packed, so at least if I don't give her my full attention, it's not completely rude.

"Oh my goodness, it *is* you, isn't it? Goodness, I never thought I'd see you again!" Working a bar, you learn faces and I know this one. Fake smile, fake eagerness. Digging. She wants to get the gossip to share at book club on Thursday.

"Here I am. Been here for almost two years now." My stomach churns admitting it. This wasn't supposed to be a permanent move back. Just for a few months, I had told myself. Until I can make sure things were good here.

Two years ago, my dad made the call no child wants to receive: your mom is sick and you need to come home.

So I packed up my admittedly small belongings and moved my then five-year-old son and me here to help out as much as I could. Just long enough for things to settle.

Something I'm still waiting to happen, apparently.

"You been working here at Luna's the whole time?" She has the eyebrow raise, another look that says a thousand words, a thousand judgments.

I'm not ashamed to be here. Not at Luna's, not as a bartender, not in my hometown, not helping my parents.

Not as a mom. God, *never* that.

But having people question me in this way, tugging at the scraps that are left of the beautiful ideal I crafted all those years ago? Annoying, at best.

"Yup," I say, reaching under the bar to pop a top off a beer and slide it to Zander, Luna's brother, before he even asks. He accepts it with a wink before shifting his eyes to Becca and widening them. I smile and shake my head. I love the Davidson kids, but they can't keep a damn secret on their faces.

"Well, I guess it's been a while since I've been to a bar. So busy, you know." She wants me to ask, wants me to ask why she's been so busy, but I really don't care. Becca was a nosy bitch in high school and it's pretty clear she's one now too. After a few beats, as I tip my chin to another regular, grabbing her drink, Becca starts again. "You know, this is my first time out since the baby." I pour the vodka over ice and cranberry before sliding it over, nodding to Becca. I gotta wonder why she's digging though; I don't think I had any... "With Tommy." Ahh, there it is. Now I remember. Becca Mayfield is Becca Davis now, having married Tommy Davis.

The football player who took *me* to Homecoming, regardless of the not-so-quiet campaign Becca ran to catch his eye. We split amicably not long after but it seems good ol' Becca hasn't forgotten it.

"Congrats," I say.

"He's just the sweetest. Works so hard, he's rarely even home for dinner, but I always make sure he has a hot meal when he gets back." I fight a cringe. I open my mouth to say, *He's never home because he's always here, hitting on me and any woman who even breathes in his direction.* But I don't because that's none of my business. Luna likes to get her hands messy in the drama, secretly thrives on it. Me? I'd rather stay far, far away.

But then she gets a catty look and opens her damn mouth

"So, what have you been up to? Since you left?" This also happens often when you come back to your hometown when you swore you'd leave.

What have you been up to?

Where were you?

What was it like?

Sometimes, it feels like talking to someone in prison who wants to know what the 'outside' is like.

But in this case, she's asking to compare her life to mine, to see if those scales she deemed unfair uneven back in high school have finally tipped back into her favor.

And for some reason, I just don't have it in me tonight to play the game, especially not as I watch Tony Garrison, Luna's boyfriend and all-around good guy walk, in the front door, eyes locked on his girl. The smallest kernel of jealousy rolls through me. *I want that.* Not Tony, but someone to give me that look.

So as another regular waves an empty in the air, I say, "Oh, I got knocked up and the baby daddy didn't want a kid, so I moved home. Now I work at a bar under my apartment and rely on tips from my regulars, like Tommy, to help keep my kid in Swedish Fish and Doritos."

Zander laughs out loud, choking on his beer, and I wink at him. "Great talkin' to you, Becks," I say before I turn around, serve beers, and make tip money for Doritos.

# TWO

-Dean-

"KNOCK, KNOCK," a sultry voice says from the doorway of the break room, but I refuse to lift my head. I know who it is. It's the second Wednesday of the month. This means Mr. Stefano is out on his monthly business trip, leaving Mrs. Stefano home alone and on the prowl.

Every second Wednesday, Michelle Stefano, mother to Ava Stefano and overpaid housewife, comes by with some kind of treat, well overdressed, and clearly looking for someone to, ahem, keep her company while her husband is out of town.

I have to wonder how many other stops she makes on the second Wednesday of the month. This is the third for her since I've been here in Springbrook Hills as a counselor at Camp Sunshine, and so far, it's like clockwork.

I've talked about it to Zander, my new buddy here, before, and apparently, she also stops at his office each month. No one has ever taken her up on the offer—that he knows of.

"Just thought I'd bring you a little something, Mr. Fulton." She's dressed in a skintight black dress and a pair of heels, an outfit befitting a night out, not a stop at the summer camp your daughter attends to drop off... cookies. It's cookies this week.

Well, at least when I leave them here for the other counselors to enjoy, she'll have made *someone* happy today. "Hi, Mrs. Stefano." I make an honest attempt at sounding as uninterested but still friendly as possible. It's a fine line I'm forced to walk.

Over the years, I've worked at seven different summer camps across the country, and there's always at least one. One parent, usually a mom, though, not always, who thinks with enough flirting, enough coy smiles and special deliveries, I'll end up in their bed, satisfying them because their husbands clearly don't.

I never do. Never even felt tempted to.

And truly, most parents are fine. Most understand boundaries well. Others will be honest about their intentions, try to flirt, drop a suggestion, or ask to go out for a drink. I'm fine with that, so long as they accept the very firm 'no' I give every time. Most understand I'm here to do a job, to make sure their kids have the best summer of their lives.

"We've talked about this before! Michelle, please, call me Michelle, Dean." I smile at her. It's a forced one showing I really, really don't want to be here right now. The one that universally tells the recipient, 'please go away. I don't want to be talking to you but I'm kind of stuck here.'

Too bad she doesn't get the hint and keeps standing there, looking at me expectantly, a hand on her hip.

"What can I do for you, Mrs. Stefano?" I don't even try to make it sound friendly or like I want her to stay because I don't. I get thirty minutes to relax without people bothering me. She's cutting into it. I love my job, but I also live for the quiet, for the peace.

"I just wanted to come see my—"

"Bullshit, Michelle, you came to hit on my counselors again." The voice is sugar-sweet but tinged with annoyance and I instantly know who it is. When dark hair pulled into an effortlessly messy bun appears, my assumptions are confirmed. It's my boss, Hannah Keller-soon-to-be Hutchins. Michelle turns her head and a strange mix of annoyance and... fear overcomes her. "I guess some things do change, huh? I thought the babysitters were so far below you? How *is* Ava? We haven't had any play dates in, gosh, two years now?" She blanches, but Hannah looks like she's very much enjoying this.

"I uh... I should go," Michelle says, turning around, cookies still in hand and leaving.

"Bye, Mrs. Stefano!" I shout happily behind her before I meet Hannah's eyes, sparkling with the same humor I'm sure is in mine before she plops into the seat next to mine. "Story there?"

She contemplates what to say, how much to share with an employee, crunching her face and staring at the ceiling. "A couple of years ago she came over with her daughter for a play date with Rosie."

Michelle's daughter is a sweet girl, if not horribly spoiled. Rosie is Hannah's soon-to-be-official niece and one of the two little girls she nannies for.

"Hunter and I weren't together yet, and she kept hitting on him in front of me. He's Hunter, so he likes to push my buttons and let it happen, but then he realized it was bothering me. But then she said something to him along the lines of them going to get to know each other better. She said I could just watch her kid because I'm 'just a nanny.'" My eyes go wide and she nods.

"Anyway, he blew up on her. I never saw her again until she brought Ava this summer." I can perfectly picture the not-so-silent partner slash owner of the summer camp telling off some snobby woman in defense of the woman he's head over heels for.

"Wow."

"Yup. She's... a piece of work."

"That sounds about right."

"Not your type?" There's a laugh in her voice as she kicks her feet up onto the table.

"God, no. Plus, I don't date parents. Too fine of a line." She nods, her eyes on the pile of chips before she picks a bag out, opening it and popping one in her mouth.

"So you've never hooked up with a parent before?" Hannah asks, looking around the room. It's not in a nosy or awkward way. She just loves to ask people questions and learn things and I'm an open book. It also helps Hannah met her now-fiancé because she was the nanny to his nieces. He was staying at his sister's place a few summers back when they started dating. If the answer was yes, she wouldn't judge me. But I just laugh at her.

"Nah, too complicated. Plus, never want to give someone the wrong idea. Someone with kids is bound to want something more. I always leave at the end of the summer. Parents... they want more than a hookup. There's too much on the line for them."

"So you avoid all attachment when you're at camps?" she asks with a smile. "You and Zee are pretty close."

Zee is Zander Davidson, nephew to Maggie, one of two head counselors at Camp Sunshine. He's also the only single one in his group of friends. Whether I wanted it or not, he dragged me into being his wingman, roping me into his friend group and giving me a genuine connection for the first time in years.

He's also the coach of the peewee football team and somehow convinced me to stay in town longer than normal to help coach the team with him.

So this is the first time in seven years I'll be in one place longer than four months. For seven years I've spent my summers at a new kids camp and winters teaching snowboard lessons at a different ski mountain, never staying in one place too long and never going to the same location twice. It's not exactly the life I foresaw when I was a kid or when I was in my twenties getting my degree, but I've oddly come to love this strange nomadic life, seeing new things and meeting new people.

"Zee is good at talking people into things," I say, and Hannah laughs.

"Yeah, so I've heard. So you're staying here through...?"

"Winter, actually. I usually head somewhere new after my camp contract is up, but this time around I'm staying in Springbrook Hills and commuting to Mount Blizzard for my ski school lessons. The drive isn't too bad, and this way I can help with the team this season."

"Maybe you'll be able to help at the Center—we're always looking for more counselors over there during the school year." Hannah's eyes light up. The Center is the community center in town with services, programs, and after-school care for kids. It's underfunded, despite the donations Hunter adds, and from what I know, always looking for more help.

But the suggestion hits too hard, too close to what I've been avoiding for seven years. Too close to my old life. There's a reason I never stay long enough to form connections, with adults *or* children.

Thankfully, before I'm forced to dodge her question carefully without insulting her and thus her rich fiancé, a loud yell rings out in the field across from the cabins.

"What was that?" I ask, looking out the open cabin door towards the field. I stand, Hannah already heading out the door behind me as we jog towards where a circle of kids has grown, yelling and crying accompanying the cheering.

Just another day at camp.

# THREE

-Callum-

TODAY SUCKS.

Today, Robby, the only kid I don't hate and who doesn't hate me, is out because he's on vacation. That means during free time I'm walking the fields alone like a loser.

I'd never tell Mom because she'd get that sad look, but I *hate* it here. Just like school last year, this camp is filled with kids who know each other. They all grew up in this small town just like Mom did. But I *didn't*.

I grew up across the country in a city, where something fun was always happening and we walked everywhere and lived in a cool apartment and I had *friends*.

Here, I'm just the random kid who moved to town right after kindergarten and still hasn't made any friends.

Sure, some kids are cool. A few have even asked me to hang out, to get my mom's info so their mom can set something up. But I never do. She already feels crappy enough about everything, and there's no way she could take me to someone's house after camp, not before she has to work.

So instead, I just stay the weird outcast kid with no real friends.

But when I see Joey walking up with his two cronies, as my mom calls them, I tense up.

If this were a movie, they would be the mean kids who kick dirt at me. They're older, eleven or twelve to my almost eight, and bigger, meaner for sure. And they've decided I'm a good person to pick on. Probably because I'm the only new kid.

*Again, I hate it here.*

Mom says I shouldn't hate things, that I'm too young to know what that means, but I do. I swear it.

"Hey, *Callum*." His voice is mocking and my belly flips. I'm not scared of this jerk, but I don't feel safe around him.

"Hey, Joey."

"I saw your mom dropping you off this morning."

"Okay?" I continue to toss the ball I've been playing with from hand to hand, bouncing it once or twice.

"You're such a momma's boy, Callum." The kids laugh as if that's some kind of hilarious joke.

"Okay." That's all I say. Another thing my mom taught me—if you give the bullies anything, they'll take it and make it worse. *Just ignore them.*

"I saw your mom too." *Crap.* "She's hot for a mom."

"Ew, gross. She's my mom," I say, both trying to avoid the conversation and move on. This isn't the first time Joey and his crew have come up to me during free time to start something, to tease me. They also conveniently do it when no counselors or grown-ups are looking, but I know if I try to retaliate, they'll make it seem like I started it. It's happened to other kids before; I've seen it.

So instead, I just endure it and keep my mouth shut whenever I get sent to the principal or the guidance counselor.

I might not be the cool kid, but I won't be a snitch.

"My dad says she's a skank. I heard him talking to my mom about it." Tick, tick, tick, up goes the temperature of my insides. I fight it, fight giving him what he wants but… "He says she got pregnant with you and you *don't even have a dad.*" My blood is lava inside me, burning me up, but I keep my eyes on the ground.

*Let them think they won. Who cares? You know the truth.*

"He said that she's a loser, left to do something cool, but then she had you, and you ruined her life and she had to come back here."

"Stop it." The words slip out, but somehow he's saying exactly what I've always wondered.

*If my mom hadn't had me, would she still be back in Seattle, having fun and living a normal life?*

I know she left here because it was boring and she wanted something more fun. But then she came back here because of Grandma and got stuck here because of me, not wanting to move me around a ton. I wish she would.

"Stop what?" Joey asks, his friends giggling.

"Stop talking about my mom." My teeth grind and I drop the ball, my hands now fisted and pushing into the pockets of my shorts.

"Or what?" He elbows one of the kids, Jackson. But it's then I make a mistake. I stop ignoring them the way I know I need to, the words leaving my mouth without me telling them to.

"Or I'll punch you." *Why did I say that?* They all laugh like I told the funniest joke ever, and I feel myself getting angrier and angrier.

"I bet you can't even hit. What are you going to do?" I don't respond. "God, you don't even know how to hit someone. You don't even have a dad. I bet you hit like a girl."

And then I snap and show Joey Masters that I can, in fact, hit. And not like a girl.

That's the thing about living in a city versus a stupid small town. When you live in a city, kids teach you things, even if you're a little kid. I know how to throw a punch and I prove it when my fist collides right with Joey Masters's nose.

# FOUR

-Dean-

"Hey, hey, hey! Break it up!" I shout, pushing my way towards the group of kids. They scatter, trying to avoid trouble, but there are other counselors around us to grab the co-conspirators, to make sure we get the full idea of what on earth is going on here.

When I get to the center, Joey Masters's two little minions are blocking what's going on, too scared to jump in and help but also brave enough to keep it from me.

All three of them are little shitheads, spoiled brats who are growing up as big fish in tiny ponds with parents who think the sun shines out their asses. I expect to see Joey pounding on a kid his age, maybe a bit younger.

What I don't expect is what's happening in front of me.

The kid is small. I think he's about to turn eight if I remember right. Scrawny, but tall—he hasn't grown into himself yet.

Callum Hernandez.

Sweet kid. Always says please and thank you, always nice to the other kids, but...

He's almost always alone, sometimes with one other kid his age, but he always has an air of sadness or frustration about him. Like he's putting more than any seven-year-old should have to on his own shoulders. I know from Hannah and Maggie that his mom is a single mom, lived here, and moved back as her elderly parents needed more help, which explains a lot. I've lived that life and know it ages you faster than the other kids.

Callum is straddling Joey and absolutely *pounding* him. For a kid so little versus a kid nearly four years older than him, it's impressive. So impressive that for a long moment, I just watch.

And then I snap out of it, grabbing the kid around his belly and pulling him back. Like in a movie, his legs kick out, his arms flailing, and I half expect a 'let me at him!' to come from his mouth. Instead, he comes to reality quickly, going limp in my arms, and when I catch a look at his face, it's clear he's realizing what he just did.

"Oh shit," he says, and it takes everything in me not to laugh.

-Kate-

My phone rings and the screen sends a jolt of dread to my stomach.

*Camp Sunshine Calling*

This could be one of two things.

And on my *one day off* this week when I have so much to catch up on and so little time and energy to do it, I dread either answer.

Either Cal is sick and I need to come get him or he's gotten himself into enough trouble that intervention is needed. Every other time he's gotten into an issue with the mean brats at camp, I've gotten a note and a quick text from Hannah to let me know. A call seems to be a bad omen.

"Hello?" I answer hesitantly.

"Hi, yeah, is this Mrs. Hernandez, Callum Hernandez's mother?" The voice is deep and rough. Not Hannah and not Maggie.

*Definitely* not a good omen.

"Ms."

"I'm sorry?"

"Ms. Hernandez. I'm not married. But yes. This is she." The one thing I did right when I became unexpectedly pregnant to a man I knew didn't want a baby was to cut ties and give Callum my last name. No strange reminders of a long-ago mistake every time I sign a pediatrician document, no name mix-ups or questions when my name doesn't match his.

Unfortunately, it also means I am constantly reminding people I am not a Mrs. It doesn't normally bother me; it's just the reality of my life. But sometimes it makes things extra sticky and uncomfortable.

One time at the pediatrician's office when Cal was two or three, I mentioned needing to keep Cal in daycare despite his near-constant ear infections. The doctor asked why my husband couldn't take off work and help out.

When I quietly and embarrassingly informed the doctor I was, in fact, not married and Cal's father is not in the picture, I got *the look*. The one of judgment and ridicule. He didn't say anything else, but I knew.

I always know.

Things like that have been happening more and more, and while I wouldn't change my decision for the world, it gets grating to continually have people assume I'm married. To have the constant reminder that I'm doing this alone.

"Yes, sorry about that. This is Dean Fulton, a counselor at Camp Sunshine."

"Hi, Mr. Fulton. Is Cal okay?"

"It's Dean."

"What?"

"Dean. You can call me Dean." I need him to speed things up. I'm panicking over here.

"Oh. Uh. Okay. Is Cal okay? Does he need his inhaler or—"

"Nothing like that. He's totally fine." *Then why are you calling me?* I want to shout. I look both ways as I hold the three leashes for Mrs. Ferguson's dogs and walk them across the quiet suburban road.

"Well, mostly. Cal got into a bit of a scuffle today at recess with an older boy."

"A scuffle?" I ask, watching as one of the corgis stops to pee on someone's lawn.

"Well, a scuffle isn't the right word, I guess." God, can this guy get to the damn point already? "He got into a fistfight." I stop walking in the middle of the sidewalks, the dogs jolting in their collars and looking back at me, annoyed by my disturbing their lovely morning walk.

"I'm sorry, *Cal* did? My Cal? Callum Hernandez?"

"Yes. He was arguing with another kid and punched him, then continued to hit him once he was down." Dean pauses, thinking. "It was actually pretty impressive; the kid's twelve. I heard it and ran to break it up as soon as possible, but he had the kid on his back, pinned down. The kid's got a pretty good black eye." *Oh, my god. I cannot believe this!*

Cal has always been a sweet kid, quiet and mindful, but he's got a temper and he's also got a killer protective streak. He wouldn't just start a fight for no reason. That means...

"What did the other kid do?"

"Excuse me?"

"The other kid. He's older. Cal's not even eight. You said this kid is twelve? What did he do to make him hit him? Cal's smart. He wouldn't start a fight for no reason, much less do it where he'd get caught easily." I probably sound like a shit mom saying that out loud, but it's the truth.

"We haven't been able—" Of course, they haven't. If I know Cal, he's sitting in a corner, pouting and refusing to talk. Mom mode activated because I will go down fighting for this kid. He's a *good kid.*

"We've been having issues with this for weeks, Mr. Fulton. I've sent multiple notes in and I've spoken with Hannah multiple times since it started. Those kids have been teasing him for *weeks.* Some days I have to force him to go in. He loves it there, but those kids are making his life miserable."

"Mrs.—"

"Ms." It comes out angry, but fuck, I am. I have enough guilt from taking Cal from the only place he knew, away from friends and familiar places, and dragging him back to this sleepy small town I grew up in. It's been over a year since we moved here and every day the guilt eats at my stomach, knowing he still hasn't settled, still isn't seeming to fit in.

"Look, I know my kid. He wouldn't just hit another kid for no reason. But I also know, if *he knows* he's in trouble, he's going to be quiet and keep to himself."

"I think you need to come down, Mrs—I mean, Ms. Hernandez. We should have this discussion in person. It's clear you're passionate about this and Cal has been upset and frustrated. But I'm not getting through to him, and I think we should try to figure out how to work together to find a solution." His voice has gone from joking and, when he mentioned Cal beat a 12-year-old, *almost proud,* to professional and assertive.

I sigh because yelling at this man won't get me anywhere, and even more, it won't help to figure out what to do with Cal.

"Okay, I'll be down in ten minutes."

# FIVE

-Kate-

THE DRIVE to Camp Sunshine is bumpy and windy until you reach the summit where the actual camp sits. It's the summer camp Hunter Hutchins built mostly because he fell in love with Hannah Keller and this was her dream. It's huge and the primary goal is to give kids of all incomes the chance for a memorable summer.

They subsidize the tuition cost for families who might not be able to afford it, work around various work schedules, and offer a few weeks of 'sleep away' camp each summer. This is our first summer attending Camp Sunshine, and while we've had a few issues, it's been a lot better than the treacherous school year last year.

I grew up in Springbrook Hills, leaving right after college, hoping to never come back, but here we are. In all honesty, it's a great place to raise a kid. It's small and close-knit, filled with friends and family to care for Cal and, despite my fighting it, me.

It's the kind of town a kid can get into just enough trouble to learn not to when it really matters, but small enough that your mom will hear about it when she goes grocery shopping because Lorraine has a big mouth and can't keep anything to herself.

But the problem is, most of the kids here have known each other since they were rolling around together on the floor at Ms. Suzanne's Mommy and Me music class. They all did daycare and preschool together, no new kids joining the crew with any regularity, so they became some kind of mega clique.

When a new person joins the fold, like Cal did in first grade, it's hard to break in. Add in being anxious, to himself, and a bit angry about the move, and you've got the recipe for a loner.

When I park my car in the gravel lot, I press my head to the steering wheel and breath deep. These days, guilt is a regular part of my day, my incessant emotions, and this is no different. The balance of trying to raise a good kid, be a good daughter, and make sure my bills are paid is a tightrope I find myself slipping from almost daily.

And I'm exhausted.

Most mornings I wake up at the crack of dawn with Cal, get him ready and out the door to camp before I complete one of the many side jobs I've picked up to help cover bills, my college loans, and a bit for savings so we don't have to live in an apartment over a bar indefinitely.

These side jobs range from dog walker to grocery shopper to house cleaner. Basically, if anyone needs something done, the town knows to call me up because I can always use the extra cash.

After that, I run errands, from groceries to cleaning the apartment to checking in on my parents before I pick up Cal. Then we get home, have dinner, and either I take him to a sitter, my parents' house, or have someone come over to keep an eye on him while I work downstairs at Luna's.

Any night I'm not working, I'm trying to spend with Cal or my parents, who are both in their seventies and the reason I had to come back home.

When I finally fall into my bed, all that goes through my mind is what I need to do tomorrow, the bills I need to pay, the forms I need to remember to sign, the lunch I need to pack, the appointments I need to make, and, most of all... the things I should have done differently.

These are also the things going through my mind as I sit in my car, hyping myself up before I walk into the camp.

"Deep breath, Kate. Brush it off, let's go," I say to myself, sitting back and unbuckling before reaching over to grab my bag and walking out towards the main building. Kids are everywhere, laughing, running through sprinklers, playing tetherball.

A group of girls is sitting at a picnic table in matching camp tees, making what I assume are friendship bracelets. It reminds me of summers at the community center downtown, but better.

As I walk up the steps, a familiar face comes into my vision and I smile. Maggie has a way of making everyone around her feel welcome, and when she smiles that big smile at me, ease and warmth run through me,

Maggie is in her 70s and went to school with my mom back in the day. Her long grey hair is braided down her back, a leather headband holding back wispy hairs that have gotten free.

Bracelets run up her arms, some jangly, some fraying friendship bracelets the kids have made her. She's wearing a camp counselor tee shirt, tied like someone a third her age, and a long, flowing skirt, her own personal brand of uniform. She's the hippy aunt of my boss, Luna, and the most amazing person you'll ever meet.

"If it isn't my sunflower! How are you, Kate, my girl?" She walks over to me, skirt trailing in the air behind, her arms wide until she's right in front of me, wrapping me up in an enormous hug.

"I'm good, Mags. How are you?" I ask, returning the hug.

"Sun is shining, my girl. Always good when the sun is shining! But I hear you're not too good." My brows crinkle. "Little birdie tells me you're working yourself dry."

"Would that little birdie also have blonde hair and be my boss?" I ask with a smile.

"I never tell my sources." She winks at me. "Need to take a break, girl. Enjoy your life! You're young! Go meet a hot guy, fall in love, do somethin' for you!" This is Maggie. She always dives right in with the advice.

"Yeah, I'll get right on that, after I go deal with the mess my son made."

"Ah, heard about that. Good for Cal, sticking up for himself! That kid is a right little asshole. Always starting shit with the little kids, never kids his age. It's good he finally got what's been coming to him." That makes me feel better.

"I will say, I think you won't have to worry about him bein' a loner anymore. He's got a little fan club now. Had at least five kids ask me not to kick him out."

"Is there a chance of that?" I ask with worry. Shit. He cannot get kicked out.

"Pish posh, no way! I love a little drama. Kids will be kids. Gotta use it as a learning experience, I always say." Now her eyes twinkle. I roll my own, but still, I smile.

"Where should I be going? A counselor called, wanted to talk to me?"

"Oh, yes. *Dean*," she says the words dreamily like she wishes she were forty years younger. "Go on to the counselor's cabin. Cal should be there too. Right outta here and keep going, can't miss it!" A voice calls her name. "Gotta go, sunflower. You come back before you leave, say goodbye, okay?" I nod, hugging her and kissing her on her cheek before I move out the door.

"And, Kate?" She stops me once more.

"Yeah?"

"You're doing a great job with him." Her eyes are warm, always able to read into my soul where I hide everything. I just smile, nod, and keep walking because I can not break. Not today.

Walking past the cabins to the right of the main building where Maggie was, there is what has to be the older kid Cal hit, holding ice to his eye. When he takes it off, it's clear Cal got him good, the skin on his cheek angry and swollen and his eye already darkening.

*Good for you, kid*, I think

*No, Kate. You're not allowed to say that. You're a mom now*, I correct myself.

There's a strange motherly pride I'm pretty sure I'm not supposed to feel, considering my seven-year-old assaulted another kid.

At the next cabin, there's a big sign in the little yard reading 'Counselors Only' so I know I've reached the right place. I also know because Cal is sitting on a red plastic chair on the front porch, an angry and frustrated look on his face and very much avoiding my eyes.

I make eyes at my son, trying to look stern, but god, he's so cute and I'm weirdly proud, so as I pass, I give him a wink, hopefully appeasing any fears of my being angry.

Don't get me wrong, I'm furious—at that kid, at the adults in charge who didn't stop it, at myself for not doing something earlier—but at Cal? No. I don't think I am.

Walking into the counselor's cabin, Hannah's standing, leaning on a counter filled with snacks and eating from a bag of chips, chatting with some guy sitting in front of her, his side to me.

"Hey, Kate!" Hannah sets the chips aside and comes to me, pulling me into a hug. I wasn't friends with Hannah when I lived here—she was older than me by four years—but I was friends with her little sister Abbie. Now that I'm back in town and working at the bar owned by a good friend of hers, we've gotten close. She is the sweetest mother hen you'll ever meet. "How are you?"

"Been better, all things considered," I say, looking over my shoulder where Cal is pretending not to listen in. I roll my eyes at her and shake my head.

"Ah, yes, the fight of the summer." She looks in the door's direction and lowers her voice. "Good for him, though. Those boys, bad news. They're always messing with younger kids, trying to get them in trouble. About time it came back and bit them." I smile at her insight.

"Maggie told me he has a fan club now."

"Mags is a gossip. But yeah, I think sticking up for himself broke whatever barrier he needed to break. Kids have been stopping by and waving. A few even made plans with him to be on the same team for soccer tomorrow." Relief washes through me.

This isn't ideal, of course, my son punching other kids. But if it means that he finally gets comfortable and is making friends?

Well, I'm calling that worth it.

"Still need to figure out what's going on with him," I say, quiet, too quiet for nosy ears.

"Yeah, you do. We do. We'll work with you, Kate. You know that. Just need to ask." She gives me the same knowing look all the girls do when I refuse their help, but I just roll my eyes. I refuse to be a burden to any of them.

"Okay, well, I'm gonna take Cal back. No reason for him to just sit here all afternoon. You come by and say hi before you head out, okay?" Hannah says over her shoulder at me as she passes, headed for my son.

"Yeah, Han. Thanks again." And then I turn to where Dean Fulton is, now in the seat Hannah abandoned, eating her leftover chips and smiling at me, a smile I'm sure drops panties every day of the week.

Uh oh.

# SIX

-Dean-

THE WOMAN in front of me is absolutely gorgeous. She has a pair of short gym shorts on and a loose tee shirt with the name of the local bar in town plastered across her tits. It's tied in the corner, letting a small triangle of tan skin show.

She's got curves for days and shoulder-length, dark hair sticking up in a ponytail on top of her head, half up and half down. Her ears are both lined with studs and tiny rings with another little hoop in her nose. It's not a rock and roll chick look, but a wild and free, wanderer at heart look I've seen before.

A kindred soul.

Her eyes are a dark chocolate brown, and though she's makeup-free and gorgeous, she's tired. The circles under her eyes say as much.

"Ms. Hernandez, right?" I made the mistake of calling her Mrs. Hernandez twice on the phone, and both times she corrected me. I glance at her ring finger anyway, seeing it bare along with her fingernails. Everything about this woman is basic, bare minimum.

"Kate."

"Kate?"

"Kate. My name is Kate."

"Oh. Well. Hi, Kate. Nice to meet you. Dean." I stick a hand out, she grabs it and I smile at her. "So, uh, Cal your son?" I don't know what I'm doing right now. Hannah told me since I broke it up, I needed to make the call and *I* needed to do the parent debrief. But from what I just saw, Kate and Hannah and even Mags are all friends.

"Uh.. yeah." She looks at me like I'm stupid and that's valid.

"Shit. Duh. Sorry. Why don't—why don't you sit. You want anything? We have, uh..." I look around and spot the pile of mini chip bags. "Chips? And sodas. Water, coffee. I think there are juice boxes somewhere..." I start rifling through the cabinets, looking for other things to offer her.

"I'm good, thank you. Can you tell me what happened?" She sits in the chair I pointed to and I sit across from her. She's pretty. Really fuckin' pretty.

I sigh.

"I uh, I'm honestly not fully sure what exactly happened. I was in the main building and it was free time. Kids get to wander. We heard a commotion. I looked out and saw kids in a circle. It was clear what was happening. Cal was pounding on Joey when I ran out." I pause.

"I shouldn't say this, but I was impressed. The kid's like, four years older than him, but he had him pinned, no question about it." Kate laughs, but it's not a funny laugh. It's like she's lost, exhausted, and has no idea what else to do.

"Yeah, just what I need, a seven-year-old who's a bruiser. God, this is all my fault." Her hands go to her face, elbows to the table.

A long-forgotten part of me is swimming to the surface: the guidance counselor who can dig deep to help people.

"How so?" She sits there for a long moment, staring at her hands and at the table like she's trying to figure out what to say. "He's a good kid, you know. Nice to everyone. Quiet, but nice. Keeps to himself. This is obviously not his normal behavior. Did...

did something happen at home? Something we should know about?"

My gut drops. Sometimes when kids snap like this, when they act out, there's a deeper, more dreaded reason. I don't think this is that, but I've seen situations where I'd never have guessed.

"Oh, god. Nothing happened. Well.. that's not right. But No. Nothing like that. Nothing like what you're talking about."

"Do you want to... talk about what the cause could be? He's a good kid, but as I said, he keeps to himself. Kind of a loner. I don't... I know kids pretty well. He doesn't seem the type to be a loner, you know? He's cool with me and really nice to Hannah and Mags. Happy and funny, just with the kids he's... awkward? I'm not sure if that's the word, out..."

"No, you're right." She takes a deep breath and I'm surprised when she continues on. "He's been... having a hard time adjusting. We lived out in Seattle most of his life, and a year and a half ago we moved here to be closer to my parents. I grew up here. My mom got sick and my parents are older so I moved back home to help... It wasn't supposed to be permanent, but you know how life is. He's had a hard time making friends. He's shy until he's not. And I work, like, all the damn time trying to keep on top of all the things."

She sniffs and I sense it happening before it does, a single tear dripping down her cheek. Then another and another and her voice cracks when she speaks again.

"I work at the bar so I work nights, and when I'm not there, I'm working side jobs. He's always stuck with a sitter, even if it's one he likes. Sometimes it's my parents and I know they're boring as fuck; they're old and were boring when *I* was a kid. The poor kid never asks for anything. I think he knows... knows I struggle. And God, I wish I could give him all the things, but I'm falling short, you know? And now look at him—he's punching kids four years older than him and winning, which, I mean, is impressive. No idea where he learned that. God, probably that sketchy after-school program in Seattle with all of those big kids. Fuck, I'm a horrible mother. I didn't even know my kid could fight! Or that he was a *loner!* I thought... I don't know. I thought maybe camp was getting better. He had a hard time last year in first grade. And we haven't had any calls home, so I just thought... God, why didn't I ever ask? Why didn't I ever ask why he never wants to set up playdates or talk about camp or... shit. Like he'd have ever told me the truth."

It's clear she's hit some kind of breaking point, the tears flowing now, and for some unknown reason, I want to grab her, pull her into my arms, and comfort her. Tell her she's not a terrible mother, she's doing great, her kid is clearly a good kid, just a little lost, and this age is hard as it is...

Instead, all I do is grab a couple of tissues from the box on the counter and hand them over.

"I'm sorry. This is so embarrassing. Oh my god, I'm an adult crying to a hot guy at a camp for kids. Holy shit, I just called you hot. Fuck. Lord. What is *wrong* with me?"

I try not to smile, to laugh as she takes the napkin I have in my hand and dots her face before looking up at the ceiling, trying to pull herself together. Minutes pass as she works to regulate her breathing before she speaks, head tipping down to look at me again. "You don't know me. You'll tell me the truth, right? Won't sugarcoat it?"

"What?"

"If I ask you a question, will you tell me the truth?" She's looking at me now, face strained and serious, her eyes glazed and absolutely stunning, regardless of the blotchy cheeks and tear tracks.

"Absolutely."

"Cal's dad isn't in the picture." I open my mouth to say... something. What, I'm not sure, but it doesn't matter because Kate cuts me off. "By choice. He wasn't interested in being a father and I didn't want to put Cal through that, the back and forth, forcing my ex to be a dad. The disappointment, any of it. So it's just us. I got rights and never looked back. But... Shit. Did I fuck up?" I stare at her.

"It's just us. I can't... I can't teach him guy things. I mean, I try. And clearly, he learned to throw a punch somewhere. But isn't that like, important? A dad? A guy?" She stares at me and I realize now she's waiting for an answer. I freeze up, too many thoughts running through my mind. Still, I force an answer.

"You didn't fuck up. A man in his life just to fill a void? That's fucking up. But this? He's a kid. He's a *boy*. Shit, I kicked kids' asses for dumb things all the time. Chances are someone said his favorite football team sucks and he lost it."

"He doesn't watch football."

"What?"

"I said he doesn't watch football."

"Why?"

"I don't watch football. It's boring. I don't get it. It takes too long and they stop all the time." I smile at her and, thankfully, she returns it.

"It's an American pastime."

"And I celebrate it by drinking and eating appetizers once a year. But beyond that?" She scrunches her nose and shakes her head and I can't help it: I laugh.

"Okay, maybe you're fucking up there." Her lips tip up. "But other than that? You did the right thing. And you're here, on a random Monday, seein' what you can do. I've seen a lot of parents all over the country. That's how you can tell the good ones."

The tension seems to melt from her shoulders, but it's still all over her face. I lower my voice. "Saw you wink at him when you came in. Some parents would glare, would yell right there. You made sure he knew he didn't have to stress anymore. You're a good mom."

"Yeah. But still..."

"You're friends with Hannah?" She nods. "You friends with her girls? Luna and Autumn and Jordan?" Another nod. "They got men. Set something up. I know they'd be more than willing. Fuck, Steve would jump for joy, all that estrogen in his house." She looks contemplative. It's also strange in the moment to realize I have a group of friends I've grown close to, gotten to know over the past few months.

Like Zander locked onto me in some kind of weird bromance move and lured me into his group.

"I don't know. I don't like to bother—" And then, for better or worse, I make a decision. I know her type—fuck, my mom was her type, wanting to do her best for her boys but not wanting to bother anyone while doing it. So I'll do the bothering for her.

"I'll do it. Talk to the guys. We'll set something up. A guys' day."

"You don't have to."

"I know that. I'm gonna do it anyway. Like I said, he's a good kid. And like I also said, I know that big kid—he's a dick. Always picking on other kids. He needed this, this knocking him down a peg."

And with that, she laughs and fuck, if that isn't beautiful too.

# SEVEN

-Kate-

"So where's Cal tonight?" Sadie asks, sipping her drink. She's with Jordan and Hannah, their men on the other side of the bar looking on while the girls sit in the spot Luna reserves for them.

Depending on the day, any of the girls will hang out with Cal upstairs in the apartment Luna rents me while I work, graciously doing it without any kind of pay. Not that I haven't offered millions of times. But on nights like this, when they're all enjoying themselves together, he goes over to my parents.

The other reason we stayed in New Jersey is I didn't have the support system I have here back in Seattle. All of my friends were young and enjoying life, unable to watch my then five-year-old while I worked or, God forbid, did anything for myself. With the expense of childcare and the pricey yet tiny apartment we lived in, it just wasn't working out. Moving back to Jersey, no matter how much I tried to avoid it, gave me a semblance of consistent help and stability.

My parents had me when they were both in their forties, meaning as I approach 30, they are now in their 70s. Watching a seven-year-old who has his own attitude issues isn't always possible. Not because they don't love Cal, but because he's so high energy, needs so much looking after and monitoring, they physically can't manage more than one or two low-key nights a week.

"At my parents'. Probably playing some brain-melting game since they don't care what he does while he's there and will let him zone out for hours." That's the other reason I try not to make my parents the only option to watch him. Most nights I pick him up to find he literally fell asleep playing one of the games he loves, the headset still on and the controller in his lap.

"You know, Autumn was telling me she wants to be added to the sitter roster," Hannah says, and Jordan nods. Autumn is Hannah's sister-in-law to be and Jordan's newfound half-sister. She's also *heavily* pregnant with her third kid.

"Autumn is about to have a newborn on top of the girls. She needs to add another kid to the list about as much as *I* need to add another kid to *my* list."

"Well, Auntie Sadie is on tomorrow, so make sure he's ready for me to bring the fun." I am so unbearably grateful for these women. When I moved back home when my mom got sick, I knew no one here anymore. I'd either grown apart from the people who stayed or they, too, moved away. Except they *stayed* away. It was a blessing to get the job at Luna's as a bartender and have the owner, Luna Davidson-soon-to-be-Garrison, take me under her wing, give me a family of friends to support me and my son.

"I'm sure he's going to be excited. I'll be out early Sunday. I think Tony's on shift, so I'm just staying until ten." When Luna had her chaos, forcing her to move in with her childhood crush, Springbrook Hills PD detective Tony Garrison, she reevaluated her priorities, making me an assistant manager. Luna and I now switch off closing nights so it's not just her all day, every day, and she works nights when her man does.

"No worries, I've got nothing better to do on a Sunday night in this sleepy town," Sadie says.

"So what's this I hear about Cal getting into a fight?" Luna says, coming up next to me and breaking my focus from Sadie. I groan at the reminder.

"Cal got into a fight?" Zee asks as Tony walks up to the bar. I didn't see him come in, but I know Luna did, her attention always on the door, waiting for him.

Since it's a Saturday, Luna will probably stay until 12 when the general chaos starts to wind down, while Tony stays and has a few drinks with the guys. Guys who are now walking over to our side of the bar so we have a small crowd in one area. Looking over my shoulder, I check on Daisy, the other bartender tonight. She has the other side of the bar covered. I put the glass I'm drying down and lean my elbows on the bar.

"Ugh, yes. He punched a fifth grader, gave him a black eye."

"Oh my goodness, why? What happened?" Jordan asks.

"He won't say. Sat in the counselor's cabin for an hour, wouldn't say a word. But we've had a few issues before with these kids picking on him. Being jerks, just being little shitheads." Everyone nods.

"Plus, you know how this town works. New kids are so rare and most of the kids grew up together from mommy and me classes to pre-k to now. So a new kid is easy pickings."

"Poor Cal. It's hard to go somewhere everyone knows each other except you," Jordan says, and she would know—she moved here a year ago and it took her a while to settle in.

"Yeah. And it's been a bit, but it's just... not getting better. And I feel so guilty about it, I literally had a breakdown with Dean, the counselor who broke up the fight. I was so embarrassed."

"Dean's a good guy, Kate. That's his job," Tony says.

"Yeah, I know. But still..."

"What do you have to be guilty about?" Zander, Luna's brother, asks. I look around the faces of these people who are now my friends, my... family, in a strange way. While I'm at work, I shouldn't spill my guts, but Luna's right next to me, also looking for my answer. So rather than keep it in like always, I let it go. Maybe it's just more catharsis from Monday's meltdown, but either way, I go for it.

"I don't know. I... I never tried with his dad. He wanted nothing to do with him and that's fine. I don't need it. But sometimes, I wonder... Am I fucking him up by not giving him that? A father figure to show him how to stick up for himself and make friends and just... be a boy?"

"You're a great mom, Kate, trust me," Hannah says. "I've seen shitty ones, and you are not that. You care so much for him and he's such a good kid. This week, since his fight? He's had tons of kids following him around, playing and chatting."

"Yeah, I don't know. It just seems like he's... lost. And he won't talk to me about it."

"Why haven't you said anything before to any of us?" Tony asks, thumbing at Tanner and Hunter. "We'd be more than happy to help Cal out, take him out for a day. I felt like a dick when Dean brought it up to me." My heart warms at the sincerity in his voice and the nods of the men. It also pitter patters a bit at the thought that the counselor stuck to his word, talking to Tony about Cal needing someone.

"I know. But it didn't seem like... a big deal? That sounds bad, but I thought it would just go away. And you all have so much of your own stuff going on, you don't need more." The ladies all roll their eyes.

"You need to ask for help," Hannah says as I turn to grab a beer for a customer.

"You're one to speak," Hunter says, winking at her. She throws a straw wrapper at him and he just smiles. And for a split second, I'm jealous. I want that. I *miss that.* Having someone to joke and tease and fool around with. My friends are great, perfect even. But that?

If only I had the time.

"You need a man," Tanner says, his hair light from the summer, stern eyes locked to me. He's the most straightforward of them all. Aside from Tony, he's also the one who comes in the most often just to shoot the shit, being close to Luna. My gut drops because I know where this conversation is going.

"You need a man in your life, a man in his life. A man to show him how to act, how to talk, to stick up for himself, showing him how to treat a partner. It would do more good than anything we could do."

"I don't—"

"You do," Tony says in agreement, and my stomach churns.

"I don't need a man. Period." For a few long minutes, they're all quiet as I turn to make a drink and hand it over to a pretty woman in a light blue shirt who smiles her thanks. I should be thanking her for the distraction.

"Why *are* you single?" Sadie asks when I turn back. Of all the crew, Sadie is the most likely to dig, to try to find the answers to whatever question she deems she needs. So while the rest have taken my hint of 'that's it, folks,' she doesn't.

"I don't need anyone," I say carefully. And I'm not lying, not fully. Do I need a man to live my life? Absolutely not. Has the last few years of watching my friends fall shown me finding a partner might make life a touch easier and more enjoyable? Maybe.

"Bullshit," Sadie says, and I sigh.

"Why are *you* single, Sadie?" Her eyebrow raises in a challenge.

"You tell me and I'll tell you." Hannah looks at Sadie, intrigued, and I have to wonder if maybe Hannah wouldn't like the answer to Sadie's side more than mine.

Fine. I'll play.

"I have a kid."

"So what?"

"I don't have time. I barely have time for Cal, with my night shifts." Sadie stares at me but must see the resolve in my eyes. It's not a lie. The biggest reason I avoid having a man in my life is because of my son. The rest of it is because I genuinely don't have the time to mother *and* date. It doesn't help that in the eight years since he was born, I've found most men don't take well to dating a woman who already had a kid with another man.

"Yeah, yeah," she says. "But we could figure something out, help with a date night. Make it a day Cal gets a guys' night, you know?" I don't say anything, but the truth is, Cal would love that on so many levels. He absolutely adores the guys, looks up to them like they are superheroes.

"It's sweet, guys, really. I appreciate it. But I don't... dating... It's hard. With Cal. I don't want him to have a revolving door of father figures and for it to not work out." They all stare at me and embarrassment for opening up at work, on the clock, in a crowded, loud bar burns through me. *Who am I right now?*

Remembering the day at Camp Sunshine, I'm forced to wonder: *who am I lately?*

I get another few customers a drink to distract and recenter myself before I'm back in front of the crew.

"You should get him into peewee."

"I'm sorry?" I say, sputtering on the water I just sipped. Hannah and Sadie cackle with a laugh, and I toss a cherry at Sadie's head.

"Peewee. It's the kid's football league. It would be good for him," Tanner says.

"We all met in football. It's great for making friends, being part of a team, letting out aggression. Hanging out with other kids your age and working towards something together. He needs that. You're right —this town is small and tight-knit. Breaking in as the new kid is probably rough. It would help," Tony says, and all the men nod.

I know most of them were on the team together in high school, but as the youngest in our little group, I never actually experienced watching them.

"I don't know..." My fingers tear at a straw wrapper, trying to keep busy. "It's... a sport is expensive. Uniform, sign-up costs, travel. Then there's getting him to practices when I'm on shift."

"We'll work around it, no problem. And we can set up a carpool," Luna says, and the girls nod in agreement.

"And I'll cover the cost," Hunter says, and I instantly shake my head.

"No, I don't—I didn't mean it like that. I'm sure I could make it work. I just need to figure—"

"Absolutely not. I'll cover it. You worry about being Kate and keeping that kid happy."

"Hunter, I—"

"You argue with him and he'll buy the whole team," Hannah says with a roll of her eyes, stirring her own drink with the tiny cocktail straw. "Trust me." Then I remember when Hunter and Hannah were first dating and he brought thousands of dollars of equipment from the outdoor adventure company he owns to the Center and then literally *bought her an entire summer camp.*

"She's not wrong," Tanner says with a smile. Tanner's company was the one to build said summer camp.

"I don't know, he might not—"

"Give it a chance. Really. It will be good for him," Tanner says and looks me in the eye, sincerity and kindness there. He's the quietest of the group, the one to take things in and mull them over rather than jump into a conversation, and something about that knowledge makes me agree.

"Okay. But I owe all of you. Not just for this, and you know it." All roll their eyes or wave a hand, but before I can argue, the lull ends and I'm swept off to help Daisy and Luna until close.

It's not until late that night, when I'm closing up with Daisy and wiping everything down, that I remember Sadie never told me hers.

# EIGHT

-Kate-

"Come on, Cal, let's go," I shout from the door, juggling his water, the jersey Hannah dropped off last night, and my own bag. "You don't want to be late for your first day."

We're on our way to the first practice of the Springbrook Hills peewee Bulldogs. The timing of the guys' intervention couldn't have been better. As it turned out, enrollment was ending the following Tuesday, meaning I had just enough time to get the forms in and sign up Cal.

My boy walks out in a pair of loose shorts and a tee shirt and, god, he looks old. It's strange, to see your kid wearing things that don't have characters or silly sayings as they grow up and realize that phase is gone. He looks like he could be a teenager or at least a preteen. It doesn't help he's definitely one of the tallest in his class, though lanky as all get out. It's like his body can't catch up to his height. But his biological father is tall and built, so I know eventually he'll grow into himself.

"I don't want to go."

"What do you mean you don't want to go?" I ask, stomach dropping.

"I just... I don't wanna go." Cal is standing in the hall, eyes on his sneakers. They're worn, already too small regardless of the fact we got them two months ago for the summer. I add 'new shoes' to my mental to-do list. But that's not what I need to focus on.

Setting down the menagerie of things beside the door, I walk over to my son. I kneel in front of him, getting on his level the way I always did when he was little and having a moment. It's barely even necessary anymore; the kid is so tall. At almost eight he's already up to my chest, and it won't be long until he's taller than me.

A small part of my heart breaks at the thought of him growing so damn fast. So fast and I feel like I'm missing it all.

A thought to dwell on another time, ideally with some wine and cookie dough.

"What's up, buddy?"

"I don't think I want to do football anymore."

"What? Why not?" He pauses, long moments where I pray he'll open up to me, tell me what's going on in his mind. It's been so difficult lately, his emotions growing with his body and no longer as simple as 'I'm sad,' or 'I'm scared.'

"What if the kids don't like me?" The words are soft, too soft. Too soft for my happy-go-lucky, loud, and excited kiddo. Shit.

"Cal, they're going to love you. You'll be part of the team. That's the best part of being on a team—it's like a big family." Or so I'm told. I adamantly avoided all sports as a kid. There's another pause from Cal but I pray he keeps it up, keeps talking so we can solve this.

"Joey is on the team." There it is.

"But so are other kids."

"I don't know..." His little voice trails off and the resignation in it kills me.

"Give it a chance. You're going to have so much fun. You know Tony and Tanner and Hunter were all on the team as kids, right?" His head lifts, looking at me with wide eyes. Those men are his idols.

I don't think I truly realized how much until this moment. God, they were right. I should have stepped up earlier, asked for help. My stomach sinks with building mom guilt, piling on more to the already heaping mound.

"They were?"

"Oh, yeah. They all were on the team together, that's why they're all such good friends." Not a lie, but not the *full* truth. "Tanner was the quarterback."

"No way, really?"

"Yup." I smile at him, standing and handing over his water. "Come on. It's going to be great, Cal. I promise. And if you don't like it after two practices, we can stop. But I want you to try it." He looks at me, but I already won him over. I smile, standing and grabbing my things as we walk out the door to my car.

———

Pulling up to the field five minutes late, I'm cursing when the parking lot closest to Field B, which is packed with little kids, is completely full.

"*Goddammit*," I say under my breath, circling the lot before moving to the next.

"That's a dime for the swear jar, Mom," Cal says gleefully, a wicked smile on his face, and I am so full of regret for starting that stupid jar. It was a whim, made the morning after another long, exhausting night when Cal dropped the F-bomb and I told him he wasn't allowed. He pled his case, saying it wasn't fair, and for some reason, I agreed. Then we made the swear jar.

Stupid fucking swear jar.

"That's not a bad word," I say, eyes peeled for a spot.

"It's not?"

"No, not really." I don't even really listen to our conversation as I glance at the clock—two more minutes have passed, making us seven minutes late now. But as I circle a second lot, it's also filled. Glancing

around, it appears there's some kind of soccer tournament going on.
"Shit."

"Can I say shit?" Cal asks, and I glare at him in the rearview mirror, but his lips are already curled into his teeth, fighting a smile.

"Don't test me, bud." There was a time, two, three years ago, when that tone, that voice would have him shaping up instantly, afraid I'd take away TV time or a toy. But with age comes brattiness, and he now gives zero shits about my threatened repercussions. I roll my eyes and head to the overflow lot on the other side of the recreational park. Cal laughs, and I remember that as annoying as he can be, I love being this kid's mom.

By the time we approach the field, we're a full 15 minutes late, jogging there from our far-away parking spot. I'm winded and sweaty and hating everything about this, while Cal is all smiles tinged in just a dash of anxiety. Let's add working out to my long list of things I should add to my day.

About two dozen kids are standing on the grassy field doing jumping jacks and counting. I'm relieved they are all dressed similar to Cal—one less thing to worry about.

"Where should I go, Mom?" he asks, eyes unsure as he takes in the field and the kids. This league is second through fifth graders, the needed age gap in order to get enough kids together for a team in this small town.

"Uh...." I look around, unsure and kicking myself for not getting things together earlier. For needing to go grocery shopping before we came here, meaning we had to bring it all home, put it away, and stuff some food in Cal before we could head out. I have no idea what he should do or what I should be doing. A set of bleachers sits to the left, dotted with parents in various states of boredom. But who is in charge...

Thankfully, my eyes hit the back of a bright red shirt with the word COACH written in big black letters across it and I sigh.

*Thank God. Zander.*

I am dying for a familiar face to help me out because once again, I'm feeling like an utter failure today.

"Come on, this way," I say, leading Cal towards his new coach, still juggling a million things.

"Hey, Zee?" I say as we reach the field. "I'm so sorry. I couldn't find anywhere to"—he turns around—"park."

It's Dean, the camp counselor I completely melted down to not a week ago.

Great. Just fucking great.

"Hey," I say, my words low, and the hot burn on my cheeks has nothing to do with the late July sun.

"Hey, it's you," he says with a smile, taking me in. *What does that mean?*

"You're... you're the coach? I thought Zander..." My voice trails off, and in the distance is my friend's brother, a whistle between his lips as he urges kids to move into different stretches.

"Zee and I are co-coaches. He asked me to help out so... here I am." He looks around me and sees Cal. "Hey, Cal, buddy!" He looks at me again for a split second before his eyes go to my son, lighting up with recognition and a huge, genuine smile. "I didn't know you were gonna be on the team!" Seeing him and the warm welcome, Cal melts a bit, his worry gone and a tentative smile on his face.

"Mom signed me up on Monday, right before the cut-off." I blush —always last minute.

"No worries, my guy. You go put your stuff over there"—he points to a bench laden with kids' sports crap—"and then go to Coach Davidson over there and he'll get you up to speed. We're just warming up now." Cal nods before running over to the bench and yelling to Zander, who looks my way with a smile and a wave.

"I'm so sorry. I meant to get here early, but it's my only day off this week and I had a million errands to do and then Cal wasn't sure if he wanted to come and I had to convince him and then there was literally no parking—"

"Hey, hey, calm down. No problem at all. You guys made it, and that's all that matters." His back is to the kids now, fully facing me. His smile is wide and trusting, the warmth of it sending shivers down my spine. *Uh, no. No, no, no, no.*

"Sorry. I'd say I'm usually more put together or on time or whatever, but from our first meeting, I'm pretty sure you know that is a colossal lie. I am a complete disaster at every turn of my life."

"No problem, you've got a lot going on." He looks over his shoulder, watching Cal drop his stuff and making sure he gets to the team okay. Why does that warm me? When Dean decides he seems good, he turns back to me. "You staying?"

"What?"

"For practice. Are you staying?"

"Oh, uh. Today, yeah. I can't for every one, but Zee said he could help shuttle, and the bar doesn't open until three so for weekend morning practices I can move things around and hang out. But for Mondays, I'll stay."

"The bar?"

"I work over at Luna's Full Moon Cafe. Zee's sister owns it?"

"Yeah, I know it. I keep meaning to come."

"It's fun. Usually one of the guys is there, keeping an eye on Lune if Tony isn't. You should stop by sometime." The words fall out of my mouth and I want to take them back because they sound like a come on, which this is *not*.

Right?

"I'll keep it in mind. When are you working next?" His eyes hold a different warmth now, one I recognize, one I should really stop. But I can't find it in me.

"Tomorrow." I tell myself he could have found out any number of ways if I avoided the answer. Might as well just give it to him.

"Got it. Good to know." He looks back at the team, now doing push-ups. "What does Cal do while you work?" His arms are crossed over his broad chest, biceps pulling at the sleeves of his tee.

"We live on top of the bar, rent the apartment from Luna. Sometimes he's up there with a sitter, sometimes he's at a friend's house, sometimes with my parents. It just depends on who I can shuttle him off to." Guilt eats me again. I hate that.

"You ever need another name on your list, you call me up."

"What?"

"If you ever need another person to call up, Hannah's got my number. I'm there." I stare for what feels like an eternity, trying to compute the words coming from him mouth with no success. "I'm saying if you're ever in a bind and you need a sitter, I can watch your kid. Cal's cool. I talked to him after the Joey incident. I like him."

"Oh. Uh. Okay. Well..." Words are not working as I stare at Dean, but then someone calls his name and we both look over his shoulder where Zee is waving him over. "You should go." He smiles, the megawatt shine once again having me blinking like I stared at the sun too long. Lord.

"Yeah, I should. Good seein' you, Katie. Talk to you soon." He winks—yes, *winks*—before he jogs off to where a group of little boys are all now calling his name, Zander laughing.

# NINE

-Dean-

ON THE FIRST Saturday morning practice, I'm out of bed and ready well before I need to be on the field. I usually use the weekends to sleep in, and I'd been dreading the early wake-ups for practice. After long days at the camp, sitting in the sun, wrestling kids all week, I'm usually shot, but when I wake up I remember who else will be at the field today.

"Hey, Kate, how's it goin'?" I say as she walks Cal over to the field. An uncomfortable rush of relief runs through me when I see her.

Meeting Kate and her son Cal has been interesting, and I'm not sure if it's in a good way. That first day she came to the camp has been burned in my brain: her curves, her tears, her desire to be good for a kid who clearly knows everything his mom does for him.

And then on the first day of practice, she strolled in, Cal in tow, and shocked me again. The attraction I have for her is not just a sweet-looking mom of a kid in my care.

No, I'm worried the connection I feel with Kate Hernandez is so much more than that. And that alone should be reason enough to stay away.

Practices work like clockwork here—Saturday mornings, Monday and Wednesdays in the late afternoon. When Zee asked if I'd be open to helping him coach, I was hesitant. Usually once the camp season ends, I'm out, gone from whatever sleepy town I stayed in for the summer and moving to a new mountain, getting ready for snow-board lessons and day camps.

It's been my routine for seven years now, ever since Jesse. But something about this town has called to me, urging me to stay at least through the peewee season. Thankfully, I found a job at a nearby mountain, barely forty minutes up north, so my winter plans are still set.

Saturday, Kate sat in the metal bleachers scrolling her phone and watching her kid. Through the entire 90 minute practice, I found my eyes drifting in her direction, seeking her and keeping tabs. It was unnerving at best.

Even more unnerving, though, was Wednesday when Sadie came to drop off Cal instead of Kate, sitting on the sidelines and laughing with Zander, chatting with other parents and just being the Sadie I've learned to love.

That girl is like a sister I didn't even know I wanted, somehow worming her way past my barriers the same way Zander did. That's been the case for much of the crew I've found myself falling in with here. In fact, this might be the first place I leave and come back to visit friends when my contract with the mountain is up and I move to a new summer camp.

The first place I'll miss when I leave it behind.

But it wasn't Sadie that had me feeling off. It was the fact that it *wasn't Kate* here.

I should say, I've had women.

Women at the towns I stay in, coworkers or barflies or just sweet girls I have a kinship with. We have fun, we talk, and when I leave, I never think about them again. It might sound like a dick move, but being nomadic, traveling without roots, it's become just another part of my life.

But I've never found myself looking forward to the next time I'll cross a woman's path. Never have I worried if she'd show up where I was, wondered what she was doing, or if she was feeling better.

If she had a man.

And fuck if that isn't a weird feeling. A *scary feeling*. Especially when it's a sweet woman, a mom who just wants to give her kid the best.

That would be a match made in hell. Sweet, twisted hell.

"Hey, Dean. Not bad, yourself?" Kate answers. She's digging in her giant bag, pulling out a small water bottle for Cal.

"Hey, Coach Dean," he says with a smile. "Look! I got cleats!" He lifts his foot and there is a pair of new black and red shoes on them.

"Awesome, man! You got good taste. Go get in with the guys for warmups," I say, tipping my head to the kids, and he nods, running off in the goofy way little kids do. I smile as I watch, noting Kate's eyes are also following her son with a similar smile.

"God, he looks like a goof," she says, mostly to herself. I laugh and she looks at me with a cringe. "Sorry, that sounded mean. He's in between growth spurts and his proportions are off. He just... looks goofy."

"Nah, I get it. I was thinking the same thing. He's not my kid, though, so I can't say that out loud," I say with a laugh. She shrugs.

"Hey, if it's true, it's true." She smiles at me, looking once more at Cal and laughing when he nearly trips when he reaches Zee. "God, *goof*. Poor thing got my coordination."

"Nah, he's actually pretty good on the field." Her eyes go to me.

"Yeah?" I nod.

"Yeah. Wednesday he was helping other kids, teaching them how to move. He's quick. When he grows into himself he'll be even better." I would know—I went through a killer awkward, lanky, clumsy stage that reminds me so much of Cal.

"Good to know." She pauses, pulling her lip into her mouth, and for a split second, I think how I want to do that, bite that lip.

*Fuck. No way, Fulton. No fucking way.*

"I worry about him. Fitting in. I... I hate I had to move him. But seeing him hang out with other kids and be happy? It's a relief." We watch as Cal puts a fist out to Joey of all kids, getting a fist bump and a smile.

"He's doing good. You're doing good, Kate," I say, and she smiles, a pretty blush blooming on her cheeks. Then Zee blows the whistle and my time is up. "Gotta go, see you later." And then I jog off, jog away from the temptation that is Kate Hernandez.

# TEN

-Kate-

THE NEXT SATURDAY PRACTICE, I'm up early, before Cal is even up, pouting about my starving him. It's a shock considering I worked a night shift and Cal is literally always up at the crack of dawn, looking for fuel for his little body.

For some reason I refuse to look too closely at, I put a bit more effort into my appearance, curling my shoulder-length hair instead of leaving it in a wonky bun like always and putting on a bit of makeup.

"Why do you look like that?" Cal asks, staring at me as I put in a pair of silver hoops while he's at the table eating breakfast. I avoid his eyes.

"Like what?"

"Like... a girl."

"Uh, because I am a girl." Cal rolls his eyes,

"You're a mom."

"Believe it or not, I'm both, Cal."

"You never look like a girl," he says. He scrunches his little nose up in confusion.

"Yeah, well, today I do, I guess."

"But why?" *Yeah, why, Kate?*

"Hush." Cal takes a bite of his cereal before he speaks again, keeping his eyes down the whole time.

"So, Coach Dean is pretty cool."

"Uh, yeah. He seems cool."

"You know... some kids on the team said he doesn't have a wife. Or like, a girlfriend." My stomach flips. I wait to see where he's going with this. "And he asked where you were on Wednesday." My belly flips. Why does my belly flip? Of course my kid's coach would ask that. That's normal.

*But why wouldn't he have just asked Zee or Sadie?* I flick the little voice in my head asking these unnecessary and leading questions away.

"Makes sense. I'm your mom."

"He's like... really nice to me."

"I'd hope so." *Change the subject, Kate. Change the subject before—*

"You know, I would be okay if you got a boyfriend." What the—

"Cody's mom has one. He says he's super cool and they play video games together and he watches Cody and his sister sometimes." Cody's parents are recently divorced. Seems there's more than one reason Cal's become such quick friends with the kid.

"Well, that's good to know, bud."

"And like... I'm just saying, Coach Dean is probably good at video games." Oh, god. Nope, this needs to be nipped *now*.

"I'll keep that in mind next time I need your opinion on grown-up things," I say, giving him *the* look.

"I'm just saying. Since, you know, you're obviously not doing so great at looking for a boyfriend. Thought I'd help you out." His smirk makes him look seventeen instead of seven and I hate it. I toss a piece of cereal that fell from the box onto the counter at his head.

"Hush and eat your damn breakfast, you little turd," I say, pouring coffee into a to-go cup filled with ice.

"That's a nickel, Mom," he says, and it takes everything in me not to curse out that damn jar.

Cal runs off nearly instantly when we get to the field, early enough this time to snag a spot in the first parking lot. Another thing I don't read too closely, since I'm perpetually late to everything. But even though Cal runs off with a shout and a wave, headed towards the gaggle of kids, Dean nods to Zee before wandering over my way, ruffling Cal's hair as he runs past.

"Morning," he says with a smile. His smile is nice—warm and welcoming, showing all of his white teeth.

*Why am I analyzing this man's smile?*

"Hey, Dean."

"He seems excited to be here."

"Every practice he gets more and more excited. I'm so grateful to you all. I haven't gotten a note home from camp with any issues since he started and his attitude is worlds different."

"Sometimes kids just need some friends to blow off steam with."

"Apparently so," I say, watching Cal instantly chatting with his friends. My entire body seems to relax when I see it, the confirmation I need that he's getting more acclimated here. So what if it took nearly two years?

"So, where were you Wednesday?" Dean asks, and then the sweetest pink tinges his cheeks. Is he... embarrassed? I smile.

"Work. Bar's closed on Mondays and we open at three on Saturday so I can come to most practices. It's just Wednesdays that I have to organize someone taking him from camp to here." I sigh. "But I gotta get a better schedule for it. Zee's gonna take him here next week because he's off shift, but I don't want it to be a regular thing. It's out of his way, and—"

"I can take him." *What?*

"What?" I parrot my own thoughts.

"I can take him to practice on Wednesdays. I'm already at the camp, and I head here right after. Easy as that." I stand there in shock. Is he offering... no. That's... that's weird, right? I barely know him. And why would he help me with Cal? It's fine when my friends do it, though I still feel guilty. But... Dean?

"Oh, God, no I couldn't—"

"Not a burden at all."

"No, I mean—" I pause, my hand going to my hair. I can't accept this offer, right? I try to explain without sounding like a total dick. "I don't know you. That's weird, right? Stranger danger, all of that?"

"I'm a decent guy, promise. Great driver." His smile shines, and it's an easy-going smile, matching his easy laugh. He uses it a lot. Not just to get his way or to charm people, like some might, but because he's genuinely happy and carefree.

I wonder what that's like.

"I don't know..."

"Look, you call up Mags. She's got my record, can prove I'm a decent guy." I trust Mags's opinion with my soul. If he's confident she'd approve... But I'm sure this man has way better things to do than cart a seven-year-old back and forth.

"No, that's not necessary. I trust..." I pause, trying to decide how to answer this. Because rational or not, I do trust this man. He's good and kind—I can feel that in my gut and I always trust my gut. Instead, as seems to happen around Dean often, I go with the truth. "I don't like asking for help."

"The crew helps you all the time."

"That took a year, and it's still mostly forced on me." Another smile. Okay, this one might be to charm me. It's clear it would undoubtedly get him his way with anyone. Every time. Period. My mind wanders to the conversation Cal and I had at breakfast. Maybe it's time to look for someone to add to our little duo...

But sure as hell, not this man, the man who won't be staying longer than the winter and has heartbreak written all over him.

"Fine, I'll force my way in too," he says. I stand stunned for a moment before replying.

"I'm sorry, what?"

"Dean! You coming'?" Zee shouts from across the field.

"You need me to force my way in, baby, I'll do just that." Then he smiles at me and winks before he's jogging backward toward where he was summoned, like he's in some cheesy college sports movie, and I stand there for much too long, trying to figure out what on earth just happened.

# ELEVEN

-Dean-

"WHAT DO YOU KNOW ABOUT HER?" I ask Tony, tipping my chin to the bartender on the other side of the bar. It's an enormous rectangle in the center of a large room, so there's plenty of room on all four sides for customers.

This corner seems to have been claimed by Tony Garrison. Even more, it seems everyone here knows it since when we walked in, although the bar was busy, no one sat at this corner.

The few times I've come for a drink, it's been a night that Luna is working and there is *always* a handful of the crew here. I know most of them from working at the camp, and I've gotten close with Luna's brother, Zander. But tonight it's Tony and his partner at the security firm they work for, Mitch, Tanner Coleman, and Sadie.

Sadie's a wildcard, best friends to Luna and Hannah, single and absolutely insane. She's always smiling in a way that tells you she's scheming. I've been to a lot of places and I've seen her type before. It's a shock to me that she's settled in her tiny hometown and not a wanderer like me.

Though, that's been losing its shine lately, so who am I to say.

"Who, Daisy?" He looks confused as he eyes the bubbly but mildly annoying blonde bartender. I know her type too—the cunning kind that acts dumber than she is for whatever her reason is. Here it seems to be tips, and you can't fault her for a tactic that's working.

"Nah, Kate."

"Oh, Kate. She's cool. Grew up here, left for a bit, now she's back. Cal's on the team, right?"

"Yeah, thanks for that. He really needed something to give him some confidence. He's doing awesome, connecting with the kids. Seems happier."

"Good. Kate was worried after that fight. He's having a hard time settling into town, making friends. Springbrook Hills is a great town to raise a kid, but it's hard to fit in when you're new here."

"Nothing to worry about there. Kids love him on the team. Good call with it." We both sip our drinks in silence. My question wasn't really answered though. "So, what's up with her?"

"Huh?"

"What's up with her? Does she have a man?" Shit, I should have been more subtle. Tony smiles at me, a knowing smile.

"Kate? No, not that I know of. Hey, Lune!" He calls his woman over and goddammit, this is going to be a thing, isn't it?

"What's up, babe?" Luna asks, wiping down the bar in front of us with a damp towel. Tony leans in on his elbows like he's about to tell a secret.

*My* secret.

"What do you know about Kate?" His voice is lower than before but not quiet to be heard over the noise of the bar.

"Kate?" Luna looks confused, eyes flitting to where Kate has a hip leaned against the bar, her dark brown, almost red hair up in a messy bun at the top of her head, jeans and a white tank, a small apron tied around her waist.

She's gorgeous.

*Shit. No. Not gorgeous. She's the mom of one of your players.*

But still...

"Yeah, our boy Dean is asking."

"You're asking about Kate?" Luna looks me over, an eyebrow raised like an older sister, scanning me for imperfections and excuses as to why I'd break her little sister's heart.

"Cal's on the Bulldogs. I guess they've crossed paths. Asked me if she had a man." It's a joke now, the smile on Tony's face telling me as much.

"Shut the fuck up man, I was just..." I trail off because I don't know what I was 'just.' Wondering? Intrigued? *Interested?* Luna just smiles at me, a wide, shining, *mischievous* smile. It's clear why the two of them work.

"Kate's single." She pauses like she wants to see my reaction, but I guard it. "Doesn't date. God, the woman doesn't have the time." She rolls her eyes. New information. I'll take it. Why I want this information, I don't know. Or at least, I don't *let* myself know.

"Why's that?"

"Works like crazy." I screw up my face. "Not cause of me, calm down, lover boy. She closes for me, opens other days. I keep offering to cut her back, but she refuses. When she's not here, she's up early, gettin' Cal to camp and then working a million and seven side jobs."

"Side jobs?"

"Yeah, Dog walking, cleaning houses, delivery, tutoring. Swear the woman doesn't stop until she crashes."

"Is she short on cash or something?"

"Don't think so. She just has to take on Cal by herself and refuses help. Won't even apply for grants or anything, so she's paying for camp out of pocket completely. Last I heard, she's saving for a house for Cal. She wants that, wants something stable for him. She's got a lot of guilt, moving him from Seattle to back here, you know?"

"Why'd she leave Seattle?"

"Mix of things, I think. It's expensive out there. She grew up here, in the Hills. Her parents still live here, but they're older, in their seventies. I think her mom has some health issues, and she came home to get them settled and just... stayed." I hum, mind reeling. "So, why are you asking? You interested?" I pause, once again, not knowing what to say. Am I interested? No, right? I can't be, I... But before I can answer the question, whatever that answer was going to be, Kate is sidling up to Luna.

"Who's interested?" she asks Luna, checking her hip on Luna's.

"Oh, Dean here was just—"

"Asking if I'd donate some time to show the kids some throwing skills. We all know Zee is shit at it." Tony cuts off his woman, glaring at her in a way that says he'll handle her when they get home. She smiles, the same devious smile as before, but different, only for Tony. Mitch laughs from Tony's other side.

"Yeah right. I've seen your throw. It's shit."

"Fuck off, Mitch," Tony says. "Or I'll tell your wife that you've been eating burgers on shift again." His eyes go wide.

"Don't you fuckin' dare."

"Gotta watch your cholesterol, buddy," Tony says with a smile.

"She finds out, I'm getting rabbit food until I die. And you're gonna be suffering alongside me."

"The fuck I will," Tony says and they continue bickering as Luna turns to Kate, chatting about bar things, and I just look on, watching this mysterious woman work as if I could make a job of it.

———

When I get back to the apartment I rent month to month on the outskirts of town, I prepare for bed before lying down, my mind going a million miles a minute, thoughts flying in and out.

Normally, it doesn't. My mom told me from the day they brought me home from the hospital, I was a good sleeper. My older brother once joked I've never had a worry in my pea-sized brain since day one. I punched him for that the first time and he never said it again.

I've always been able to shut off my mind, shut off my fears and anxieties and thoughts and sleep as soon as I fall into bed. It's a great skill to have, but it seems to have gone missing tonight.

Tonight my mind is stuck on a pretty woman with dark hair, lots of curves, and a killer smile.

She's all I can think about.

And rationally, my mind should be stuck on her kid or the meltdown she had that first time I met her. But instead, it keeps going back to the sway of her hips as she lost herself making drinks and listening to the loud music in the bar, the way that ass moved and the places staring at it took my mind.

It's then I know that there is no way I'm going to sleep without some relief.

Before I know it, I'm reaching down and my fist is around my hard cock, gripping it hard. But it's not my hand my mind is seeing. No, without my permission, my mind conjures a vision of Kate, all curves and smooth tan skin kneeling beside me on the bed, her throaty voice asking me if this is okay as if I'd ever object. I imagine she'd be hesitant at first, biting her lip like she does when she's watching practice from the bleachers but doesn't think I know.

"Faster, baby," daydream-me says, and the order has her eyes going hooded. Fuck this woman is beautiful. My hand—no, her hand —grips tighter, speeding up and flicking her thumb over the head. I'm pumping fast now, the vision so perfectly real that I have to fight opening my eyes, fight facing reality.

"Can I..." She licks her lips, eyes flicking to my hard cock.

"You wanna suck my cock, baby, I'll never stop you." A blush burns her cheeks before she's kneeling between my legs, now spread. I put my hand into the crazy bun she always has her hair in, watch it fall, and tangle my hand into it, using it as a guide as her mouth covers me, sucking me perfectly.

"Fuck, baby, you're so fucking good." Her wide brown eyes look up at me, almost innocent except for my cock in her mouth, and I groan, loud. That's when I feel it, her wet dripping onto my thigh she's now straddling, so turned on she can't help but try to find some-thing for herself.

"You want something too, baby?" She nods, moaning with my cock still in her mouth.

My vision continues as I get closer and closer to the edge, picturing Kate climbing on top of me, straddling my dick and sinking her sweet cunt on to me. "Fuuuuuck, Kate, so fucking good. You ride that cock like a good girl, make your man come, yeah?" She nods, eyes hooded, and leans back, fucking herself on my cock.

Eventually, she'd get to the point where she doesn't even care about me, about getting me there, totally consumed by getting herself there. One hand is on her tit, squeezing the nipple hard, and she nearly screams. I move a hand to her clit, rubbing it.

"Need you to come on my cock, Kate," fantasy-me says, urging her on, so fucking close to spilling in her. And that's all it takes, my demand, before she's screaming my name and riding me, riding my cock as I explode in her. I'd hold her by the dip in her hips so I could bury deep, and we'd lay like that long after, catching our breath.

Except now I'm panting alone in my bed, the vision of Kate Hernandez still burned on the back of my eyelids, my stomach covered in my cum, and wondering what she'd taste like if I made her come on my tongue.

*I am so fucked.*

# TWELVE

-Dean-

THE FIRST WEDNESDAY I drive Cal to practice, he's quiet and polite. He hops in the backseat, and into a booster Kate transferred into my car after she dropped him off this morning, and quietly stares out the window, his sports bag at his feet.

"You excited for practice?" I ask.

"Yup." Silence for a minute. It's not a rude silence, a snotty kid silence, just one where he's either trying to be conscious to not annoy me or he's trying to be polite. I try again.

"What team won the water balloon fight?" The kids broke up into teams today and had a massive water balloon fight. We spent over two hours filling up literally thousands of balloons using one of those fast filling kits, and it took less than 10 minutes for them all to be gone. But they laughed and had a blast, which is the point. It made it all worth it.

"There wasn't a winner, not really. We were all soaked." A small smile is on his lips this time and I take it as my sign to keep going. It's been a while since I've worked one on one with a kid to build his trust, get him to know me, but right now it's a skill I'm glad to have. Cal needs someone in his corner, someone who can talk to him and guide him. While he has his mom and the guys, it's clear he hasn't opened up to any of them.

"You seem to be getting along with the kids better. Even Joey. That true when no one's looking?" Finally, he looks up at the front, catching my eyes in the rearview mirror. He's been going to practice for a few weeks now, and I'm not just saying that. He's getting more comfortable with the kids on the team, and they seem excited to see him when he runs onto the field for practice. I've also noticed him hanging out with teammates at camp.

"Yeah. They're cool. Cody invited me to his birthday party next week." He looks away again. Cody is the cool kid on the team, a nice kid though, and he's in the same grade as Cal. His parents are also divorced, meaning they have something tough in common. Relief washes over me. This is good. This is actually *great* for him.

"Oh yeah? Awesome. When is it?"

"Saturday. After practice."

"Nice. You gonna go?" He's avoiding my eyes like he isn't as excited about this as I think he should be.

"I don't know."

"Why wouldn't you?"

"It's a sleepover."

"Okay?" I turn into the practice field and Zee's truck is parked there, but no other kids are here yet. That's expected—I head over a bit early so we can get things set up for the kids ahead of time. I figure Cal can help us out today.

"Mom would have to pick me up Sunday morning, probably early."

"Okay..?" He sighs, not like he thinks I'm dumb but like he doesn't want to talk about it. I don't push, just sit in the parked car quietly. Waiting. Waiting to see if he'll open up.

*Come on, kid. Let me help you out.*

And then he does.

"My mom works late on Saturdays. She's tired on Sunday. Sleeps in. I usually make my breakfast on Sunday mornings. It's the only day she sleeps in, so..." God, he's a good kid. A really fuckin' good kid. And fuck, it sucks that's where his mind goes first, what his mind is on instead of normal kid shit.

It's not Kate's fault—not by a long shot. But it's a lose-lose for everyone.

I get it. My mom was a single mom, working three jobs to make ends meet for my brother and me so we'd never want for anything. Knowing that, we always did whatever we needed to make life easier for her. It wasn't much, of course, but still. We missed birthday parties knowing it would be more work for her to take us and hid permission slips for class trips we knew she would have to scrimp to afford. We knew how much she was sacrificing for us and never wanted to make it harder on her.

And seeing it now in this awesome kid, as an adult? It brings back a lot of memories and it fuckin' sucks.

I don't want that for him.

I pause, thinking.

"Your mom would be more than happy to pick you up, you know that, right?"

"I know. And if I told her, she'd be mad I was even talking about this, mad I was thinking about not going. But she deserves to sleep in." The knowledge of how he is feeling is what makes me sit there, gut-churning. I've been this kid, had these thoughts, fought to protect my mom in the same way.

"What if I talked to the guys, had Zee or Tony pick you up?"

"What?"

"Yeah, one of them should be able to." I'm mentally calculating how to make this happen, what kind of favors I can call in, what IOUs I can give out. "Yeah, we'll iron it out first before you ask your mom. Then she won't have to pick you up but you can still go. Yeah?"

A long moment passes as he looks at me in the rearview mirror in silence.

"You'd do that?" He seems shocked.

"What?"

"You'd do that? Help me out?"

"Yeah, dude. We're friends, right?" Another long moment passes before he smiles. Big.

"Yeah, we're friends, Coach Dean." And then he's hopping out of the car, grabbing his bag, and running onto the field, leaving me in the car, confused as ever but also feeling warmer than I have in years.

————

The next week, Cal is chattier. I made the mistake of asking him how the sleepover went on our ten-minute drive to practice today and he hasn't stopped jabbering since.

"Your mom figure out our plan?" His smile is huge and smug.

"Nope, she was totally oblivious."

"Oblivious, huh?"

"Yeah, it means she didn't know it was happening." I smile to myself. We sit in peace at a light, about a minute from the field, before he speaks again. "She's pretty." Cal's voice is hesitant, and when I look in the mirror, his eyes are on his lap.

"What?"

"My mom. She's pretty." He's silent like he's waiting for me to answer, but I'm older and wiser so I can stay silent longer. I wait until he finishes his thought. "For a mom. She's pretty. Don't you think?"

"Uh, yeah, she's pretty."

"So like... You think she's pretty?" Oh shit, this is going in a dangerous direction.

"Kid, this isn't—"

"And if you think she's pretty you could like, take her on a date, right?"

"Cal—"

"I mean, not right now, of course, because we're going to practice." God, this kid is too much. It takes everything in me not to laugh
out loud at him.

"Well, of course." I can't fight the small chuckle that comes out
of me.

"But like. Maybe another day?" He sounds so damned hopeful
and it kills me to break this to him.

"Look, Cal, I know you mean well—"

"She's lonely." I stop any effort to change the conversation.

"What?"

"My mom. She's lonely. She doesn't say anything, especially
since she has me and she works like, all the time. But she is." I try to
break in but he keeps on, and I have to give the kid credit—he's going
for it. "Kids know these things. Grown-ups think we don't but we
notice things. I see Luna and Tony, and Tanner and Jordan. And like,
they seem awesome together. They're always happy. Same with
Hannah and Hunter. My mom... My mom should have that. I mean,
sometimes Autumn and Steve watch me and I hang out with Rosie
and, like, she tells me her mom and dad hang out *all the time*." God,
the fact that's a surprise to him says a lot about Kate and her past
dating life. "And Rosie's dad, like, helps her mom out all the time. My
mom needs that."

"You're right, kid," I say, pulling into the park where the field is
and dying to get myself out of this conversation.

"So, like, you should take her on a date."

"Cal..."

"Just think about it, okay?" We're parked again, and he's looking
in the mirror, his eyes serious in the way only a seven-going-on-eight-
year-old can look.

And I can't do it.

I can't break this kid's heart.

So it might be fucked, to give him any kind of hope, and it might
be selfish and stupid, but I like the kid. I like him and I want him to
think he's doing good by his mom. So I nod.

"Alright, kid. I'll think about it." When I say that, he beams and opens the door, looking back for a split second.

"Thanks, Dean."

And I don't think he just means for the ride.

# THIRTEEN

-Kate-

ON MONDAY I'm scrolling on my phone, trying to find a good present for Cal's birthday next month, when a whistle blares and the team breaks up, Cal running my way with a paper in his hand.

"Hey, bud, how was practice?" I ask, stomping down the metal stairs and grabbing the sports bag he insisted he needed because 'all the other kids have one' last week.

Cal asks for absolutely nothing, so you know I damn well went right out and got him that bag.

"Good! Coach Dean says I have a great arm and I'm *fast*. So I'm going to be *starting* at the first game!" He's nearly bouncing as we reach the car, skipping ahead of me and waiting at the door for me to unlock it. Once I do, he throws his stuff in the car before scrambling in, stuffing the paper in the pocket on the back of the seat. Knowing Cal his entire life, I know he's hiding it.

I get into the car, turning the key in the ignition and waiting before asking, "What's on the paper?" I try to catch his eye in the mirror, but he fiddles with his seatbelt, his pants, his water bottle.

Shit.

I've seen this before.

Many times since he's been going to school.

Cal is smart. So damn smart, he's picked up on things I hoped he'd never have to realize. Things like his mom is a single mom without the same time or money or freedom as some of the other kids. It's why, regardless of the fact he tries to hide it from me, I know he never asks for play dates.

It's why, when he actually asked for that dumb sports bag, I bought it the same day. He's a good kid, means so damn well, but a huge part of me grieves the fact he isn't getting the normal experience where he can be a kid, greedy and with blinders on to the real world. Instead, he's always worrying about saving me from having to tell him no, saving me from feeling guilty.

"Cal." There's a long pause, but I haven't moved the car, still staring in the rearview mirror at him, adjusting it to make sure he knows I'm watching him.

"It's paper for a fundraiser."

"A fundraiser?"

"For the team. There's a tournament in Pennsylvania, so the fundraiser is to... help. With that."

"Can I see it?" I put my hand back to grab it, waiting for him to put the paper in my hand. When I don't feel it there, I wiggle my fingers until he does as I'm asking.

I pull it forward and see a copy of a flyer with a tear-off section on the bottom with name, hours, and a player on it. On the top is a giant slice of pizza with sunglasses. Skimming it over, it's a call for volunteers to come help man a pizza fundraiser. They're getting the pizza donated and selling slices at one of the high school games to raise money for a tournament next month.

"They're looking for parents to help." Cal's voice is low.

"Do you want me to volunteer?" He doesn't look at me and it breaks my heart.

"It's a Friday. You have work."

"Cal, I asked you a question." I stare at him, but he still refuses to look at me. Another few moments pass before he answers.

"I mean. It would be cool, I guess. But you don't have to. I don't want... Cody's mom will be there. And uh... so will Joey's." Ahh, Joey, the little asshole who I finally found out got punched because he teased Cal about having no dad. It took quite a bit of bribery and cajoling for Cal to explain what happened.

To be honest, knowing it all now, I'm kind of annoyed Dean stopped him when he did.

I'd love to see what kind of person is raising that kid.

"I'll be there."

"But Mom—"

"I'll be there, Cal. Lune usually works on Fridays and so does Daisy. I can come in late or switch some things around. It's no big deal." I turn the key in the ignition to give myself something to do as I try to mentally figure out the logistics.

But no matter what, I'm going to this stupid fundraiser.

"Are you sure?" he asks, and the hope in his voice seals the deal.

"Yeah, babe. I'll be there, okay?"

"You're awesome, Mom." And he says it in a way I know he means it, not because he just got his way and he's being a little turd. It makes any favors I need to cash in totally worth it.

———

Later that night, after Cal is in his room, dinner is done, and the dishes are cleaned, I sit on my bed and take a deep breath.

Why am I so nervous about this?

God, this is so stupid.

I stare at my phone with the numbers typed in. They look huge, like they're taking over the screen, jumping out at me. Once more, I check them against the sheet of paper in my hands.

Fuck it.

I hit send, calling Coach Dean, holding the phone to my ear and putting my big girl panties on. It is *so dumb* to be nervous about calling this man. Who cares if he's hotter than any man I've ever seen and gives me butterflies every time he's near? He's just another dumb guy. Right?

"Hello?" Oh shit. My stomach drops to my floor because, despite all of my self hype, I *am* nervous. Terrified, even. My eyes go wide as I stare at the mirror across from me, at the small smudge in the corner I need to clean, my mind lingering on that.

Blank.

Stupid, stupid! Answer, Kate!

"Hello?" The voice says again. *Shit!* "Anyone there?"

"Uh. Yeah. Hi. It's uh..." *Oh my god, what's my name? Why can't I think of my name?*

"Kate?" Does his guessing make it more or less embarrassing?

"Uh. Yeah." A long pause. A long pause where I question everything I've ever done or said ever in my life.

"Is there... a reason you're calling?" I think he's laughing.

I mean, of course he's laughing. This is funny and I sound really dumb, but... shit. This is so unbelievably embarrassing. "You okay, Kate? Cal okay?" Now he sounds worried. Crap.

"Yes, yes, sorry." I choke on my spit stumbling to get the words out, any words so I don't sound like a moron. "Oh god, he's totally fine, just dandy. All good here." *Just dandy?!* So much for not sounding like a moron.

"Glad to hear it. You call for a reason? Or you just tryna talk?" My face is on fire. He can't see it, thankfully, but it is. Beet red with harassment and I might barf at any moment. "Not that I mind just talking. Not even a little." His voice goes down a bit, just a tiny fraction, almost imperceptible, and it sends a chill down my spine. No, spine. No way. No chills allowed.

"No, uhm. Cal came home with a flyer. For the fundraiser? I wanted to volunteer." Phew. Finally. A semblance of the point.

"Oh, no way? For sure. Are you working, though?" I tip my head from left to right, stretching my neck.

"Yes, and no. I am, but Cal really wants me to help out, so I told him I would. I'm gonna make it work."

"Got it. You're a good mom." I know in theory I'm a good mom, but hearing it from someone who isn't necessarily loyal to me is... nice. "He talks about you all the time." I relax. This is easy. This I can do, even if I don't take compliments well.

"Yeah, well, won't be winning mom of the year any time soon. Moving him across the country, shuffling him from sitter to sitter—"

"Giving him a community of different people who love him and want to help take care of him? That's worth everything to a kid like him."

"A kid like him?"

"I was like him as a kid. Shy but loved people. I would have loved what he has now."

"Yeah, well, a father figure would be better, I'm sure." *Why on earth am I saying this? Why, when this man talks to me, do I start word vomiting everywhere?*

"It's his loss, not Cal's. Cal will be just fine. He's a great kid."

"Yeah," I say then pause, unsure what I should do. The silence is comfortable, or as comfortable as a silence with a mostly stranger you find strangely attractive can be.

Dean Fulton is not my type. Not that I have a type these days. Or that I have the time for a man. But if I did, it sure as hell wouldn't be him.

He's too carefree. A wanderer. Sunshine and summer days and zero stress. I mean, I'm sure he has his own stresses. He's human after all. But from what I understand, he spends his life hopping from summer camps to ski mountains and back again, traveling all over and never staying in any one place too long. Basically, one long vacation.

My reality is working endless odd jobs to make ends meet and make it so Cal never has to want for anything. It's never having a true day off, and when I do have one, I'm dragging my kid around to errands.

Stability. That's what I want. I want surety and stability.

"So, what are you up to?" Dean's voice breaks through my mental rambling.

"What?"

His voice is a laugh when he repeats himself. "What are you doing right now?"

"I uh... I'm calling you." Another deep laugh, the kind you can tell comes easy and often.

"Got that, Katie." *Katie.* Why does that sound so damn nice? "What are you doing? Or what should you be doing?" Loaded question. I *should* be cleaning or folding laundry or paying bills or making Cal's lunch for camp tomorrow. I should *definitely not* be thinking about how much his voice gives me shivers. I stick to a safe answer.

"I'm uh.. sitting in my room. Cal just finished playing some game, now he's getting ready for bed."

"Yeah? What game?" And that starts a conversation that goes easy, chatting about everything and nothing until I'm lying in my bed on my belly, kicking my feet over my head like I'm a teenager and I want a boy to take me to the dance.

An hour later, Dean's telling me about the time there was a rattlesnake in the counselor's bunk in Texas, both horrified and laughing at the mental image of a group of brave camp counselors trying to corner it in their pajamas when I yawn.

"You tired?"

"No, no, I'm fine. Finish your story." But my damn body betrays me, and I yawn again. *Shit.*

"You're exhausted. When you gotta be up tomorrow?"

"Cal's usually up by seven." I look at the clock. It's not even 11. "I'm usually up way later than this. Bartender, remember?"

"Yeah, but you're not tonight. You should sleep when you can." I don't know if it's talking to him all night and hearing his goofy stories or just because he's a new adult who isn't a friend or the man of a friend, but I open up.

"I like talking to you though." My voice is breathy with sleepiness. Dean says nothing for what feels like an eternity. Now shit, why would I say that?

"I like talking to you too, Katie." The nickname sends a thrill through me, the name only my mother has ever called me. "But you need your sleep." He's got some kind of rough, determined voice now, and it's pretty clear that no matter what, he's gonna force me off this call. Better not to embarrass myself further and throw a fit.

"Alright, Dean."

"You go to sleep, yeah?"

"Sure thing."

"Sweet dreams, Katie." And then the phone clicks, no drawn out high school 'you first' which makes sense because he is *not* that, but still...

The feelings rushing through me aren't far from it.

———

The next time we talk, Dean is the one to call me. It's ten on a Wednesday and my exhausted ass is lying out on the couch, Cal asleep in his bed as I try to convince myself to get the energy to get ready for bed and not just sleep here. Today's schedule was camp for Cal, cleaning Mrs. Desmond's house, then opening the bar and working until 9:30. Dean took Cal to practice and then dropped him off at Hannah and Hunter's to hang out with Hunter's nieces until I got out. Around nine, Hannah drove Cal back here and watched him until I was off the clock.

"Hello?" I answer when his name pops on my screen. There must be an issue, something wrong. But it's late...

"Hey." *Hey?*

"Uh, hi?" He laughs.

"Hey, Kate. How are you?" *How am I? What the hell is going on?*

"I uh... I'm... I'm good?" I'm also wide awake now, sitting up on the couch.

"Good. How's Cal?"

"He's... fine? Asleep." I pause. "Is everything... Is everything okay?"

"Yeah, why wouldn't it be?" He sounds at ease and just a bit confused.

"Just... Uhm.. Why are you calling me?" He laughs, the sound deep and rich.

"Don't know. I was bored and Hannah told me you were off at ten today. I figured I'd call you up. Chat."

"Chat?"

"Yeah, Katie. Chat. Talking?" I blink then look at my phone to confirm this is, in fact, Dean calling me.

"Uh. That's nice and all, but... why?" Oh my god, am I being a bitch? I am, aren't I? I'm being a total bitch. I should apologize, take it back, I should—

But instead of being annoyed or offended, he just laughs.

"I enjoyed talking with you on Monday."

"Oh. Well. That's... nice."

"Nice, huh? A resounding encouragement."

"God, no, I didn't mean it like that."

"I get it. I'm just messing with you. I do that." He's quiet for a moment and I feel like I need to fill the silence.

"Did you... uh.. How was your day?" *Good, Kate. Normal conversation. Polite questions. You've got this.*

"Not bad, not great. Can't have a perfect day every day, though, you know?"

"Oh. Did you... have a rough day or something?"

"No. Not at all. Love my job. Even when the kids are a pain, I love it. I'm practically a kid myself, which helps. I tend to understand them the way other adults don't always. Sometimes it just means I get to deal with more of the drama though."

"That's a good skill to have in your line of work, no? Being able to talk on their level?"

"Yeah, it comes in handy. Look at Cal—kid was silent that first practice I took him to. When I drove him to practice this week, he was jabbering non-stop, telling me all about his day at camp, about the birthday party, about the fundraiser." Seems he knows even more than I do.

"Yeah, thanks for that, by the way. You set that up, right?"

"Set what up?"

"Tony picking him up from the party?" He's quiet again, but this time I stay quiet too, waiting for him to fill the silence.

"He's a good kid. He was bummed about not going, said he didn't want to ask because you deserved to sleep in on your morning off to pick him up." My gut drops, my fears and assumptions proven right. Crap.

"I never tell him—"

"I know that. Trust me. I've been Cal before, when I was a kid. It's all on him. Know if he asked, you'd bend over backward to make it happen. He knows it too, though. And it's you two against the world." Warmth fills me.

"Are you close with your mom?" He doesn't answer right away, and I wonder if maybe I went too far, maybe if that wasn't my place.

"Growing up, very much so. She was a single mom. A lot like you. I was like Cal, but I had a brother which helped keep me busy. But we worked nonstop to make things easier for her. Now I see I probably made some of her guilt worse. She had to have known what we were doing." I hum on the other end of the line, knowing that the chances of his mom *not* knowing are slim. I always know. "But we'd avoid sleepovers and field trips and all of the things so that she didn't have to worry about it or take off work or scrape together the money. I'm sure Cal does the same. He wanted to go to that party. I know you wanted him to go to that party. Knew you wouldn't ask the crew outright for any extra help and Cal wouldn't ask you to do that. You two were going to dance around it and no one would have been happy. So... I was the middleman. No big deal."

"To him, it was."

"Yeah."

"And to me. To me, it's a big deal," I say. He stays quiet. "You're a good one, Dean Fulton. Your mom did well on you." He laughs.

"I'm sure she disagrees."

"Why aren't you close any more?"

"It's not that. It's just... hard. I'm not home often, so I don't see her very much. But there's... a lot. There. In my hometown. So I avoid going there. But I love her." I wonder what 'a lot' is but know better than to push.

"She knows."

"What?" He sounds confused and, in a way, I am too. This conversation is much deeper than I would have thought possible with the carefree camp counselor, but he seems to surprise me at every turn.

"She knows. Your mom? She knows you love her."

"I hope so."

"Any kid who worries about his mom like that? Who helps a single mom and her kid the way you do? She knows you love her, that she did well with you." And I mean what I say. I just hope he knows that too.

# FOURTEEN

-Dean-

THE PHONE CALLS have been an interesting turn of events.

The first one, when Kate called to volunteer, had me staying up long after I'd forced her off to sleep, thinking about her.

Tuesday, I resisted calling.

But by Wednesday, I needed to hear her voice again, especially when I didn't get my fix at practice.

*What is it about this woman?*

Friday morning I wake up early, spending more time than needed getting ready to go work at a kids camp. I catch her eye for two minutes as she drives down the camper drop-off lane, she and Cal doing this crazy routine I've seen them do before when he essentially launches himself from the car with lightning speed and they yell goodbyes at each other as she drives off.

Each time it makes me laugh.

She showed up to the fundraiser, shockingly, on time—something I've learned is not a common trait for Kate and Cal.

Hannah, apparently the fundraising queen in town, ushered Kate off into a corner to help take money for slices, and Cal and Cody instantly paired up to hound attendees of the game to come buy pizza.

About halfway through our shift, Michelle DeStefano comes by with Ava, who ran off to play with some other girls from camp. While I understand why Hannah would be here, being, well, Hannah, Michelle has no true reason to be at the peewee football fundraiser.

"Hey, Dean," she says, sidling up to my table where I'm taking slices from the boxes and putting them on plates for Hannah and Kate to sell.

"Hey, Mrs. DeStefano," I say and quickly do the math to realize that, yes, it is in fact the second week of the month, meaning Mr. Destefano is out on his business trip.

Great.

I look to my left, making wide eyes at Hannah, dying for a rescue. Her eyes mimic mine, but there's a huge, teasing smile on her face. I try to mime a subtle 'help!' but she just shakes her head and ignores me.

Rude.

"I told you, Dean, Michelle! Please, call me Michelle." To her credit, her eyes flit over to Hannah and look just a bit anxious. That woman's got some power over her.

"What can I do for you, Mrs. Destefano?"

"Just came to support our town!" Her smile is big as she looks down her body to show off her outfit. It's orange and black, the high school football team's colors, but the orange tank top is so tight her modified breasts are moments from falling out and the skin tight leather shorts can't be comfortable to wear.

Who looks in the mirror and says, 'yes, this is the look I'm wearing to a high school football game'?

Before I can comment on it, a hand comes around my waist, small and warm, a shock to my system. I look down to see a tiny deep-red, nearly black ponytail sticking up, Kate's short hair.

It's Kate.

And fuck if the fit of her there at my side isn't perfect.

She looks up at me with a smile, telling me she's my rescuer.

It would only be right to go with her ruse, right? I put my arm around her, pulling her in further. Yeah, the ruse. That's why I do it.

But shit. The fit is perfect.

"Hey, Michelle, how are you?" Kate says, feigning friendliness, but something in her tone says otherwise.

"Uh... Kate. Wow. I haven't seen you in... years." Michelle's face looks even more put off than when she saw Hannah. "I thought you left town."

"Oh, I did. But I'm back now," she says, but there's a cattiness to her words I don't expect. It's like some kind of oos teen movie where each word holds a completely different meaning than the dictionary. "You've met Dean, right?"

"Yeah, uh, Ava goes to Camp Sunshine." Kate smiles again, sweet and demure.

"That's so wonderful. Isn't Dean just the best?" Her hand goes up to touch my cheek and she stares at me with a smile I return. Hers is taunting, but I'm sure mine holds a million and seven questions. "Can I get you a slice? All proceeds go to the Bulldogs."

"I, uh, I... I have to go, actually. I... uh.... Ava..." she looks around and starts to walk off. "It was... great seeing you. Again." Michelle stumbles, her foot catching as she goes. "Bye!" And then she turns and leaves, getting lost in the crowd.

I watch until she's gone before turning to Kate. She tries to pull away, but my hand stays in place, holding her there.

"What was that?"

"What was what?" she asks, innocence dripping from her words.

"With Michelle?"

"We went to school together." Avoidance.

"And?"

"And what?"

"He wants to know why she's scared of you," Hannah says with a laugh. "Wasn't there a thing with you two? Your freshman year? Or something like that." Kate looks away, not confirming or denying. "Wait. Oh my god. That was you, right?" Finally, Kate looks at Hannah, a small proud smirk on her face before she nods. Hannah's mouth drops open as she laughs.

"Oh my god, I would give *money* to see that!"

"See what?"

"Nothing," Kate says quickly, too quick for it to actually be *nothing*.

"Kate kicked Michelle's ass in high school." Kate glares at Hannah, but she keeps going. "It was something about cheerleading, I think? She said something bitchy to one of the freshmen, right?" Kate stands there silent, arms crossed over her chest. But I now am committed to hearing this story and hold her tighter in place.

"Michelle told a freshman she was fat and needed to go on a diet. I told Michelle she could diet all day, but Tanner Coleman would still never want her skanky ass." We all blink at her. "She was a bitch." More staring.

"Anyway, she said something snarky back to me, I don't even remember what, and I lost it. Beat her ass. She never called anyone on the team fat again though." Kate shrugs and then inspects her nails, painted alternating black and red colors. A surprise, since it seems like she never has time for herself, much less time to do her nails.

"Like mother like son, huh?" I ask, and in that moment, Kate's walls drop and she smiles, real and true and blinding, and I decide I want that for myself.

# FIFTEEN

-Kate-

WHEN MY PHONE rings Friday night after Cal is in bed, exhausted from running around with Cody at the high school game, I answer without hesitation.

"Hey, bruiser," Dean says with a smile in his voice.

"Shut up."

"I can't believe that story hasn't come up sooner, especially after Cal. No wonder he beat Joey's ass."

"This is why I tried to get out of small-town life," I say with a laugh. "Everything lives in infamy." I'm lying in bed and put my hands over my face like I can hide.

"It's fun though. Plus, there are worse things to be remembered for than kicking someone's ass in defense of another girl."

"I guess."

"You're lucky, growing up here. You might have to deal with everyone remembering everything, but there's definitely more good than bad about small towns. I've been all over, remember?" I sigh. He's not wrong.

"Yeah, yeah. Growing up in it is different from moving to it, though. I always thought I'd be able to rewrite my story when I moved away." I remember when I went to college, I mapped out my new personality. There was no one to argue it, so why not make myself be who I thought I wanted to be? I partied and stayed out late and nearly failed my first semester, but I had a blast.

It never stuck though. Turns out, it's not the town that makes you who you are. At least not completely.

"So why'd you come back? Or why'd you stay? I know you came back to help with your mom."

Answering that question is harder.

"What, no softball questions today?" I ask with a laugh.

"If it's too personal—"

"No, no. It's fine." I sigh again. "My dad called me almost two years ago now and told me my mom was sick. Really sick, hooked up to monitors, not breathing independently, the whole nine yards. We thought that would be it. She's had a life of breathing issues and she's not young. I was born when they were older, in their forties—a medical miracle, my dad always says. She had a really severe case of pneumonia that was resisting antibiotics and showing no improvement. By the time my dad called, they had sedated her to help her body heal. They knew I'd come home as soon as they called, so he didn't until it was almost too late. I packed up everything and drove across the country with a nearly six-year-old to help."

"That must have been fun."

"Not in the least." I laugh. "I planned to stay a few months then figure it out from there. But while I was here, I realized how much help my dad needed. They refuse any kind of in-home care but they can't keep up with the cleaning and the care and everything else. On a good week, they're totally fine, can do it all. On a bad week, I have to stop in every morning to help. So between not feeling comfortable leaving my only family here with no real help and feeling guilty about moving Cal a third time... we just stayed."

I shrug, even though he can't see it. "It's a good place to raise a kid though. So I'm not mad about it. I just... I mourn it sometimes. What could have been."

"I get that," Dean says, and it means more. He went for more today, so I will too.

"So, what about you? Why are you the way you are, traveling and never settling down?" I ask, spilling it all and not even sugarcoating it.

A deep sigh comes through the line and I wonder if I pushed too far.

"I'm sorry, that was way out of line. I should—"

"No, it's fair. You told me about your parents and coming home. I can tell you about leaving mine." Another sigh.

"When I was in middle school, my dad left and I acted out. I was the bad kid—the really bad kid. Smoking behind the school in seventh grade, ditching school in eighth, getting into fights, all of it. No one thought I'd graduate high school. Not a soul. My mom tried— she tried hard, but I don't think even she had high hopes for me. I think for the most part she just prayed every night I'd make it out alive and with a GED."

"Bar was set high for you," I laugh to break the tension I already feel building and I'm slightly relieved when he laughs as well.

"The highest. So when I was a freshman, I snuck into the school and spray-painted a bunch of lockers. The guidance counselor caught me. Didn't know it, but he'd taken a liking to me, decided he'd keep an eye out. I thought that was it, I'd go to juvie and become some piece of shit kid for the rest of my life."

"But..."

"But I didn't. He forced me to call my mom and tell her what had happened. It was eight, maybe nine at night. I don't know what I was thinking, to be honest—it wasn't even late enough for true criminal activity. I was a dumbass." I laugh at his own assessment. "So once he calls my mom, he tells her he's going to have me stay there all night and clean up my mess. I thought for sure she'd say hell no, but fuck, she was at her wit's end too. So she agreed." Another laugh for both of us.

"I stayed and scrubbed lockers, cleaned walls, anywhere I had painted. I wanted to be mad—so damn mad, especially when the clock hit two am. But then I realized he wasn't calling the cops, wasn't reporting me. After that, he earned my respect and my loyalty. I started going to his office when told, rather than just ditching. Started to actually talk to him. At first about dumb shit. Music and movies and sports. Then about girls and school. And then I opened up. Talked about my dad leaving and being there for my mom. How I felt and how it all affected me. He gave me strategies and methods to heal myself, to learn to handle my emotions."

There's a pause and a part of me knows he hasn't talked about this experience in years. Maybe ever.

"He changed the path of my life. I know that, looking back now. I see the changes he made in my life. See where I could have ended up if he hadn't taken an interest in me." There's a chance for me to talk. To slip in, to say something—anything, but I wait. I wait to see where he'll go next. Something tells me that's not it, there's more.

And I'm right.

But what I'm right about damn near kills me.

"I went to school to be a guidance counselor for elementary kids. By the time I was 25, I was done and I was lucky enough to get a job right off the bat." There's another pause, and a part of me knows that what comes next is painful. That what comes next will change the way I see this man forever.

"In my first year, I met a kid. His name was Jesse. Sweet kid. He loved everyone he met. He was... so kind, so fun to be around. Everyone he met fell in love with him. Cal reminds me of him a lot." His voice is softer now and my gut is sinking with each word. This conversation isn't going well. I hate it. I want to back out, erase it all before my mind can fill in the blanks, but something tells me he needs this. It's another story he hasn't told in some time.

"That November he was diagnosed with advanced leukemia."

"Oh god." The words are a whisper as the blood in my veins turns to ice.

"Yeah. It was bad. He came to my office a lot to talk about it. I became close with his parents, counseled them as a family when I could, referred them to professionals. I shouldn't have—looking back, I crossed so many lines. But... I was young and his circumstances were extreme and..."

The breath he takes is deep, like he's trying to fill his lungs up all the way before proceeding. "He'd come to my office and nap when he wasn't feeling well but didn't want to make his parents pick him up. We were friends. It sounds weird, I know. He was eight. Being friends with an eight-year-old, that's weird. But he was one of my students and I saw him more than any of my kids and, like I said, he was a *good kid*. So good. Pure. The best, even."

I hate where I know this is going. My eyes are already welling, picturing a different nearly eight-year-old in his place. My stomach churns at the mere thought. "We thought he was doing better. Scans were coming back with improvement. He was planning to do peewee in the fall"—his voice cracks before he moves on—"and I kept one of those foam balls in my office to practice throwing. I was the coach there too." God, the similarities. How do they not eat at him? He sighs.

"One day, his mom called me and I knew. She was a mess. A complete mess. Hysterical. Told me I needed to come down to the children's hospital. It wasn't looking good. He was asking for me. I left the school without saying a word to anyone, not a teacher, not the main office. I just left. I made it in time. In time to see him smile, talk to him for a few minutes, and then something happened and alarms were going off and people were screaming. I was forced from the room. I never asked what happened. What made him turn, nothing. But he... didn't make it."

He sniffs and I think he might be crying. The thought of this strong, cheerful man crying by himself in a room kills me almost as much as his story.

"God, this is embarrassing, huh? Fuck, I haven't.... I haven't talked about him... Shit, I'm sorry."

"Dean, no." My voice is soft, the same one I use on Cal when he feels dumb for having a nightmare or being afraid of something. "No, Dean. This isn't embarrassing. How many... how many people know this story?" I know the answer before he gives it.

"None." God. *How?* "At least, not all of it." How is he so happy every day with this in his past?

"I never went back. To work, I mean. I know it was wrong. I left everyone hanging, but I couldn't... I couldn't do it. To see the office he basically shared with me? Memories of him were everywhere. It hit me hard. I went back once, thinking maybe I could... But I couldn't. I packed all of my stuff up and quit on the spot. His parents would call me daily and give me updates on the services. Shared stories about him. He was a *good* kid. Didn't deserve that. I just keep thinking about how, if this is how *I* feel, a near stranger, his parents must be destroyed."

"I can't even think about it. How it would be." We're both quiet, contemplating his story in different ways before he breaks the silence.

"I can't get attached. To people, I mean. I can't do that to myself."

"I can see why." He stops for a moment, and I think it's in surprise, surprise of my agreeing.

"So now I do this. Go to camps for a few months out of the year, do snowboard school. It's long enough to make an impact, to better them, because I do think that's my purpose. But not enough to connect with anyone. I can't... I won't do that again." He can't see, but I nod. Then I speak instead.

"It makes sense." A long pause.

"What?" There's surprise clear in his voice.

"I said it makes sense. Not attaching yourself to the kids you help."

"What?"

"I said it makes—"

"No, I heard you. I just... No one ever agrees. Like no one agrees it was the right move."

"If something happened to Cal, I'd never be the same. I'd

completely cut myself off for everything, everyone. I've thought about it. More than once, actually. I'd start over. I couldn't deal with that. People who knew him, who could bring him up in conversation, who knew his sweet soul. I couldn't... I couldn't do it."

The thought alone tears at my throat, my heartbreaking for those parents who feel that every day now, feel that loss. Dean is quiet for what feels like days.

"You get it."

"I do."

"You don't think it's weird? He wasn't my kid."

"No. Not really. I mean. Other than his parents, you were probably closest to him. It's different, but... it's not, you know?"

"Different, but it's not." The words are a near whisper. Silence takes over the line again.

"I think it's great, what you do, though."

"What?"

"Going around, helping kids still. Look at Cal. He was miserable all last year. School starts next week and he's jumping off the walls. Cody's in his class, so that's a huge win. He's already planning his birthday party in October. Zee may drag you in to help me plan it. He wants a football theme. He's told me this already. But I have no idea how football even works, so..." I make an effort to get to solid ground, to give him space to breathe.

"I'll help."

"Good," I say with a smile, happy his voice sounds less sad, back to the happy, sweet Dean I've come to know. *Sweet?* I don't have time to dwell on that before he's talking again.

"Thank you."

"Thank you?"

"Yeah."

"For what?"

"Listening to that. I needed it." I want to push, want to ask why he's thanking me, why it meant something, why he needed it, why...

But my gut tells me I shouldn't. I should let it be. I should drop it and be gracious that he opened up to me.

"You're welcome, Dean," I say instead and I think that was what he needed too.

# SIXTEEN

-Kate-

THE SATURDAY BEFORE LABOR DAY, my phone rings.

With the holiday weekend, I took off both Saturday and Sunday morning to prep for school starting Tuesday and to spend some time with Cal. I should have known planning literally anything would mean the worst for me.

*Dad calling.*

I glance at the time: 6:45.

Shit.

There's no good reason for my dad to be calling me at nearly seven on a Saturday night.

When I came home to help with Mom and monitor things, at first, Dad helped by babysitting Cal. It was fun, Cal loved it and my parents loved having him there. But soon watching my growing in both size and energy kiddo was taking more and more out of my parents.

Now he mostly only heads over there for a few hours if he doesn't have camp so I can run errands, or occasionally my dad comes here at night to watch Cal while I work downstairs. But even that isn't ideal, considering my dad can't see for shit in the dark to drive home.

I stop in a few mornings a week typically, but with trying to pack in more work in less time this week, I haven't made it over there.

Staring at my phone, I'm wondering if that was a mistake.

"Hey, Dad, how's it goin'?" I say when I answer, stomach in knots. Cal's head turns towards me from where he's sitting on the couch, finishing a slice of pizza. He probably also knows there's no good reason for his grandfather to be calling. Instead of worrying him, I just smile and wink at my kid before turning to my room.

"Hey, Kate." He sounds tired. Tired and scared.

"Dad?"

"Shit. I don't want to bother you"

"Dad, what's going on?"

"It's your mom. This week she's been... sick. Hard time breathing. Pneumonia again. The doctor sent her home with some meds on Tuesday but it hasn't been getting any better. You know your mother, though, refused to let me take her in." He's not lying. My mom is even more stubborn than I am when it comes to accepting help.

"This morning I made her promise to let me take her in tomorrow if she didn't get any better, but I should have forced her to go in today. Fever shot up and her breathing got bad... An ambulance just came."

"What?!" I say, a shout, but then I remember Cal is watching my every move. He doesn't need this stress or anxiety. "*What?!*" I repeat in a whisper yell.

"Calm down, she's fine, just had a little trouble breathing, and when I called the doctor, he wanted to get her in as soon as possible. But you know I can't drive at night, my eyes..."

"Why didn't you call me?"

"I didn't want to stress you out. You have enough on your plate, plus you've got Cal..."

"But..."

"But I need to go to the hospital to get information and see your mother." *And he needs me to take him.*

"I'll be there in twenty minutes," I say, already sorting through my mind who I can call, who can watch Cal so he won't be stuck at the hospital too. Unfortunately, my options are slim.

"You don't have to—" I want to yell at him because that's a dumb sentence people say to relieve guilt when they know for a fact that who they're talking to does, in fact, *have to.* What other choice do I have? Fuck, I moved across the country with my kid to my hometown to be closer to my parents when things like this began to happen more often. Now guilt is taking over because I've been too busy to even go to my parents' house and check on them.

"Stop, Dad. I'll be there in twenty, thirty max."

The problem is, when I hang up, I realize the corner I've backed myself into.

Luna is closing tonight and she can't leave Daisy to take over, especially on a Saturday night. Tony and Zee are both on shift with a big case that broke in Bridgeville and leaked over here. Hannah and the rest of the girls are in the city.

I have no one to leave Cal with, which means I'm going to have to take him with me. I really don't want that for so many reasons. For one, God forbid something bad happens, I don't want my seven-year-old son to witness that. For two, who knows how late we'll be? While he's not new to staying up late, I can't have him falling asleep in a hospital waiting room.

Shit.

I do have one option though.

I flit through all of my others once more in my mental Rolodex, but the benefit (or downside, depending on how you look at it) of being on a time crunch is you can't overthink stupid decisions. So I scroll through my phone, finding the name I need, and stare at it. Not long enough to change my mind, just long enough to remind myself how dumb this is. Then I tap the name, bringing the phone to my ear and trying to convince myself I'm not making a horrible decision.

"Hey, what's up?" Dean asks when he answers within two rings. Our nightly calls have been nice, a strange comfort for two weeks now. Both of us have made the call, just to chat, to waste time together.

But somehow he knows that's not what this is. His voice is concerned, but I don't even give myself the time to dwell on it.

"God, Dean, I promise I wouldn't be doing this if I had any other choice, but Luna's got the bar, and Tony and Zee are both on shift. Hannah's in the city with the girls going dress shopping and I don't want to bother—"

"Katie, honey, calm down. What's going on?" His voice, his words, *Katie*... It all brings me out of my whirlwind and into my rational mind. I go into manager-mom mode.

"I don't want to bug you on a Saturday night, but I need someone to watch over Cal and everyone is busy. Luna would offer to shut down the bar, but I can't do that. She's already helped me out way too much." I pause, taking a deep, steadying breath.

"Is there any way you can come here and watch Cal?" I fill my lungs once more, my emotions reaching an equilibrium. "I don't know how long I'll be. I'm hoping not long at all, but who knows. An ambulance just took my mom away with breathing troubles and my dad... He can't drive there alone." There's a single heartbeat in between my words and his answer, and I'm regretting my decision to make this call. Sure, we've been talking nearly every night, and he's been such a help with Cal, but this is too far, this is—

"I'll be there in five," he says, the words succinct, and relief rushes through me.

"Thanks, Dean."

# SEVENTEEN

-Kate-

I'M PACING my living room, staring at my phone every five seconds for updates, when the knock comes. Looking through the peephole, Dean is standing there in jeans and a flannel shirt, hands in his pockets, looking around.

Luna must have let him in the back and through the landing since she's the only person who has those keys. Seeing him, I unlock the three—yes, three—industrial locks on the door before opening it. After the apartment was broken into during Luna's stalker experience, Tony and Luna spared no expense before renting it to me, ensuring it was as safe as can be.

"Hey, Dean, thanks so much for coming, I can't even—"

"Is everything okay?" He steps in, looking around.

"Yeah. Well, no. I mean, yes? I don't know." I'm a mess, as always, and can't help but wonder if that will ever change or if I'm forever doomed to this life.

"Calm down. Is Cal okay?"

"Yeah, Cal's good. Playing some stupid game."

"You? Are you good?" I ignore the warmth flowing through me at his words. He asked about my son first. *It's because he works with kids.* I try to convince myself, but it doesn't sit right.

"Yeah, I'm good, Dean. It's my mom. My parents are older—"

"Cal told me. Said they let him get away with whatever he wants." He smiles and I fight the urge to roll my eyes at further proof Cal steamrolls my parents when they watch him.

"God that kid. Menace. Well, they're older and my mom has some health issues. My dad called me, said she wasn't breathing right, and an ambulance took her. It's late, he doesn't see well at night and can't drive by himself. I need to get him and bring him to First Presbyterian and find out what's going on there." I sigh, seeing my relaxing night off burning into a crisp before my eyes.

"I don't want to take Cal. My dad... he's a mess, I'm not sure if he just didn't want to tell me how bad it is or if he's too scared to say it out loud, but it sounds bad. If something happens.... He doesn't need to be there for that. But he's still too young to leave by himself—"

"It's no problem, Kate. I'm happy to help. I'll stay as long as you need me to." I stare at him and stare and stare, my eyes unfocusing as I curl into my happy safe place, trying not to break. I can't break, not now. "Where is he?" he asks, breaking the moment. It's like he knows.

Before I can answer, Cal walks in from the living room, wearing the jersey Tony gave him and holding a controller.

"Hey, Coach! I didn't know you were coming over!" Cal's face lights up and relief fills me. He's going to be okay. God, this is probably going to be a vacation compared to hanging out with Mom for the night. Much needed guys' time.

"Hey, bud. What's goin' on? Your mom needs to run out, so I'm the lucky one that gets to hang with you for a bit. Is that cool?" Dean steps around me, putting a fist out to Cal, and he looks so old bumping Dean's fist like they're some kind of old bros instead of a kid and his football coach.

"Of course! Mom got me *Madden*. Wanna play?"

"Definitely. You go get it set up. I'm gonna talk to your mom really quick and then I'll be over there." Cal nods and happily skips back to the living room. He must unpause his game, blissfully ignorant to the chaos because the loud soundtrack starts playing again.

"You good?" Dean asks, and when I turn my head from where Cal disappeared to, Dean's face is full of concern, worry. For... me? I'm too tired—physically, emotionally, spiritually—to argue or try to hide it.

"No. I'm tired and anxious and wish I could catch a damn break, but here we are." His hand goes to my arm and the warmth burns through the ratty hoodie I threw on over my leggings. I don't even have the energy to worry about the fact I look like a slob and he looks... like Dean. "Thank you for coming. I hope I didn't ruin any plans or..." My voice trails off and I wonder if maybe I *did* ruin his plans. Maybe he had a date or...

"Was just sitting around. You go, get your dad. Keep me updated, yeah?" I nod, grabbing my bag and fiddling with my keys in my sweatshirt pocket. "Anything I should know before you go?"

"No, not really. No scary movies or he'll never sleep. I try to get him into bed by nine on weekends, but honestly, I don't care tonight. Just keep him alive," I say as he walks me towards the door with a laugh, the sound easing some tension in my soul. A feat I didn't know was possible tonight.

"I think I can manage that. Stay safe, Katie," he says. Before I can turn and walk out the door to the hall, his hand is on the back of my neck pulling me in, pressing a soft, sweet kiss to my forehead. It lasts a heartbeat, maybe less, but it burns the skin there, warmth and reassurance radiating from the spot before he rests his own forehead on mine.

"Go, Katie," he says, pushing me out the door and shutting it behind me. Thankfully, I don't have any time to overthink. Instead, I take the small kernel of reassurance and safety with me through the night like a security blanket.

———

It's nearly three when I pull into the parking lot of Luna's.

The night was a miserable mess at best, but it looks like my mom will be fine. After I picked up Dad, we spent nearly two hours being moved from department to department, trying to figure out where the ambulance took her.

When we finally landed in the Intensive Care Unit, the thought alone forcing a tendril of dread to curl in my belly, we waited almost another two hours until a doctor came out to talk to us. My mom has advanced pneumonia, pneumonia that should have been addressed by a professional days ago, at the very least. But instead, their stubbornness means she is going to be spending at least a week in the hospital on antibiotics and breathing treatments.

I want to rage at my dad for not forcing her to come. I want to rage at myself for knowing my mom was sick and not checking in more. I'm so mad I moved here to help during times like these and I can't even be on top of it, I'm so busy with... everything. When we got to see her for a few precious moments, she was hooked up to tubes and lines, a nose cannula delivering her oxygen as she continued to gasp for breath.

My mother, who spent my childhood strong and happy, living life to its fullest, looked tiny and weak, and it broke my heart. It took little to recognize the sight also broke my dad's.

We left not long after. Since it was late, nearly midnight at that point, I walked my dad in and my heart further broke, a crumpled mess in my chest. Disarray was everywhere, on every surface: piles of laundry and mail and a sink full of dishes. On the kitchen table was an empty pizza box and a pile of over-the-counter meds my dad had clearly been administering. The cabinets were nearly bare of food, the fridge the same.

"It's not that bad, Kate. Just couldn't keep on top of it and take care of your mom. I'm gettin' old, you know," my dad had said, trying to make a joke of it, but the words cut me. He's right—they're getting old.

Maybe it's time to push for extra help once more. They'll both fight it—it's a battle I've been fighting for nearly five years now—but I think it's time I make that executive decision. They need help and I need to come to terms with the fact I can't be everything to everyone —I need help too. I need to create a team around me to make things easier. For me, for Cal, for my parents.

A decision, an internal war for another day.

Today was a wake-up call.

Instead of stressing or arguing, I just smiled at him before urging him to get ready for bed. Once there, I said goodnight, telling him I'd lock the door behind me. He fell asleep almost immediately, clearly worn from the chaotic day and the stress of my mom.

But I couldn't leave it like this. Instead, I spent another hour cleaning, starting a load of laundry and then a second one, cleaning dishes, organizing the clutter, cleaning the house. Once done, I ran to the 24-hour grocery store in Bridgeville and got the basics, essentials to tide him over until I could do a bigger shopping trip, trying to find a balance of easy-to-make foods and things that will fuel him appropriately.

By the time I brought it all back, finished the laundry, and felt the house was clean enough to appease my guilt, it was two-thirty in the morning and new guilt started to eat at me. Poor Dean was stuck in my apartment watching Cal. Typing out a quick, 'On my way' text, I hopped in my car, fighting both the tears that needed releasing and the exhaustion the entire ride home.

The bar is closed and Luna is already home by the time I park out front, right next to Dean's car. Looking at my apartment above the bar, the window in the living area pointing to the street and parking area is dark but flashes with the lights of a television. Walking to the rear entrance, I unlock the door before locking it behind me, heading to the next door.

The apartment upstairs has two security doors before the main door. It's a pain, but a precaution insisted on by Zander when Luna first bought the bar. For years she lived upstairs before she got with Tony and moved into the house they renovated together.

The extra security is great, especially considering I have a little boy who is hopefully fast asleep upstairs, but right now it just means I have three extra doors to unlock and relock behind me, plus a flight of stairs to trudge up, my legs already like cement.

Although I'm often up early because of Cal, working odd jobs during the day and then working a bar until close at night, I am more tired today than I have been in years. I'm not sure if it's the emotional toll, the cleaning binge, or the fact this is typically my day to catch up on sleep, but I am absolutely beat.

I also know in the morning when Cal wakes up at the crack of dawn, he's going to wake me up to go get breakfast, since I am in desperate need of a grocery shopping trip.

*Let's just add Mom of the Year to Daughter of the Year today, huh?*

Sighing, I walk into our little apartment, placing my bag quietly in the kitchen before heading to the living room. When I walk in, Dean's head turns my way, a game on the TV, light flashing on his face in the dark, highlighting the handsome curves of his face.

"Hey," I say in a whisper, leaning against the wall.

"Hey." His eyes rake me over from top to toe, and then they get a dark look I almost don't see in the dim lights. I don't blame him. I look like shit, a complete mess.

"Cal okay tonight?" He moves over on the couch, giving me space and silently telling me to sit next to him.

I shouldn't.

I should say thanks, say goodbye, urge him to leave. But I'm exhausted. So I sink into the soft, cushy couch Luna left behind when she moved into Tony's.

"Yeah, we had a blast. Played games and he talked my ear off." A small smile plays on his lips.

"God, I'm sorry. He can talk to a brick wall."

"It was fine. Gotta admit, he didn't go to sleep until like, 11. I put on a movie, told him to get ready, and just waited for him to pass out on the couch. Then I carried him to bed."

"He probably thinks you're the coolest person alive."

"Well, I am, so..." I laugh at him, with him, and the lightness feels good. It feels good to have something light in my life right now.

"How was it?" The question comes quick like he's been wondering since I left, worried since I left...

"It was... not great." My head hits the back of the couch as my eyes drift to the ceiling, trying to get my brain together.

"How's your mom?" Still a whisper, still gentle, like he thinks I'll break. Or even more, like he *knows* I'll break.

"She's... okay. Pneumonia. She's hooked up. Dean... she looked... so tiny. Frail. I can't figure out if it's because she's sick or just things I haven't noticed before. I'm so busy, all the damn time." I take note of a dust bunny I need to clean. *Add it to the list.* But Dean doesn't say anything, doesn't reply, he just listens. I turn my head to him, back still on the couch, and he's just.. staring at me.

Listening.

A sounding board.

I don't know the last time I've had that. An ear that doesn't jump to give input or advice.

I've been a single mom for almost eight years.

I'm an only child, a fertility miracle to my older parents.

I have friends—great ones, ones I now consider family—but I've never been that person. The person to vent about my issues, to spill it all, to let another person take a piece of my verbal burden. I've always been the sounding board, the one people vent to, the one my friends can talk to with no shame, no worry I'll judge them.

And with Cal... I need to be. I need to be the sponge for his fears and anxieties and burdens. It's my job. But no one ever tells you how draining it can be to be the only one shouldering the weight of a child, regardless of how much joy it brings you, the honor you have in being that to them. And while I would never in a million years give it up, I'd be lying if I didn't sometimes wish I had someone to share that burden with.

Yet here Dean sits, an open ear, willing and able and, quite literally, trained to do so.

So for the third time, I dump everything onto his lap.

"I'm so fucking busy all the time that I didn't see my parents can't keep up. The house was a mess, Dean. Dishes and laundry and clutter were everywhere, my dad trying to keep it together to take care of my mom. He could barely change into pajamas, he was so tired when we got there.

Once he was asleep, I cleaned the house—it was a disaster, and the fridge was bare. Nothing for him to eat. He's too old to drive home in the dark. But they're so damn proud, they never asked for help. Never asked for a thing. But, Dean. He can't live like that. *They* can't live like that. It's not safe. I can start checking in more regularly, but for how long? If something happens, god forbid..." I stare off again, the tears building, the fear taking over, the exhaustion breaking the barrier I keep my emotions behind.

Or maybe it's him, maybe it's Dean who does it. It seems that way, with how I always melt down, make a fool of myself in front of the man.

"I'm so damn tired. I never get to stop. Today was my day off, and I still did a million things. I need to go grocery shopping. Can't sleep in because Cal will need breakfast. I have a damn pile of laundry that needs to be done, which means I'll need to drag Cal to the laundromat with me.

The poor kid never gets a chance to be a kid. No wonder he's struggling so much. I'm *failing him*. The fights, the kids being mean... it's all my fault. He's stuck here, being watched by people all the time, and I'll rarely even see him once he's back in school. I used to get the days.

When he was in kindergarten, it was fine. Half days, and then we'd hang out and then I'd work but now..." Tears rip through my throat now, falling over my eyes, and I cover my face with my hands. A minute. It's all I need. I need a minute to cry, to dwell in this, to mourn that this life isn't going how I once daydreamed it would before I get up, brush myself off, and keep moving. Because if I don't, who will?

But then there are hands on my waist.

Warm hands, strong hands. Those hands lift me, moving me on to a solid body, comforting arms wrapping around me. One hand goes to the back of my head and pushes it down into the chest.

And I'm free to fall apart.

"Shhhh. It's okay. It's going to be okay." His words are a balm, coating my rough edges where the sandpaper that is my life has been slowly grating, adding protection so it can heal. "Let me help you, Katie. It's going to be fine."

"He's going to hate me one day. I'm never here. We're always doing something boring. I'm dragging him to my jobs, someone else is watching him, and I'm dumping him places. God, I moved him all the way across the country because I couldn't even make it work in Seattle with him. He knows no stability, no home. I'm *failing* him, Dean." Sobs are breaking free now, but they're cathartic, like the tears are cleansing me as they leave my body. Tears of thoughts I've never let free, never spoken aloud.

"The fact you think you're failing him proves you're not," he says, his mouth to my ear, low and calming as that hand holds me to his chest, the other rubbing up and down my back.

"A shit mom, one who *would* fail? She wouldn't care. Wouldn't work herself to the bone to give him what he wants, what he needs. And Kate, you do that. Even when you're not there, you've created a safety net around him, people who love him, who want to see him succeed. You've given him a group of people who would bend over backward to help him." I shake my head to disagree, bumping into his chin now nestled to the top of my head.

"Luna came up after close. I had to fight her to be the one to stay, to watch Cal. She wanted to make sure everything was okay. You need to text her, by the way. Then both Zander and Tanner sent me a text, asking if they could take over, if you needed anything." My heart warms. I know he's not wrong. I have amazing people around me. People who would drop everything to help me if I just asked. My sobs begin to slow.

"Why do I always cry around you? You probably think I'm crazy. A fucking mess. All I do is cry." I sniffle. "I have it good, I know. But here I am, again, crying about how hard I have it. God, I'm so selfish." He pauses like he's weighing something, deciding what to share.

"I grew up with a single mom." My body stills, not sure how to respond. He's told me this, of course, but this feels... different.

"Not unlike you. Worked hard as fuck, did it all herself, made sure everyone was happy. It was just me, my brother, and her for years." His hand goes to the tie in my hair, tugging and then running his fingers through. A small noise leaves my throat—the feeling sending ribbons of warmth through me.

"She was amazing. I never wanted for anything at all. We fought, of course. She wasn't perfect, and I was a little asshole, but I never felt unsafe, unloved, uncared for. There were days when I was passed from sitter to sitter, where I'd go with her while she cleaned houses or we'd do nothing on winter break, but that's not what I always remember. I remember her breaking her damn back to make sure life didn't touch us. And looking back, I sometimes feel guilty for making it harder on her, feel bad she sacrificed everything for me. She eventually found a man, when I was 19 or 20, married him. They're happy enough. But she... she wanted more. For herself, for my brother, and for me. She wanted more kids, that much I know. She wanted to find love that made her crazy but never wanted us to get hurt. She wanted to go out for girls' nights and enjoy life. Wanted freedom, but she never let me feel that yearning." I sniff, but a kernel of dread is building in my belly because this story...

I moved to Seattle to get out of this tiny ass town where everyone knows everyone and everyone is always in each other's business.

Back then, I hated it, hated I couldn't go to a CVS and get medication without Joanne from the pharmacy telling everyone at church I had a UTI. I hated that if you went to the movies on a Friday, it was guaranteed you'd see your ex with his new girl. Hated that everyone remembered every damn thing you did in elementary school because there weren't enough kids, enough embarrassing memories to blur it all together.

I *hated it.*

So when I was accepted to the University of Washington, I ran. I didn't even come home for the summers, instead, I stayed in an off-campus apartment with four other girls, scraping by and waiting tables and loving that I could get lost in the hustle, lost in the crowd.

I always figured I'd start my career, get married, move to the suburbs, and have kids—at least three. I always wanted a sibling and never wanted my kids to feel that longing.

But then Cal's father and I got pregnant, and I was stuck in that city where I knew no one, couldn't afford anything, and was pregnant with a baby that the father wanted nothing to do with. A baby that I wanted more than anything.

So I had him sign off his rights, protecting his growing career from any child support requests and ensuring I would have full custody and say in Cal's life forever. But Seattle is expensive.

I had to move to a tiny, sketchy studio apartment and beg what friends didn't instantly abandon me to help, to babysit, to keep me afloat. I got Cal into childcare, but again, it was unbearably expensive, and because of it, my hours were restricted to daycare hours—not great for waitressing or bartending.

And then my dad called to tell me my mom was sick, really sick, in the hospital sick, just like today. Fuck, today was like deja vu. I took it as my sign. I didn't plan to be here long, just a few months until things settled, until things could be good for them and Cal and I could figure out our next steps.

I had to suck it up, pack up what little we had, and drive my piece of shit car across the country with a pouting five-year-old in tow. New Jersey isn't much cheaper to live in, small town or not, but at least here we have a community of people to help, people who can take over while I work nights, people who can refer me to odd jobs. People to keep an eye out for Cal.

And somehow, before I could stop it from happening, I'd rooted myself in this town. Whether I wanted to or not, I was, for lack of a better word, stuck here. Some days I want to scream at the thought.

"You're a good mom," he says, disturbing my existential crisis with his hand in my hair, directing me to look at him until my eyes meet his. The bright light of the TV in the dark room flashes on his hazel eyes, but in them, it's clear he's not just saying that; he truly means it. "And you're so damn strong, holding everything together for him, refusing to take more than the minimum of help. You're not a failure. Everyone who meets you loves you and wants to help in whatever way you'll let them."

He pauses like he isn't sure if he should continue on. "And you're absolutely gorgeous." Butterflies in my belly erupt, hitting the walls and trying to escape. Butterflies that are in a frenzy because I think... "And I'm going to kiss you." This he says as if he's telling it to himself, like he's shocked by it, and then he stares at me for long, drawn out moments before I realize he's looking for my permission.

Permission to kiss me.

Kiss me at three a.m in my living room with my kid asleep in the other room after dropping everything on a Friday night to watch him.

So I smile, a small thing, my lips barely even moving to tip up, but that's all the reassurance Dean needs before his lips press to mine.

It's tentative at first, sweet even, the butterflies settling in quiet excitement as our lips touch, and for a split second as I sit in his lap, his body warm around mine, his lips warm on me, I regret never doing that lip scrub Sadie gave me because his lips are so damn soft on mine but then—

Then his lips are moving on mine, his hand tangled in my hair, putting pressure on the back of my head and forcing my lips to open. Just a bit, just enough so he can press his tongue between them, and then...

A mewl, tiny and quiet, breaks from my lips when his taste hits me, when his tongue touches my own and dances and that's what breaks him.

The normally calm, cool, collected Dean snaps. Another arm

comes around my waist before he flips me on the couch so my back presses to it, his body lying overtop mine, and then he's *kissing me*.

Lips and tongues and heavy breathing, small moans from me, and quiet grunts from Dean as he barely, just *barely* brushes his groin to my own, the hardness there proof he's enjoying this as much as I am. As we kiss, making out like teenagers on the couch, he moves us so we're both on our sides. I hitch a leg over his hip and start to grind on him, the move sending shock waves through my system.

"Jesus, Katie," he says, and now that nickname no one else calls me holds another meaning, not just sweetness but heat. I pull his lip into my mouth, tugging with my teeth, and he bucks his hips into mine, making me smile into the kiss.

The hand gripping my hip moves, dipping under my shirt. Slowly, so slowly it's near torture, his warm hand creeps up, up, up until it's on my back, fingers on the clasp of my bra. Waiting. Waiting for the okay.

*God, this man.*

There is something so unbearably sexy about a man who knows what he wants but also wants to make sure you undoubtedly want it too.

Instead of answering with words, I arch my back and give him a small moan as I continue to move against him, pressure already somehow building into magic between my legs.

Deft fingers unclasp my bra in one move before his hand is moving towards the needy flesh. And when his thumb hits the underside of my breast, my moans go from quiet and sweet to deep and needy. He laughs into the kiss, and part of me wants to be annoyed, but the other part... I keep grinding on his hip, his own hardness brushing against me and pushing me further.

I should be embarrassed. Embarrassed to be this wound, to be this wet, but I can't find it in me as his thumb keeps moving and brushes my hard nipple. I moan at the sensation before he adds another finger and gently pinches, pulling on the taut flesh, and *oh my god.*

"Dean, oh my god," I say in a panted whisper.

"Do you like that, Katie?" he asks, his voice low and gruff, the rumble on my chest urging me higher, so much higher. The seam of my jeans has shifted, so it's pushing my panties into my pussy and rubbing against my clit with each movement.

"God, yes, I think... oh, god, Dean, I think..." Panic takes over because if he keeps this up, *I think I'm going to come.* That's embarrassing, right?

"Please tell me you're going to come on my leg just from my hand on your tit and kissing me. Please tell me because you are so fucking sexy right now and I *want that.*"

"Yeah, yeah," I say in a murmur, lips on his but no longer kissing as I focus on the pleasure driving through me.

"Holy shit, that's it, Katie. Keep going and come on me just like that. Fuck, you're beautiful." His words growl through me as he pinches tight on my nipple, bucking into me, and that's it. I move my head to his shoulder. my mouth going to the flannel covered arm and using it to hold back the moan, loud and deep, that breaks from me as I shatter, fragments of pleasure shooting through me in the most intense orgasm of my life.

And I'm fully fucking clothed.

Holy *shit.*

Imagine what this man could do with...

*"That was spectacular,"* Dean says, awe and lust in his voice and I look up at him in the dark, eyes hooded, and I smile.

"Your turn," I say, because now as I'm coming down, I would do anything to return the favor, to make him come and hear him as I do. He smiles and doesn't look like he'll argue with my assertion. But as my hand reaches for him, his body freezes, his hand quickly leaving from under my bra and grabbing my wrist.

"Wha—"

"Shh."

I stare at him confused—I thought we were on the same page. But then I hear it. Little feet and then...

"Mommy?" The voice is small and quiet and it sounds like it did when Cal was little, really little, too little to know it's not cool to call me mommy. I pop up and look over the back of the couch, never more thankful to be fully dressed than in this moment. Cal is standing there, squinting and rubbing his eyes, his hair sticking up at strange angles. He's in a pair of loose shorts and a tee shirt, too cool for the character pajamas I got two months ago.

"Hey, bud." I don't say anything other than that, don't ask questions. You learn as a parent you can get away with a lot more if you just ignore the elephant in the room.

"Coach Fulton?"

"Hey, man. I was just about to head out. Thanks for hanging out with me tonight," Dean says, and I look over at him, trying to hide my blush. He just smirks at me, knowing, adjusting himself from behind the couch cushion. My eyes widen.

"Go back to bed, bud. I'll come to kiss you in a minute, okay?" Cal looks from me to Dean and back before the big kid shield comes back up.

"I don't need a kiss. Night, Mom. See you later, Coach." And then he's shuffling back into his room like it didn't happen.

"What a little fart," I say under my breath, mostly to myself, but Dean laughs, a deep chuckle no longer cautiously quiet. "It's not funny! I was about to..." I look down at him, at his lap, and in the dim light from the television, his eyebrow quirks.

"About to what, Katie?" A chill runs down my spine as he stands, putting a hand out to me. When I take it, he pulls me into his arms and I relax. I don't worry about Cal or work or my parents. I'm just in the arms of a hot man who just made me come on my living room couch.

"Uhm... well... you know..." I stutter the words, but he just laughs again.

"Gonna take a raincheck, babe. But hold on to that fuckin' thought, okay? I know I will." My eyes go wide and his smile mimics their stretch. "I'll call you tomorrow, yeah?" he asks, and what else can I do but nod. "Walk me out?" Once again, I nod and watch him put on his shoes and jacket before walking him through the apartment door, the security door, and down to the bar's exit.

"Bye, Kate." His words are warm and his breath brushes my lips as he pulls me in. Before I can say anything, he kisses me once more, this time casual and smooth, like we do this all the time. Like he always kisses me when he leaves my apartment after watching Cal.

I hate how much I love it.

Not the kiss, but the feelings that come with it.

When he lets me go, he plants one last kiss on my forehead before walking out with a wave. I watch, watch him walk to his car and start it up. But he sits there for long moments, not leaving.

As I watch, my phone rings in my hand.

*Dean Calling.*

"Hello?"

"Lock it and head upstairs, babe."

"What?"

"Lock the doors. Go upstairs, lock those doors. Not leaving until I see you turn off the TV and head to bed."

Warmth, pure and sweet like honey, drips through me because I don't know the last time someone cared about me, just me. But still...

"Dean, I... we should..."

"We'll talk about us another day. After you've slept. For now, you go to bed." I keep staring at his car, knowing he's staring back, and I shake my head before turning around.

"Good night, Katie. Sweet dreams. I know I'll have them," is all he says as I trudge up the steps before clicking off. And once I turn off the TV, I stand at the window facing the parking area and watch him drive off, wondering what on earth is happening.

Did I really just dry hump my son's camp counselor until I came?

Yes. Yes, I did. And as much as I want to feel shame for it, I don't. Not one little bit.

# EIGHTEEN

-Kate-

THE NEXT MORNING it's not my alarm waking me before the sun rises.

It's also not Cal coming in to quietly ask me for breakfast.

It's the sun, a sliver of it streaming through the broken blinds I need to fix moving across my face.

*The sun.*

The sun is up.

I pop up in bed, scanning the room for the clock, patting around for my phone. When my eyes hit the clock I see 8:52 in bright red blinking numbers.

*Eight fifty two.*

I can't remember when I've ever slept to eight fifty two.

I am *so fucked.*

Also, where is Cal? Is he okay? Because by now his stomach is eating itself and he's dying for sustenance.

I whip the sheets back, roll out of my bed, and run to the living room, panic in my veins.

But Cal sits at the kitchen table, happily chewing and watching some dumb show on the iPad.

Okay, Cal is in one piece, but I'm beyond late to walk the Ferguson's dogs. *I can't believe my alarm didn't go off!*

"Shit, shit, shit! My alarm didn't go off!" I look around the room, trying to remember where I threw my cell last night. It's on the table, amongst the brown paper bagel bag and a cream cheese tub. I rush over, grabbing it, and expect to see a text, a call, something telling me I missed an appointment or that the sky is falling... something.

*No new messages.*

What the...

"Your alarm wasn't on," Cal says, and I look at him, confused.

"What are you talking about? It's always on. Did we lose power last night?" I check the clock on the oven that resets at the slightest loss of power, but nope, nothing.

"Don't freak, everything is cool, Mom."

"Why was my alarm off?" There has to be a logical reason.

"Coach said you needed the sleep. He turned it off last night while you were with Grandma and Grandpa. How are they?" Instantly, my blood boils. Dean did *what? How dare he! That is such an invasion of*—but then my eyes dip to my son's hands which are lifting to his mouth where he takes a bite of a chewy bagel, cinnamon raisin with strawberry cream cheese. His favorite.

"Where did you get a bagel?" There definitely was none in the house last night. In fact, after walking the Ferguson's dogs, our next stop was just that.

"Coach brought them over." The words are muffled in bagel and cream cheese, a chunk spewing out and making me cringe.

"Ew, Cal, don't talk with food in your mouth." He shrugs, but at least he wipes up the goo. *Gross.* "But, I'm sorry, what did Coach do?"

"Yeah, he brought them over this morning. I was up, you were sleeping, and I was playing a game. He scared the shit out of me."

"Callum!"

"Sorry, poop." I sigh. Cursing is not what's important right now. I need to stay on topic.

"How did he get in?"

"Luna gave him a key last night."

"Luna gave him a key?"

"Yeah, she came up after you left. He said he wanted to lock the doors behind her, you know, because of that crazy guy that one time? So Luna gave it to him." I blink, trying to understand what the hell is going on.

"And he brought you bagels?"

"He got you some too. Last night he asked me what you like. Everything with veggie. Gross." His little lip scowls, but I'm still so unbearably confused. "He also left me a note to give you." He looks around, chewing with a smear of pink cream cheese on his cheek. "Oh, here." He hands me a slip of yellow lined paper, the thin kind they have at school, the kind Cal sometimes brings home.

*Katie,*

*I covered for you with Mrs. Ferguson. Hope you slept well. Call me when you wake up.*

*xD*

And then my night comes flooding back. Not the Mom and Dad part, not the part where I knew I needed to find a better solution for them. The part where I came home. Where Dean had taken care of Cal, where I cried in his lap *again*. Where he told me about his mom, about growing up and seeing everything in a different light as an adult.

*That damn kiss.*

What was that?

It happened, right? I didn't hallucinate that?

"There's a coffee in the microwave," my son tells me. I walk over to it, hitting the button to pop the door open, and right there is a coffee from Rise and Grind, Sadie's handwriting on the side.

*Call me, girl!!*

I sigh, knowing she will hound me until I die if I don't do just that. But I have someone else I need to call first.

"You good, bud? I gotta make a call." My son nods, chewing and watching his show, not even paying attention to me anymore, but that's fine. I don't want him paying attention to this. Grabbing the still-warm coffee and my phone, I walk to my room and shut the door before opening my contacts and scrolling to 'Dean.' He picks up on the first ring. He'd been waiting for it, expecting it.

"Morning, Katie." His words flow over me, that *name* I never let anyone call me. When I was a kid, I was determined it made me sound like a little girl when all I wanted to be was a grown-up, and when I was an adult, it always felt... off. But now, every time the name comes from Dean's lips, a shiver rolls down my spine. The *good* kind.

"Did you turn off my alarm last night?" I don't bother with hellos because, as nice as the name feels, I'm pissed. But Dean just laughs.

"Yes."

"When?"

"When you were gone. Cal showed me where it was."

"But you didn't even know if I had to be up early."

"Babe, everyone in town knows your crazy ass schedule. Everyone knows on Saturday mornings you go to the Ferguson's and take their demon dog to the dog park for an hour. How that tiny ass dog has energy still after all that running around, I have no idea." I pause.

"They do?"

"The dog? Yeah, it was tugging me on the leash the whole walk back. I swear, the thing is 15 pounds, but it has some force behind it. He doesn't tug for you?"

"No, I mean everyone in town."

"Well, I don't know about everyone, but a lot of them. You do a lot, babe. For a lot of people. They notice. I had to ask around a bit since I'm not as clued into the Springbrook Hills life unless it's involving the elementary kids, but yeah. I knew. Plus, Cal would have told me your social security number last night if he'd known it."

"Traitor," I mumble under my breath.

"I know all of your secrets now, Kate," he says, lower now, more seductive, and damn if my body isn't responding.

"What kind of secrets?"

"All kinds." I can hear the smile on his face.

"I'm gonna kill him." Dean laughs again, and another chill runs through me before I remember I'm mad at him. "I'm mad at you."

"Mad at me?"

"Yes."

"I brought you bagels and let you sleep in."

"I'm still mad at you."

"You gonna tell me why?"

"Because you turned my alarm off! And brought me bagels! You have a key to my apartment?!"

"I dropped it back off at Tony's this morning."

"Oh." Why does the idea of him *not* having a key make me bummed when three seconds ago I was pissed?

"I also gave Tony money to make me a set of copies."

"What?"

"You need help, Kate. Period. I'm the only one in your crew who doesn't have conflicting work hours, a social life, or a partner to spend time with. Plus, Cal likes me."

"Dean, this isn't—"

"You need help, Katie." He's not saying it nice now, though it's low. It's almost like an order. "You need help and you refuse to take it, so I'm forcing you to. I'm gonna help you. Help you with Cal, get you some free time. I called around and have some options to go over to help with your parents. I think I found a good solution, but they're your parents, of course." I breathe, trying to say something, anything.

"You're running yourself ragged. Absolutely dry. Cryin' in my lap every time I see you, always exhausted. You need help. And I'm going to give it to you whether you accept it readily or not." I don't say anything for long moments until I finally break the silence.

"Why?"

"Why?"

"Yeah, why?" My voice is soft now, almost embarrassing with the strain of the tears I'm forcing myself not to release.

"Why what, Katie?"

"Why help me? Why worry about if I'm tired or run dry. Cal, I get. Taking him under your wing like you and Zee have? I so appreciate it. But I get it. You're a teacher. That makes sense. But me?"

"You're no good to me tired."

"What? What does that mean?"

"I don't want to do this over the phone."

"What does *that* mean?"

"It means we have to talk and I don't want to do it over the phone."

"That doesn't make me feel good." My belly is in knots, dissecting and overanalyzing what that could mean.

"Fine. You're no good to me tired. I can't take you on a date if you're too tired to move. I can't do *other* things with you if you're too tired, if your mind is stressing about everything else. There's more Kate, but I think that's the gist of it." I'm silent. What the... "You get me."

"What are you saying?"

"I'm saying I'll be over at four tonight to take you and Cal out to dinner."

"What?"

"Gotta stop asking questions when you know the answers, babe."

"Why are you coming here to take me to dinner?"

"We're going on our first date, Katie." His voice is low and soft and those butterflies come back, wings tickling my belly.

"What?"

"Dinner. Me. You. Cal. Tonight." The flutters explode with his clarification. But...

"Dean, it's sweet, really, but... I have work tonight. At the bar."

"Talked to Luna. You're comin' in at eight. We'll eat at four. A little early, but we can be early birds today. After I'll watch Cal until you get off shift."

I'm speechless.

"You there?"

"Yeah, I... You talked to Luna?"

"Yeah."

"About taking me on a date?"

"Yes."

"And she... what, told you my schedule?"

"Pretty much. She seemed pumped to have someone taking you out. Guess you don't date much?" I don't. Never, actually, not since I got home from Seattle.

"No." The words are low, embarrassed.

"Like that, Katie."

"What?"

"I said I like that. That you haven't dated. Like being the man to take you out."

"Look... this is... sweet. Really. But I don't know... this might not... Cal..."

"What about it?" I sigh. I don't want to have this conversation because it scares everyone off, every time.

"Look. This is nice. But there's a reason I don't date. Cal... he's young. I don't want to have a revolving door of men in his life. Don't want him getting attached and then they... go." He pauses for a moment and I'm sure that's it.

"God, you're perfect."

"What?"

"Great fuckin' mom. I've seen shitty ones. Ones that try to get me into their bed, don't care about how it might affect their kids. But not you. You'd lay it all on the line for him. For your family. Fuck, for your friends. Sacrifice yourself to give them everything. You're perfect."

"That's kind, but still—"

"Take it day by day. I don't want to hurt Cal either, but fuck, I like you, Katie. A lot. More than I should. More than I can remember ever liking a woman. Let's..." Now it sounds like he's nervous, like he's weighing things. It's a strange sound to hear coming from him. "Let's try. See what happens. I'm here for a while. We can.. test it out."

"That's great, Dean. But Cal. He comes first."

"We don't tell him. I'm just his coach, that's it. We'll keep it like that. The other men help out, right? Tony and Hunter and Tanner? Sometimes they throw in, watching him. I'm added to the roster for all Cal knows. That's it. But me and you? We'll know we're testing things out, testing the waters. Okay?"

I weigh it in my head for long moments, then in my heart. And then, just for good measure, I weigh it a little lower, remembering how it felt last night, kissing a man for the first time in years, having a man hold me and make me feel good...

And even though I can tell it will end in disaster, even though I know Cal is too smart to not understand the difference between Tony watching him and Dean taking us both out, I make my decision.

"Alright."

# NINETEEN

-Kate-

My first date with Dean Fulton was dinner at the crazy burger place in Bridgeville that has killer burgers but also has an arcade. While we waited for our food, Dean gave Cal five dollars and told him to have fun in the arcade. Once he got his quarters, Dean followed him around the arcade, giving him tips from how to move his wrist to kill it at air hockey to how to hit the clown to get the most tickets to the right corner to hit to make the baskets with the Hoops game.

I wanted to cry the entire time, watching Cal light up, glow from Dean's attention.

When our meal was ready, Cal's name shouted over the loud-speaker, we went to the pick-up window and sat down to eat. That's when the true test came.

I love Cal. More than anything in the world, I will sacrifice over and over until the day I die to give him the best life I can, but... he's seven. And he can be beyond annoying.

Because I love him and because I'm his mother, I can tolerate it most days. But when he gets excited, it gets worse. He *talks*. Incessantly. About just about anything. These days it's football and camp and more football. But really, it can be anything under the sun.

So when we sit down with our food and Cal gets that gleam in his eyes, I know. I know we're in for his jabber fest, and I brace myself for the dead-eyed, absent-minded head nods most people who don't absolutely adore this boy give him after about two minutes.

It never comes.

Instead, Dean joins in, giving insight on teams and passes, players that I didn't even know Cal knew. They talk plays and upcoming peewee games before moving on to normal things like favorite foods and favorite movies. And with each word, Cal glows more, having someone other than me to chat with about all of his favorite things.

With each word I see it happen, see Cal fall deep with Dean.

And with each word, with each grain of confidence added to his quickly growing pile, I can't help but wonder for the millionth time if not having some kind of male influence in his life other than my dad or the men of my friends is hurting him. If maybe all these years avoiding any kind of connection with the opposite gender solely for Cal's benefit was actually more damaging in the end.

After dinner, we head to the movies. Dean lets my son choose some weird kid-friendly action movie I have no desire to watch but they both chat about it with excitement—apparently, Cal has been dying to see it, all the kids at camp have, but he 'hasn't gotten to it yet.'

That's sweet kid code for, 'I didn't want to ask my mom because she has no time and it costs money."

God, this kid.

We need to have a serious talk soon about being honest and opening up.

When we hit the snack counter, much to my hemming and hawing that we just had dinner and don't need anything else, Dean forces Cal to pick out whatever he wants, ending up with a bucket of popcorn, a soda I cringe at, and three boxes of candy. This man is pulling out every stop to make sure my kid has the absolute best time ever and I have no idea how to take it.

We settle into our seats, the theater shockingly empty, and Cal demands we sit as per his own seating chart—Cal, Dean, then me.

"You don't want to sit next to me?" I ask.

"No. I want to sit next to Coach," he says with a finality that has me almost offended, but Dean just laughs, taking the soda and popcorn from my hands and forcing me to sit as per Cal's demands.

The movie plays, the sounds loud, the crashes louder, the jokes as dumb as can be, but Cal and Dean keep leaning over to each other, telling each other quips and commentary on the movie that in any other situation you could not *pay* me to watch willingly. But again... the joy on Cal's face, the way he excitedly punches Dean's arm when something cool happens... It's amazing.

We're about halfway through the movie when Dean takes the popcorn bucket from my hands and places it on the floor before lifting the arm of the seat between us, locking it in place, and putting an arm around me. I look up at him in surprise, but his eyes are locked on the screen. His arm just tightens around me until I place my head on his shoulder and settle in.

After that, I couldn't tell you how much longer the movie was. It could have been an hour, it could have been three days, it could have been three minutes. But I would have stayed there for an eternity, held by Dean, the man who made an entire night revolve around my son and making him feel happy and welcomed. A man who forced a first date on me the day after I dry humped his leg on my couch. The man who required that first date be with my son.

And it was magic.

When we get back to the apartment, the bar is open and a few regulars nod, Luna waving from the bar with wide eyes that say, 'we will talk about this in an hour!'

I just shake my head and smile as we head to the back door, unlocking it and moving through the next two doors.

"Dean, I gotta show you my new ball!" he says, running towards his room.

"Hey, stay there for a bit, yeah? I'll come in and see it in a few" Dean shouts down the hall. "Let me talk to your mom first."

Cal turns around in the hallway. "Are you guys gonna kiss?' His face screws up into an ew face and it takes everything in me not to laugh in his face and or melt into the floor in an embarrassed puddle.

"Callum!" I start, but Dean cuts me off.

"And what if I do? What if I kiss your mom?" His arms cross his chest in a taunting and challenging way. So much for being subtle around him. Cal eyes Dean up and down.

"Are you dating her?"

"We just went on our first date."

"Bro, your first date was with a seven-year-old kid? Lame." My mouth drops open. Who is this child?

"You and your mom are a packaged deal, kid. Made sense to me." Cal clearly takes a few moments to think on that.

"That makes sense. So, uh, what's your plan? With my mom?"

"Callum James!" Dean just looks my way with a look in his eyes that is half-amused, half taunting. "Dean!" Is this what my life is going to be like now? Also, what happened to not cluing Cal in?

"We just started dating, my dude. But I plan to help make her life a little easier." Cal looks like he's taking that in and then his face goes serious, not in a 'trying to be tough way' but in a worried kid way, and my stomach drops.

"Can you make sure she's happy?" The smile on my face melts, all humor gone.

"Cal, honey, I'm—"

"Yes," Dean says, cutting me off. "Yeah, I can do that. That's my new job." I look at Dean, but he's looking at Cal. They're having some kind of moment, some kind of guy talk I can't decode. Somehow, although the kid isn't even eight, he's already got it down.

"Okay. Cool." He looks between us. "Then yeah, you can kiss her. But like, not in front of me. I don't want to see it." And then he walks away like the entire conversation didn't just happen. I watch his back as he goes, noticing he needs to size up in shorts, before looking at Dean when he's gone.

"What just happened?" I ask, but he's walking my way, forcing me to move back until my body hits the wall of the entryway. "Dean?" I ask, but my voice is breathy and low as his body presses into mine. "Dean?" I say again. I can barely hear myself this time as his forehead presses to mine.

"Been wanting to do this all day," he says, then tips his face down, angling to catch my lips as my head tips up without my permission. Then his lips are on mine, soft but firm as they press. The feel of them, the urgency, it's like he's trying to convince me he has in fact been dying to do this all day.

And I'd be lying if I didn't feel the same,

He presses me deeper into the wall, his body lining up so perfectly with my own, and it takes everything in me not to hyper-focus on that, on how good he feels against me. How well he fits.

His body was made to be on mine.

Then his tongue is tracing my lips and fuck, fuck, it's all I can focus on. His taste, the small groan he lets out when his tongue tastes mine, the way his hips move so I can feel how he's already growing against me.

It reminds me of last night, of the feelings running through me, of how I felt both completely sated and completely *unsated* at the same time. We kiss there for long moments, but as soon as I move to hitch a leg over his hip, completely lost in him, he pulls away. He continues to press small kisses to my lips like he can't stop, can't resist, but eventually, he stops, pressing his lips to my forehead.

"We need to stop," he breathes.

"Yeah," I say, the world coming back to me. The universe returning.

"You need to get ready for work." *Shit.*

"Yeah."

"Want me to help you get dressed?" he asks with a smile, lips moving against my forehead.

"Yeah," I say without thought, and Dean instantly laughs, the deep rumbling shaking me as he's pressed to my body.

"As much as I'm dying to see your body, that first time will not be under the same roof as your kid and it will not be when I can't spend hours enjoying you," he says and fuck if I don't clench, dying for him. For more.

"Yeah," I say once more, and this time it's a sad 'yeah.' He laughs again before moving back from the wall, taking me with him.

"Go. Get ready. I'll be here when you get off," he says, turning my body and smacking my ass. I walk toward my room as he goes to the fridge to grab a soda and settle in for the night.

———

The night flies by, the crowd excited and chattering, gossip running free as always. We're packed, so packed Luna doesn't get to corner me until we're closed and prepping for the next day, noting bottles that need replacing and wiping things down.

I'm drying a glass when she comes up to me, bumping her hip into mine.

"So?" I play dumb.

"So what?"

"Don't you 'so what' me, Kate." I stay silent. If she wants info, she needs to ask for it. "Fine, I'll bite. What happened today? I get a call this morning asking if you can skip opening, but not from you. Oh no, it's from the hot new football coach. What's up with that!?"

"Yeah what is up with that, Luna? A hot guy asks if you can shift my schedule and you agree? He could be a serial killer for all you know."

"I was going to switch you anyway, the night you had. And I'm a good judge of character." I stare at her with wide eyes, quietly reminding her she was once kidnapped by a regular who tried to smuggle her out of the country because he was psycho and obsessed with her since high school. "Okay, that was one time. But even Tony says Dean's cool. And Tony never liked Jim." I roll my eyes. "So?!" There's no way out of it.

"Okay, things with my mom... you know that part. And then I couldn't find anyone to watch Cal. So I called Dean."

"And?!"

"And he came."

"Did he *come?*"

"Jesus, Luna!" I shout, a blush creeping up as I remember he did not, in fact, come. *I did though.*

"Oh my god, the blush! I need details. So. Many. Details."

"Luna!" But she just stares at me and, to be honest, I'm kind of dying to spill. "We kissed. And... then some. He's a good kisser, Lune."

"That's all you did?"

"Kind of?" I blush, but I'm relieved when she doesn't push. "This morning I woke up but had no alarm. He turned it off." Luna's eyes are wide. "My thoughts exactly! But Luna... he took over for me with Mrs. Ferguson and brought bagels for Cal so he wouldn't wake me up all hangry. And then he told me we were going on our first date. And his first date with me would be with Cal." Luna's mouth drops and then, to my shock, her eyes start to water.

"Oh, Kate. That is the sweetest thing I've ever heard."

"Right?! He took us to dinner and played arcade games with Cal and took us to some dumb movie and let him get whatever junk he wanted and now he's watching him, even though he was up early and went to bed later than I even did, and what am I doing?!"

"What do you mean?"

"What am I doing? I don't date, and that's for a reason. Because if Cal gets attached and hurt, that's on me. I'm a mom first, Luna. And Dean... he's sweet and all, but he's not staying here." She looks like she's thinking about what I just said.

"I see what you mean. But Kate... you can't be single forever." I roll my eyes. "I mean, you could, but that's miserable. You also can't shelter Cal forever, you know? You can't not live your life because of Cal. Is that what you want him to learn?"

"I hate that you make sense," I say, turning my back to her and wiping down the already clean counter. She laughs, grabbing the rag from my hand.

"Go. Go upstairs. And talk to him. Have a conversation about what this is. But babe, go in with an open mind. He can't promise you forever—fuck, no one can. But that doesn't mean you shouldn't be happy." I scrunch my nose, not wanting to agree but also... She points to the back. "Go. Jake and I have got this from here. Right, Jake?"

The bartender/bouncer/overall good guy lifts a hand and waves, agreeing with the boss lady. I roll my eyes but move to walk past her towards my apartment anyway.

———

"Hey," I say in a whisper as I walk into my living room, reaching up to let my hair out of the tight bun I kept my hair in.

"Hey," Dean says, stretching as he stands from the couch, taking two steps until we're toe to toe.

"Did you fall asleep?" His eyes hold the same look Cal's do when he first wakes up, a boyish tired that melts my heart when I see it. Turns out Dean's version does the same.

"Nah, was watching the game. Just dozed off." His lips press to mine, not seeking anything, just a gentle brush of hello.

"Yeah, right." I smile at him. "Thanks. For this. And for... today. And yesterday?" I say. I'm rambling now, a habit that seems to be more common when Dean's near.

"My pleasure," he says, pulling me in close and pressing his lips to my hair as I snuggle into his shirt, trying to take a breath of him without being creepy.

"You gonna head out?"

"I'll hang with you a bit," he says then lets me go and leads me to the couch.

"You don't have to. You must be exhausted."

"I'm good, sit with me," he says, pulling me down onto the couch where I land right in his lap. My belly flutters at the movement, of being so close to him. "See? This is nice." He pushes the hair behind my ear, smiling at me.

"Mmm," I murmur at the feel of his hands in my hair. There's nothing better, I swear. We sit in silence for long moments, long comfortable moments that don't feel at all like either of us has to fill the silence.

"I had fun with you and Cal today, Katie."

"I had fun with you too."

"I'd like to do it again. Both with and without Cal," he says, and a mix of dread and excitement rolls through me.

I haven't really dated in over eight years. Dating is hard as a single mom, not just because of the logistics of finding someone to watch my son, but also because I need to be super mindful of who I bring into my kid's life. Of the ideas he gets about life just by who I choose to expose him to.

From the very beginning of my pregnancy, I knew I didn't want to have a constant revolving door of new men in his life. While it might be a normal process for finding the 'one,' especially while you're young, I need to put my son first. But because of that, dating has been near impossible.

"Dean, I—"

"Please, no. Give me a chance, Kate. Give this a chance." His hand on my hips squeezes, the warmth seeping in through the thin fabric.

"Dean, look. I... shit. I like you. A lot more than I expected to. I think you're sweet and fun and, obviously, I'm very much attracted to you." He smiles a devious smile.

"But..?" He urges on.

"But... I'm a mom. A mom first, always. That means so many

things. I will never put you first. You need to know that now. Cal will always be my priority while he's under my roof. Period. The second is... I don't date." He goes to speak, but I cut him off first.

"Not because I'm against it or anything. But... it's not easy. I'm a mom first. Schedules get messy and it will rarely be just... us." I move a hand between us. "But more than that, I'm careful with what I show my kid. I don't date because I don't want that in his life. We're a packaged deal, Cal and me. We come together, but it means we get... attached together. I know... I know you're not here for good. And that's... fine. But I can't let Cal get attached, get used to you and have you break up with him too when we're done. That's why I don't date. I don't want my actions, my dating life to hurt him. You know?"

He's quiet and I think that's it. Last night was fun. The date was a blast, but that's it. Friends.

"You're a good mom, Katie." He repeats his words from earlier. Warmth and disappointment drip through me. "A damn good mom, always putting Cal first. Wouldn't want you if it was any other way. I think that's beautiful, how you put him above everything else. But do you think I haven't realized that? I haven't figured out you'd be hesitant to start things with me because of him?" My breath stops.

"I can't make promises, Kate. I can't and I won't. But... right now? I'm here through spring, bare minimum. The team plays through November, mountain is close enough to commute. There's a camp right here." He says it without saying it.

*If things are good, I could stay.*

"I love that you want to protect Cal. But know I'd never want to hurt him, either. And Kate, he needs a guy in his life. Needs a guy to show him how a man treats a woman, needs to see someone treat his mother well, help her shoulder the burden—"

"He's never a burden," I blurt out, because that needs to be clear. Dean smiles.

"I know, baby. He's not. But being a single mom? That's a heavy weight and you've been shouldering it for too long. Your back is bowing, baby. You need a break. You need someone to come help you lift it. Cal needs to see there are people out there who can do that. To see that's what a man does, so one day when he has a woman, he knows how to act."

I smile.

"You're gonna be that?"

"I'd like to try," Dean says, hand on my jaw and tilting it up to his.

"Then I'll give you a shot, Dean. Please don't make me regret it," I whisper against his lips before he kisses me again.

# TWENTY

-Kate-

"You're taking me to the beach?" I ask with a laugh as the sign reading, 'Welcome to Ocean View' comes into sight. We drove about an hour south, but the whole time I was clueless as to where we were going.

Yesterday I was told—yes, told—by Luna that I wasn't working today. I was also told my son would have a sleepover at Autumn and Steve's and I'd be picking him up the following day.

It seems Dean called in the cavalry and they were all more than happy to throw in. Now I'm in Dean's car as we drive to the destination of our first date.

Well, our first solo date.

"Yup," he says, a smile on his lips. "I've never been to the Jersey Shore. Figured this was my chance while I'm here." It doesn't sit well with me, that 'while I'm here,' but I force it back. For once in my life, I need to live in the moment. The last time I did that... well, shit, it was probably what got me pregnant with Cal if I'm being honest.

"Don't expect an excess of fist pumping and muscle tees," I say in reference to the show that gave every Jersey girl both a feeling of excitement, because, hello, Jersey, and frustration, because, hello, half of those goons weren't even *from* Jersey.

"So I hear. Tanner said this town's fun, more low-key than Seaside, though." I nod, remembering Tanner's older brother left Springbrook Hills right after graduation and moved down here. Add him to the 'never coming back to Springbrook Hills' list.

"Do you have a plan while we're here?" I ask, looking for a parking spot, which is always a nightmare if you come down this way on a weekend.

"Nope." I stop and stare at him.

"What do you mean, no?"

"I mean, I don't have a plan."

"But it's... a date. You planned it."

"I planned coming down here."

"And then what?"

"Don't know. We'll figure it out." My anxiety rises. If there's one thing that puts me on edge, it's not having a concrete plan. Somehow, Dean, as always, sees this and nips it. "Stop. Your entire life is one big plan. You live on schedules and plans and running from job to job and task to task. You need some chaos and spontaneity in your life."

"I have plenty of chaos in my life, thank you very much," I say, crossing my arms over my chest as Dean parallel parks. He does that thing guys do that's unbelievably, unbearably hot for literally no reason, his arm slinging around the back of my seat, bare bicep flexing beside my head, and shit, he's hot. This man should not be allowed to be this sexy. He's around children all day. That can't be legal, right? A hot as fuck man around young impressionable minds?

"No, you don't," he says, and it takes a moment for my brain to remember my last words. "You don't have true chaos. You have chaos you create because you overthink things and you don't let people help you." I sit stunned.

"Excuse me?"

"You don't have to be sunshine and rainbows, Katie, but chaos?

Chaos is fun. Chaos is exciting. You live... predictable and unneces-
sarily burdened because you won't take the help those who adore you
give." An eyebrow is raised and I want to argue. I'm actually kind of
mad now, his words striking a nerve that usually lies untouched. But
then his words sink in. *Those who adore you.*

"Do you adore me, Dean?" The words spill out without my
permission, and I wish I could take it back, pull the words back in.
But once again, he sees that somehow, smiling big and putting a firm
hand on my chin, tipping it up, and pulling my face to his.

"I think I could, Katie," he whispers before he presses his lips to
mine. My body melts, warmth dripping through me in a PG replica-
tion of that night on my couch. When he breaks the kiss, he stares at
me and smiles.

"Let's go," he says, the words a whisper, and all I can do is nod at
him before we're off.

———

An hour later, we're sitting on one of those recycled plastic benches
facing the water, feet propped up on the railing, each holding a slice
of pizza the size of our heads.

"Okay, you're right. This is the best pizza ever."

"You go to the boardwalk, you get a giant slice of pizza from
Three Brothers, boardwalk fries, and then end it with Kohrs soft
serve. It's a law, I'm pretty sure."

"A law, huh?" he says with a laugh, and I just smile and nod,
taking a bite of my giant ass pizza. "So, is ice cream next?" I shake my
head.

"No, next is an arcade." He raises an eyebrow and fuck, I can't
help it... I laugh. My insides are so damn free right now, like that first
time your parents take you to the shore and you get the wristband for
the rides and unlimited junk food and arcade tokens.

It's strange sometimes, having a kid young. I had Cal when I
was almost 22. I got a total of two months being 21 and unattached.

When Cal was born, I had friends, of course, but I didn't have time.

And when the time you had for your friends dwindles, so do your friends. And the ones who stick around, they stop coming around when you have nothing to talk about anymore. It's not on them—not completely. But when you can only meet between naps and the only insight you can add to a conversation is spit up and diaper changes and searching for a daycare, while they can talk about fancy new jobs and chasing dreams and seeing some local celebrity at a club... Well, you just drift.

And when you're the sole provider for a child, the person who has to be responsible and capable and... together every single day, you just become less... fun. I actually can't remember the last time I had fun. That's.... sad, right? Depressing, even.

Of course, I have fun with Cal and with the girls, but it's different. With Cal, it's kid fun, mom fun. The kind of fun I know I need to have now or regret when we're both older and I can't turn back time. And with the girls, there's always a deadline—I need to get back by X time to get to Cal or they have to be home by Y when their man gets home.

But here, hanging out like I'm a teenager on my first date with a boy at the Jersey shore? I'm having fun.

"You have to win me a prize, Mr. Fulton."

———

"Cal's going to love this," I say, staring at the giant bulldog plush Dean is holding. I'm holding an equally large plush pink unicorn and, god, as cheesy as it is, having a boy win me a prize at the boardwalk is a *rush*. It didn't take long for Dean to find one of those basketball-throwing games he played with Cal. We stood there for a couple of rounds, battling to see who would win before we moved to one where you throw a football at a moving target.

Dean took a video of me absolutely sucking at *that* one while laughing at me. He sent it to Autumn who I'm sure showed Cal. He's totally going to make fun of me tomorrow, but I can't quite figure out how to find it in me to care.

"Next time we'll bring him," he says, putting a strong arm around my shoulders and guiding me back to the boardwalk where the crowds are bigger than before There's music playing and people laughing, but that all melts away with his words.

I've avoided dating for so many reasons, most prominently the convenience and time factor, but one was most definitely that I will never put my son below a man or stop talking about him.

I always figured if I was on a date and talked about my kid, bought him up incessantly, it would be a black mark on my dating score card—and I've been proven right on that the few times I've tried dating as a mom. Men in my dating range... they're not looking for a pre-made family, no matter how cool the kid is.

But Dean...It's like he gets it. It's like Cal is a bonus, not a weight he'll endure to date me. That light inside shines its warmth through me a bit more.

"Okay, so what next?" I say, moving the conversation along so I don't get caught up in it. Dean's quiet, and when I look up at him, he's smiling down at me, not his normal huge grin, but a smaller, softer one.

"Wanna do something fun with me?" His face holds a challenge I can't decode, but his words... It's like he can hear my thoughts on not having fun, testing me to see just how much fun I'm willing to have.

And being one to never back down from a challenge, I smile back at him and nod. "Let's do it."

# TWENTY-ONE

-Dean-

KATE IS STANDING in front of Tanner's brother's tattoo shop, holding that damn pink unicorn, mouth ajar.

"Not what you expected?" I ask with a smile, watching her look it up and down like she's trying to figure out what she's seeing.

We're standing on a quiet end of the boardwalk. To the left is a gift shop, hermit crabs scurrying around in colored seashell homes waiting for some kid to trick his parents into buying one, an empty business with a 'coming soon' sign to the right. And right in front of us is a tattoo shop with a black and white awning, neon lights in the front window, and even from here, you can see the walls plastered with drawings and sketches of tattoos.

"I... I don't know what I expected?" she says, blinking again. "Is this Ben's place?" She means Tanner's brother, Ben. A strange part of me I refuse to acknowledge has a spark of jealously at the mere thought of her knowing who he is. But then I remind myself that unlike any of the other towns I've traveled to over the years, Springbrook Hills is tiny as fuck and everyone knows literally everyone, even if they left the town fifteen years ago.

"Yup."

"Oh," she says and pulls her lip into my mouth, gnawing on it.

"You don't have to. Fuck, we don't have to even go in. But I..." I lift the sleeve of my tee shirt to show her the quarter sleeve going down my bicep and across the back of my shoulder. "Need a new addition." She gasps.

"Are those... Are those real?" Her eyes are wide and glazed and she almost drops that damn unicorn as she reaches out to touch my tattoos. I laugh.

"Well, yeah, babe. They're real."

"I mean... I've never... Never seen them?"

"You've never seen me shirtless." The blush burns beneath her tan skin and fuck, she's gorgeous.

"I, I mean, I, uh.." I put her out of her misery

"I have them where I can hide them. Some places don't like them. Don't want it to be an issue if one of my jobs is anti-tattoo. Not a problem with the mountain jobs, but in the summer... you never know."

Her fingers trace over the different pictures, the feeling going right to my cock. Of course, my mind instantly remembers my daydream of her touching it, and the image of her riding my thigh until she came is burned into my mind indefinitely. Still, I get it under control.

"What are they?" She tries to take a closer look, but night has fallen, the boardwalk lit only by streetlights and the moon. I want to tell her she can see later when we're in my bed and she's too exhausted to move, but...

"They're for everywhere I've been. I get one for every summer camp and every mountain." She looks at them in awe, her eyes wide and breath hitting my skin. She's so close. God, I want this woman.

"Like a scrapbook."

"Exactly," I say with a smile. I've never thought of it that way, but it is kind of. "You have any?"

"Scrapbooks?"

"Tattoos." She blushes and looks away and holy shit. I've never seen any ink on her when she's in her shorts and tanks. They often ride up, my eyes always wandering to that exposed strip of tan skin, so I know there's nothing on the small of her back...

"I have one. It's tiny, a little heart. I got it when I was twenty."

"Where is it?" I ask, and I don't mean to, but I do anyway, the words falling from my mouth without passing my mental filter. I stare at her, silently begging for the answer. The blush, the fact I've never seen it...

"You'll have to find it." She pauses, smiling at me before taking a step towards the tattoo shop. Then she looks over her shoulder, her smile part teasing, part shy as she says, "Tonight." Then she walks into the tattoo shop and I follow behind, as always, in awe of this woman.

"Hey, I'm lookin' for Ben?" I ask the pretty girl at the front desk when we walk in. She has black hair to her shoulders and blunt bangs, big cat-eye glasses, and three piercings on her face—her upper lip like a beauty mark, her nose, and her eyebrow.

"Hey there, hot stuff," she says with a smile. And apparently a flirt. Kate tenses next to me, and I wonder for a split second if I'll get to witness a cat fight. That actually sounds pretty hot. "Calm down, girlfriend, that's just my thing," she says to Kate with a wink and a smile on her red-painted lips.

"It is," a man says as he walks in, looking at his receptionist with a chastening look that also seems like he's both used to and accepting of her behavior. Looking at the guy, I know exactly who he is.

He looks very much like his younger brother if not for a sharper jawline and the piercing in his eyebrow., His hair is similar in length to Tanner's, shortish on the sides and longish on the top, but his is combed back artfully, with more care and precision. Tanner usually has some kind of hat hair we all make fun of him for.

"You lookin' for me?" He even sounds like Tanner, and it makes me wonder if they looked like twins as kids.

"Hey, man, I'm Dean. Your brother told me you might be able to fit me in today?" I stick out a hand to him, and he takes it.

"Oh, yeah, Tanner told me about it. Didn't know you'd be bringing a pretty lady with you though." He smiles at Kate and fuck if now I'm not tensing up. I really don't want to fight Tanner's brother.

"And *that's* just *his* thing," the receptionist says, her voice smokey and laugh filled.

"Shut it, Hattie," Ben says over his shoulder. "What can I do for you guys?" I drop the stuffed animal we got for Cal into a chair, and instead of lifting the sleeve again, I reach behind me and take my shirt off completely. I glimpse quickly at Kate, whose eyes are locked on me, and it takes everything in me not to smile.

I fail, of course, and the smile is returned by Ben who seems to understand. "I need to add to this," I say, turning to show him my shoulder. It's something I started that first summer after Jesse when I went to a camp in Colorado. I saw a gecko that reminded me of this little stuffed animal he'd bring in toward the end when he wanted a comfort animal. I felt like it was sent by him to tell me he's good, he's happy, and I did the right thing by leaving. So I got the little lizard tatted on my back shoulder, to keep him close.

I didn't lie when I told Kate I got the tattoos to remember where I've been, but it's more than that. There are two mountains and one camp not represented on my body, because it's not about the camps—it's about Jesse. Everything on this arm is something that reminded me of him.

Something reminding me of why I need to work with these kids. Why I need to wander and take in the world and live the life Jesse didn't get to experience, but also why I cannot form a connection with anyone or risk it destroying me.

"Yeah, for sure. Something small?" he asks, walking around to check my arm. Some of it is done better than others, some old and fading.

"Not huge, not tiny. Keeping in line with everything else." Pulling my phone from my pocket, I swipe to find a photo. "This," I say, showing him the mascot for the peewee Bulldogs. Kate must see it and a tiny gasp comes from her lips, the sound I'm dying to recreate in a different setting.

"He's going to freak, you know," she says.

"Who?" Ben asks

"My son. He's seven, almost eight. Dean coaches the peewee team with Zander."

"No way. I started in peewee. Go 'Dogs," he says with a raise of his fist.

"I'm pretty sure every guy in Springbrook Hills did," Kate says with a tease.

"True. Too bad I wasn't as good as my pretty boy brother." He smiles and winks at Kate, and Jesus fuck, that *jealousy* comes back with a force. It's so unfamiliar to me. I usually could give two fucks who the girl I'm seeing flirts with—I won't be there for long. But with Kate...

"And what about you, sweetness?" the receptionist, Hattie, asks. "You gettin' anything?" I start to say no, that it's just me—I know I joked about her doing it too, but I wasn't serious. But as always, Kate surprises me.

"I've been dying to get my son's birth flower," she says, slipping down the strap of her tank top to reveal clean, smooth skin. "I'm thinking here," she says, patting the area on the back of her shoulder.

"What's his flower?" Lola asks, flipping through a binder she pulled off a shelf.

"A marigold. October."

"Ooh, a Halloween baby?"

"Not quite—but he was born on Friday the thirteenth, so..."

"You're living Hat's dream," Ben says with a laugh, and I wonder if they have a thing, their closeness and flirting.

"Totally," she agrees with a smile before turning the book to Kate. "What about something like this?" She shows her a simple orange flower and Kate beams.

"Yes! Exactly! Could you fit me in?"

"I have a cancellation. Ben can take your man and I'll do you, sound good?" Kate looks at me, waiting for me to agree or decline. I nod and then we're both swept off to separate parts of the shop.

The entire time I'm on my stomach, getting my new piece put on by Ben, I hear Kate giggling with Hattie.

"She always like this?" Ben asks. "Giggly?" I smile.

"No, not even a little."

"Yeah, Hat can do that, get people comfortable, even the most uptight."

"She's a single mom, a lot on her plate. It's not that she's uptight, it's that she doesn't let herself relax," I defend. Ben lifts his hands in surrender.

"Woah, not saying anything against your woman, just saying Hattie can calm people." I remind myself what a fucking moron I'm being, especially since this man has a damn tattoo needle on my skin. "So, how long have you been together?"

Another difficult question. Because, if I go by the time I saw her and some part of me decided I wanted her, two months. If we're going by how long we've been dating? Well.. a week to three hours, depending on how you look at it.

"Not long," is my response. Good enough.

"Seems sweet. Kid any good on the field?" I nod. Not because it's the nice thing to do, but because Cal really is good. It took him a week or so to get relaxed, to trust his team, and another week to nail the basics, but the kid's fast, can throw well, and takes criticism perfectly.

Ben and I have simple conversations while he does the bulldog, mostly about football and Springbrook Hills, and he gives me a few stories to humiliate Tanner with the next time I see him before Kate walks in. She still has that one strap down, and plastic is taped over her shoulder.

"Let me see," I say, using a hand to gesture her forward. She walks until she's right in front of me, squatting and showing me her back. Through the plastic covering, there's a vibrant orange flower, simple and beautiful and perfect for Kate. She stands and sits on the chair facing me.

"Gorgeous." I turn my head to Hattie. "It looks beautiful; you do great work."

"Hey, remember who's working on you," Ben says with a laugh.

"I'm sure you do great too, but you're taking your sweet time back there," I say with a laugh.

"Yeah, yeah. I'm almost done. Stop squirming," Ben says before he wipes it down and adds a layer of goo on top. "Come on, stand up," he says, handing me a mirror and putting my back to a larger one.

Looking into the hand mirror, I see a black and white bulldog, the perfect replica of the mascot for the kids. But instead of the collar with its little red 'S,' there's a 'C.' It's a last-minute decision, one I didn't plan on when I originally decided on this tattoo, but seeing it there, it's perfect. A 'C' for Callum, the most potent reminder of Jesse yet.

"Oh my god, it's perfect!" Kate says from behind me, a small squeal of excitement. "It looks so good and it goes so well with..." Her voice drifts off, her hand moving closer to the tattoo but not touching it. "Is that a..."

"A 'C,'" Ben states, but her eyes are locked on mine, knowing.

"A 'C.'" Her eyes hold awe and questions, but I just smile. Mostly because I don't have any other answer. It's just... a C. For Callum. And I don't know why or what it means other than that. I refuse to dig into it.

When we leave, we fight for a brief moment over my paying, but lucky me, they already had my card on file and I was signing before she could throw much of a fit. Kate mumbled something about paying me back and waved as we walked out, making plans to come down next time with the whole crew. For a woman who doesn't have time for friends or herself, it's clear she loves people, talking to them, making plans with them.

Normally, I find that part of her fuckin' adorable, wanna work to give her that freedom, but right now...

I pull her by her hand down the boardwalk, the soles of her Vans clumping as she struggles to keep up until I find a small alley between two buildings on this less busy side of the boardwalk.

"Dean, what are you—"

But I'm pressing her up against the brick, still warm from the later summer sun despite the slight chill of the breeze coming off the ocean.

Her eyes are wide, staring at me and gleaming in the moonlight as I press my hips to her, pinning her to the rough brick. One hand is on her waist, the other on the wall next to her head as I dip mine down, pressing my forehead to hers.

Kissing Kate is all I've been able to think about since that night on her couch. Of course, her moans, the grinding of her against me, the way she cuddled to me after, the scent of her that lingered on my shirt as I drove home... yes. That all makes me hard every time I think of it, consuming my mind.

But that kiss.

The feel of her soft lips, tentative and sweet and nervous, the taste of her, the way she just... fit with me.

It's something that both scares me and excites me in a way I can't put into words.

"Can I kiss you?" I ask, and I feel almost silly doing it, considering, again, the couch and the fact that we're on a date and, of course, the fact I didn't ask if I could press her against a wall... but when I do her eyes flare and her lips tip up and it was the right choice. The *way* right choice.

And when her head nods ever so slightly in confirmation, I move in, first with a tentative brush of my lips to hers, a gentle hello that's a sharp contrast to the feelings running through me.

Then her arms are lifting, wrapping above my neck and pressing into me, deepening the kiss and poking her tongue at me. That's all it takes for me to lose it. I'm pressing her tighter to the wall, grinding my hard cock into her soft heat, mindful only of her fresh tattoo and tangling my tongue with hers. I nip at her lip and she moans, a leg hitching to wrap against my hip, grinding to get more contact.

Never one to disappoint, I use the hand I have on the wall to grab her ass, helping her to move up and wrap fully around me. The change in position as I press her to the wall more has her fully on top of my dick, painfully hard, and she's moving now, a cruel impression of what I want to do to her. I use both hands on her ass to urge her on, setting a pace I've been dreaming of for weeks, and she moans deep.

Right as she begins to move on me, feet clump down the board-walk, a crew of what's probably teens running down and laughing and, unfortunately, breaking me from my sex-induced stupor.

Unfortunate, because I need this and know the drive back to my apartment will be nothing but blue balls. But also fortunate because I wasn't too far from making a decision to move her soft shorts to the side, unzipping my pants, and sliding into her.

Now that would have been a bad idea.

I mean, probably.

At the very least, I need to tell myself it would be a bad idea before I'm fucking her right here.

"We need to get to a bed," I say, not even specifying which because I truly don't care. I'm softly kissing her now, small pecks, and she's returning them as if we both know this needs to stop, but we just can't do it.

That's how it is for me, at least.

"Yeah," she replies, her voice breathy, but she continues her assault, tiny kisses between panting breaths and slight wiggles of her hips. I hold them tighter, my lips curving up into a smile.

"Yeah, Katie. We need to get to a bed. As soon as possible."

"Yeah," she breathes again and I laugh this time.

"To do that, you need to stop kissing me and let me put you down." And then the woman pouts—uptight, serious, overworked, and overtired Kate pouts. It takes everything in me not to laugh at her, but something tells me it wouldn't help my mission of getting into her pants tonight.

"Okay," she says and slowly unwraps her legs from around my waist until I set her down, her body sliding down mine in the most painful torture imaginable.

"Let's go," I say, grabbing her hand and walking her back to the car.

# TWENTY-TWO

-Kate-

I'VE NEVER BEEN into the apartments on the edge of town. I had friends in the ones on the other side, the smaller apartments close to the school, but the Bridgeview apartments are larger, newer, and, from what I can tell, fancier. When we walk into the apartment, I look around, trying to take in the large and surprisingly tidy space. Dean's leaning against the wall, arms crossed over his chest. "It's, uh, nice. Your place. Bigger than I thought. I've never been on this—"

"Get over here."

"What?"

"I said, get over here, Katie." My feet obey before my mind does, slowly taking me to him, but not fast enough for his liking. When I'm maybe two feet away, an arm reaches out, curling around my waist and tugging me. I let out a squeal as he drags me into him, giggling until I hit his chest, his other arm wrapping around me. When I tip my head back, the look on his face registers in my mind, and I stop giggling.

The look is wild heat.

"Hey," I say, nerves taking over.

"Hey." His voice is low and growly, reflecting the look in his eyes.

"Your apartment is, uh, really nice." He smiles.

"Don't want to talk about my apartment, Katie."

"Oh." My eyes scan his face, but his are zeroed in on my lips. "Then what do you want to talk about?"

"I don't want to do any talking." He notes the confusion on my face. "I have a night with you, alone, in my apartment. The only talking we're doing is me telling you how to move." My eyes go wide, my pussy clenching.

"Oh."

"Yeah, oh. You good with that?" His lips graze mine, his hand in the back of my hair, keeping me in place. My urge to look away, to distract myself from the intensity kicks in but... I'm stuck.

"Yeah," I whisper.

"Good," he says and then he's kissing me, turning me and walking me back until I'm walking through a doorway into a hallway. His hands are on my hips, tugging down my shorts as we kiss, both of us beyond the line of flirting and kissing.

I need more.

So I help him, kicking off the shorts, my hands going to the bottom of my shirt, tugging it up and over my head. We break our kiss for just a moment as he continues to back me up until we're in a room, his room, I think.

Then his hands are on my bare waist and he tosses me into the air, and I squeal as I land with a soft bounce. Then I'm lying across his bed in nothing but a tiny pair of panties and a bra.

I should have worn the nice ones.

*Why didn't I wear my nice ones?*

I drape my arm over my belly as I watch Dean shuck his pants and do that thing guys do where they reach behind them, muscles flexing, and tug their shirt off. His tattooed shoulder is on display now, flexing as he palms himself through the dark grey boxer briefs. He's already hard and fuck, and this man does not disappoint.

He looks like what every flighty fuck boy hopes they look like, but grown up. All tanned from working in the summer sun, defined abs, and broad, broad shoulders I really want to lick.

When I realize I might actually get the chance to do just that, my belly flutters.

Then he takes a step closer, eyes roving my body and all thoughts leave my mind. "Gorgeous," he murmurs under his breath, as if it's not meant for my ears. He's crawling up the bed, kneeling between my legs before his hand circles my wrist, tossing it to the side.

"Dean, no—"

"Don't play that game." I'm confused.

"What?"

"This body is mine now. Don't hide it from me." I can feel my eyes widen, my mouth open.

"I have stretch marks." The words drop from my mouth, and once again I have to wonder wtf is wrong with me. This is not the moment for this, Katie.

"Good."

"Good?"

"You're not a little girl, Katie. You're a fucking woman. This body? All woman. A woman who created something so amazing with this body. This body I've been dreaming about for fucking weeks." My arm which was tensed to cover my belly again goes limp. "Since I saw you in that tee and those tiny shorts, all I could think about was slipping into this cunt." His fingers move to the edge of my panties where they meet my thigh, grazing the wet beneath the fabric and making me shiver. He smiles, having seen it.

"I want to see it all. Don't you hide what's mine."

I think a small part of me falls in that moment, when he's not paying attention to my face and reaching behind me to unclip my bra, removing it, and tossing it.

But I am. I'm thinking about all those times I looked at the body that was so foreign to me, so changed after Cal, and wondered if a man would ever find it attractive again.

And this man isn't just attracted to it, to me. He's claiming it as his own.

I breathe deep, my emotions stifled as his mouth goes to my newly revealed nipple, pulling hard, no gentle lick or caress to ease me into it. My back bows, hands moving to his hair as his other hand goes to my hip, thumb grazing right beneath the fabric there. When he sits back, he just smiles that boyish Dean smile, watching my chest pant, watching my body move with aftershocks.

"So are we going to hide this body from me again?" he asks, voice low, reassuring and also teasing. I just smile at him, eyes glazed with lust. "Good," he says before moving down my body, pressing kisses to my belly.

It takes several seconds before I realize what he's doing.

A kiss for every mark.

Every cluster where my skin stretched too quickly, growing up and getting curves. Where it changed when I was pregnant. He's pressing a kiss to each one, intuitively knowing where they are, where I need his lips.

I want to cry.

His face looks up at me, the teasing gone, serious in his place before he whispers, "Beautiful."

And then his lips are pressing right above the line of my panties, tongue coming out to taste the skin there, and I no longer feel the awe. Instead, there's an ache. An ache that grows as his thumbs hook into my underwear, tugging them down, his lips kissing a short line down, down, down. His eyes catch on the tiny heart to the left of my hip bone, low enough so my parents would never see. They flash to mine as his tongue licks it. "I like this."

I'm about to reply, say something witty or fun or... anything. But then his mouth is *there*.

And once he's there, all he does is kiss me. Gently, like he's just saying hello. My hips buck up, trying to get more, but once again, his smile is directed at me.

"Still." His words send a shock through me. "Stay still," he orders, and my body obeys without my mind's permission. "Good girl." I let out a moan, and he lets out a chuckle, but it's not the sound I hear, not the sound I react to.

It's the vibration of it as his tongue slowly circles my clit.

My hips buck.

He stops.

"Uh uh. Be a good girl and stay still, Katie. Let your man taste you." The sound I let out is childish and annoyed, but I stop moving all the same, breathing deep as his tongue returns. "Sweetest cunt I've ever tasted. So fuckin' good, baby." I fight bucking my hips as his tongue drags down to my entrance, curling to lap at me and move back to my clit.

"Dean!" I shout as his lips circle the spot I need him most.

"Being such a good girl, Katie. Should I let you come?" he asks, a thick finger entering me, instantly curling up to stroke the spot only I have ever found.

"Please, please."

"I like that, you begging," he says. Who is this man, this devious, controlling man in my bed?

And why am I so fucking turned on by it?

"Please, Dean, let me come."

"I will, baby. I want to have my fun first," he says, eyes glinting with humor before his face is in my pussy, eating me with vigor. The finger pumps as his teeth nip tender flesh, my hips working to stay still, trying not to stop this before he's done.

"Dean! I'm gonna—" I start, my pleasure climbing and climbing until—

He's gone.

And then he's not, kneeling before me, his hard cock in his hand as he strokes it, his boxers having disappeared at some point...

"I'm clean. Please tell me you're on something. I need to be in this cunt right fucking now."

All I can do is nod and say, "IUD." And then he's slamming into me, both of us making a loud noise, a satisfied noise, an all-consuming, life-changing noise.

"Perfect," is all he says as he pulls out again, watching where he disappeared and slamming in again. I wrap my legs around his waist, urging him in deeper. Out and in, out and in, slowly building me again.

"Fuck, look at you take my cock, Katie. Look at that. Fuckin' made to take this cock, yeah?" I nod. "Tell me, Katie," he says, one hand to my hip, one hand hovering over where I need him, eyes locked to me now.

"I was made to take your cock, Dean!" I shout, and god fucking dammit, in this moment it feels like I was. It feels like I was put on this earth to be fucked by this man.

"Yeah, you were," he says, his hand going to my clit and rubbing. My back arches, my hips moving to take him deeper, and that's all it takes to explode around him. "Fucking gorgeous," he murmurs. After I come down, it's clear the games are over, his eyes going dark and dangerous as I try and catch my breath, my body continuing to quake, his thumb continuing in lazy passes on my clit as his thrusts slow.

But not for long.

Just long enough for my eyesight to return, for my mind to come back to me.

And then he reaches behind him, unhooking my legs from around his hips and moving them up, up, until they're straight up his chest.

*Oh my god,*

I may have just come harder than I can ever imagine.

I may still be catching my breath, still dazed from said orgasm.

But the look in Dean's eyes tells me that was an appetizer. That what comes next is the real thing.

"Gonna fuck you hard, baby. You good with that?" His words are a growl, eyes hooded, mirroring how mine feel. My mouth drops open, my pussy clenching around him with his words as his lips tip up on one side. "Yeah?"

I can't speak.

He seems to know that.

He also doesn't seem to care.

"Katie, answer me," he says, a demand, and his arm goes out, coming back to slap the tender side of my thigh. My entire body is oversensitive, the move making my back arch, a moan drop from my lips. But all the same, I answer.

"Fuck, yes, Dean. Fuck me," I beg and that's all it takes before he pulls out, every thick inch dragging inside of me, before he slams back in, groaning out loud.

"This fucking cunt. Better than I dreamed. Fuckin' dream woman, Katie." The words are both unbearably sexy and shockingly sweet, but when he slams into me again, this time tilting my hips up to hit my g-spot, my mind goes blank again, pleasure shooting through me, drawing out another moan.

He does this again and again, targeting that spot, the power behind his thrusts impressive, sweat dripping off him to land on me. Seeing it, one hand leaves my hip to swipe the drip with his thumb before moving to my nipple, rubbing it in there.

"Pinch your nipples, Katie. Tell me how good I feel inside of you."

Another demand.

Another demand I give into.

My hand grazes up my heated flesh, moving from my waist to my breast where I grab it, pinching the nipple he primed for me between my pointer and thumbs. My back arches as an inhumane noise falls from my lips, pleasure overtaking me once again.

"You gonna come for me again?" I nod, no longer capable of words. I am. I'm shocked, but I am. "Come on my cock, Katie. Come on my cock and drain your man."

Those are the words that do it.

*Your man.*

And then I'm screaming, pulsing around him, this one stronger than the first, if not shorter. And through the chaos that is my body on fire, shattering beneath Dean, I feel my legs drop and wrap around him as he bends forwards, groaning his own release into my ear.

As I catch my breath, his weight strangely comforting me like one of those weighted blankets, I wonder if I'll ever be the same.

―――――

The sun is up when I wake.

It seems to happen a lot these days.

What doesn't seem to happen too often, though, is waking up wrapped in strong, warm arms. Dean's arms. I breathe deep and blink a few times, trying to clear my head of the fog of sleep or wake myself from this very lovely dream, but only one of those happens as the arm around my (bare!) belly squeezes and then begins to roll me to face him.

By the time my (bare!!) chest is to Dean's (BARE!!) chest, my nipples are already hard as they graze the light dusting of hair there. My mind is no longer in a morning fog but a Dean-induced one that is even harder to escape from.

"Morning," he says with a smile, pushing hair from my face.

"Hi," I say and a blush burns on my cheeks.

"Slept good," he says, his hand gliding down my back to my ass and back up. I *never* sleep naked. Ever. Not only do I live with an eight-year-old, but it's just... weird. And uncomfortable. Any time I do, I wake up regretting it in the middle of the night, throwing on a tee and sleep shorts.

But tonight?

Tonight I had the best sleep since Cal was born.

"Me too," I say, moving a bit to get closer, to feel him, to...

Graze his morning wood.

My eyes go wide.

And then my entire body goes gooey, the memories from last night still fresh.

"Get that look off your face," Dean says.

"What?"

"Would love nothing more than fuckin' you first thing in the morning."

"Well, then..." I start, my hand creeping across his chest.

"We gotta go get our boy."

My body stops.

"Our boy?"

"Cal's at Hunter's. Told Hunt we'd be there at 10. It's almost nine thirty."

*Our boy.*

Cal has never been anyone's but mine. Always us against the world.

But the thought of sharing that with this man, this man who would bypass morning sex in order to care for him?

The idea is intoxicating. So I smile, not fighting him, and we get ready together to go get our boy.

———

"Can we go to Lighthouse for lunch?" Cal asks as we walk down the winding walkway of Hannah and Hunter's home. Lighthouse is a classic Jersey diner that, as far as I know, stays open all hours of the day and makes the best of everything, from eggs and home fries to greasy burgers and disco fries to full turkey dinners. Oh, and everything can be ordered at any time of day. It's the magic of a Jersey diner. When I moved back home with Cal in tow, he instantly fell in love with the staple, and whenever it's his turn to request a meal out, we go to Lighthouse.

"Yeah, bud," I say, my mind still on another planet. *On another night.*

"Is Dean coming?" I stop walking.

"What?"

"Is Dean coming with us to lunch?"

"Mr. Fulton." A warm hand comes to my back, pushing me along, the sparse of it warming me through the late summer air. "Or Coach."

"He can call me Dean." I look up at the man in question with what I know is my angry mom face, the face Cal withers at when I throw it in his direction. But, of course, I am not Dean's mom and he just smiles at the look.

"At camp, I'm Mr. Fulton. On the field, I'm Coach. When it's us? He can call me Dean."

"Sweet," Cal says, and the words sound so *old* on him I almost don't argue with Dean.

"You're an adult. He should call you Mr. Fulton."

"Are we together?" The words are low in my ear, not for Cal to hear, but it doesn't matter—he's run ahead, hand on the handle of Dean's car, looking back at us impatiently like we're holding him up. Still, a blush burns my cheeks and a chill runs down my spine.

"Are we together, Katie?" I know he means more than just in *that* way. I also know he's shown me that's what he wants. So I nod, the burning blush reaching wildfire heat levels. "Then when we're together, when it's us, he calls me Dean." I can't argue with him. I wonder if that will change ever.

We reach the small black car and a bleep hits my ears, pulling me from my daze, and the doors unlock.

"So *Dean* is coming with us to lunch?" Cal asks as he hops in the backseat of the car, his voice clearly trying to make a point, but I don't hear him.

"What's that?" I ask, face screwed in confusion.

"What's what?" Dean replies over the hood of the car, door open, and staring at me like this is normal. Like we do this often, chatting while Cal gets in and he's annoyed because I always take forever.

"In the backseat."

"A booster."

"Why is there a booster in your backseat?" It looks new, a small black booster Cal is sitting his butt in and buckling into as if this is normal. As if he always leaves a sleepover, gets into this car, and buckles in while requesting his favorite diner for lunch.

"Cal needs a booster." I stare. "Technically, he could go without, kid's tall, almost eight. But I feel more comfortable with him in one." My eyes stay locked on him. "State law says 57 inches or eight years old."

"I know that. How do you know that?"

"Google is free, babe."

"Why did you google that?"

"Knew we'd be pickin' up Cal. Figured there was a chance I might be driving him more. No reason to keep moving his booster from your car to mine when I take him to practice."

"What?"

"And after school. No busses in town, not sure how you know he always gets where he's going. But you can add me to the list. Better to be prepared than always borrowing your booster."

*"What?" I'm so confused.*

"What aren't you getting?" He looks at me with an annoyed stare.

"Uhm, all of it?" I stare at him with a 'duh' look.

"Mooooom, get in the car! I'm starving!" Cal whines, and I look through the still-open door to him, buckled up like this isn't blowing his mind the way it is mine.

"Hush, you."

"Get in the car, babe." My eyes go back to Dean, confused and overwhelmed and oddly feeling like I'm the only one not in on this conversation. "Get in, Katie." His voice is lower now, sweet, and it's all it takes. I do as he asks, slamming Cal's door, slipping into mine, and letting Dean take us to the diner for lunch.

# TWENTY-THREE

-Kate-

I'M STANDING IN A DOORWAY, shocked.

This is because I knocked at the front door of Dean's apartment, heard a shouted, "come in!" and did just that. Now I'm standing in the doorway, watching my kid and Dean, who are sitting on the living room couch, shouting at a TV together, holding controllers, and... ignoring me.

It's been a month of Dean watching Cal after practice, of him lessening my burden, our duo slowly becoming a trio, and it feels... nice. I no longer wake up each morning filled with dread, with an unnamed weight holding me down. Instead, I wake up and, more mornings than not, I'm wrapped in warm arms, pulled against a bare chest.

"Hey, Mom!" Cal shouts, finally taking a moment to greet me. I still don't move.

"Hey, babe! No, go left. Left Cal! Your other left!" There are greasy paper plates on a kitchen table, a box of pizza half open with two slices sitting inside and an untouched salad next to it, the plastic lid still crimped to the foil container.

*"Get a salad. You guys need the veggies,"* I said when I texted Dean this afternoon after he told me he'd take Cal back to his place after practice.

"Yeah," he texted back.

To be fair, I never said they had to *eat* the salad. Just told Dean to get one.

Note to self: be more specific for future boys' nights.

I won't nitpick too much, though—it's our first sleepover here. Dean's slept at our place many times since we got together, but we've never slept at his place. But tonight Dean made the final executive decision to hop the last wall separating us. I dump my bag on the ground, picking up a cold slice before walking to the couch and sitting next to Dean. He leans over, hands still on the controller, eyes on the game, and presses a kiss to my cheek.

I'm shocked by how easy this is. Really, how easy it's been since that first date. It's like this is how we were always supposed to be, a mini unit of three outcasts.

"How was practice?"

"Good." They both say, and I roll my eyes. In some ways, dating Dean is like dating a bigger version of Cal, but in an obviously less creepy way. He really is a big man child. It should be a huge turn-off, this adult who loves to goof off, has no stable life or plans, but somehow it works for him. I love having this carefree energy in our life after spending years constantly stressing about what happens 'next.' Dean stays firmly in the present, and somehow it is so unbearably attractive to me in a way I never saw coming. It's like he's the perfect counterbalance to my own mentality.

*Slow your roll there, Kate,* I think, because words like future and perfect balance should not be in my vocabulary right now.

Or, maybe ever, if I want to keep a shred of my heart intact.

"Did you guys do more than look at that salad?"

"No," Dean says, and for a split second his eyes leave the game, meeting mine, and a smile graces his lips. I roll my eyes at him before standing and grabbing the second cold slice of pizza and the salad and plopping next to Dean on his comfy couch that came with the apartment he leases.

We spend the next half hour like this, Cal staying up way, way too late, but I let it pass because I'm not sure of the sleeping arrangement and I'd rather he be absolutely exhausted when he goes down for the night. But at around ten-thirty, Dean hits pause and turns to Cal, putting his controller down.

"Alright, kid. Pajamas, get ready for bed." And then a miracle happens—Cal smiles, nods, and prances off like he wasn't just told to put down his game and move on. I'm sorry, what?

Dean must see the confusion on my face because he laughs, pulling me in once my kid is out of the room and planting a kiss on my lips, a kiss that lasts longer than the normal three seconds when Cal is in our presence.

"I told him if he went to bed easy, I'd buy donuts in the morning," he whispers into my ear, and I laugh out loud because it's so *Dean*. Moments later, Cal runs out in his little shorts and tee shirt, looking excited and like his age, a pleasant change to his normal way-too-old-to-be-my-baby look.

"Mom! You have to see what Dean did!" he shouts from the hall.

"What?" I turn my head to Dean, who's smiling softly.

"Follow him." Cal turns around without a word, running into a small hallway across from the bathroom. When you walk into the apartment, you enter a large living space and kitchen combo. To the left is a small hallway with Dean's bedroom. To the right is a small hallway with the bathroom and what I assumed was a hall closet of sorts. But it looks like...

"Come on, Mom!" Cal shouts, and I try not to laugh at his excitement or give into the shiver running down my spine as Dean's hand sneaks under my shirt, pressing into the bare skin on the small of my back, and we walk toward the room.

But no amount of pushing, no level of excitement from Cal can prepare me for what I see when I walk into what I now realize is a second bedroom.

Inside is a small twin bed, the same as he has in the apartment. The walls are painted a bright green and covered in big posters of football players, individual Eagles in jerseys, and one of the entire team.

There's a small dresser with a football light on it and a frame with a team photo of the Bulldogs. An area rug of a football squishes under my bare toes and the bed is covered in Eagles emblems.

It's a boy's room made for a football-loving little boy.

And I know it wasn't like this before. He definitely didn't move into it like this.

"What... How did..." I ask, looking around.

"I asked him what he'd like last week. He said football. Luna helped me paint, had to pay her and Tony in beer but it turned out pretty good. Apparently, she painted their entire house." His hand goes to the back of his neck, rubbing there. A nervous tick that my brain can't place him ever doing before. My mind goes to Luna coming in with bright green paint on her hands and dodging my curiosity with a smile.

"You... you did all of this. For... Cal?"

"Isn't it *awesome*, Mom!?" Cal says with a shout, jumping on the bed.

"Callum! Get off that bed!" I say, mom mode going into effect.

"He's fine, Katie," Dean says into my ear, the heat of it sending chills down my spine.

"This had to have been..."

"Don't. Doesn't matter. Have no one to spend my money on besides Cal. And you. That's it." Warmth flows through me and, for some odd reason, I feel like crying. To hide that, I turn to Dean, burying my face into his shirt, sniffling and fighting a full-on sob.

"Katie, no. What's wrong?"

"She does this. When people do nice things for her," Cal says matter-of-factly, panting as he jumps on his bed some more.

"Don't jump so much that you have an asthma attack before bed," Dean says, and that's it. That's what does it.

In the past eight years, I've had no one to worry about Cal with me. No one to warn him not to eat too fast, no one to tell him to be careful of an asthma attack. No one to put him undeniably first. We have so many people in our lives.

More than most could ever dream of having. But I've never had someone to share this burden with, no matter how beautiful the burden is. And this. The room. Watching Cal and making him feel welcome, not like he's an inconvenience. The warning of a stupid asthma attack. God. *God.*

I realize then I could fall. I could fall hard and probably never recover.

I also realize that after tonight, the chances of me not having fallen are slim.

And finally, I realize I'm not sure if I care.

———

I close the door to Dean's bedroom, having brushed my teeth and washed my face, ready for bed. Except, not really.

"Did you really have to check on him again before coming in?" Dean asks, a smile on his face as I stand in the doorway. I put my hands on my hips and smile.

"How did you know?"

"White noise machine got real loud, then quiet again."

"You gonna be able to sleep with that on?"

"I have every night I spend at your place, babe."

"Yeah, but it's... different."

"Cause we're here?"

"Yeah."

"Only different if we make it so." God, he's so logical and straight-forward sometimes. He lies there, broad chest on display, sheets pulled right up to his lower abs. One muscular arm is behind his head, propped up on an abundance of pillows I always make fun of him for having on the few nights I've stayed here. He's absolutely perfect. In more than one way.

"You made his life today."

"Nah, just gave him a space of his own." I think back on all the times he's begged me to decorate his room in the various apartments we've lived in. Luna wouldn't care, but between the added cost and the fact that I never planned on staying for longer than six months, I never got to it.

"Trust me. You did something big tonight."

"Yeah, well, he deserves it."

"And you? What do you deserve?" I ask, my voice going low and husky, and the corner of his mouth tips up alongside his eyebrow.

"What do I deserve?"

"For being awesome. Watching Cal. Being there for him. Giving him a man to look up to. The room. All of it." I take a single stride towards the bed, bare feet whispering against the hardwood floors.

"What do you have in mind?"

"I think you know," I say, stepping closer again.

"Do I?"

"Oh, yeah." He sits up, the sheet falling down to the waistband of his boxer briefs. With his challenge, I jump onto the bed, a giggle on my lips as he grabs me by the waist, rolling me so I'm caged beneath him. I start to laugh, the sound happy and free before his mouth is on mine.

# TWENTY-FOUR

-Dean-

KISSING KATE IS an experience in and of itself, but kissing Kate when she's happy and free is euphoric. Knowing I gave her that? There's no word for it. My lips are on hers, pressing and melding, my tongue slipping between them to dance with hers, my arms nearly going weak at the feel.

She is everything.

She is so much more than I want to admit, than I can admit, to myself or otherwise.

So instead, I kiss her. I kiss her and kiss her until her hips are lifting to get some kind of purchase, some kind of relief, always ready for me. At some point, she wiggled out of those loose sleep shorts, and when I break the kiss to look down at her, they're stuck, hooked around her ankle. I'd laugh, but the look in her eyes...

Instead, I sneak a hand up her shirt, an old camp tee of mine that looks way fuckin' better on her than on me, until I reach her tit, tweaking her nipple with my fingers until her back bows, a deep moan falling from her before my mouth is on hers again.

"Quiet, baby," I say once I stop, moving to take her shirt off and toss to the side. "Can you be quiet for your man?" Her eyes flare, her mouth open, and she nods, but I know the truth.

There's no way in hell she can stay quiet without some kind of assistance. This woman is pure sex appeal, telling me what she likes and what she loves with the sounds she makes, and each one makes me unbearably hard.

I've been looking forward to getting creative for a month now, crafting fantasies that keep me up at night, my hand pumping my cock as they flash behind my eyelids. When I creep a hand down her belly, her pussy is soaking wet, and while I want to make this last, I need to be in her more.

With one quick pump of my fingers, I pull them out before putting my hands on her waist and flipping her, positioning her the way I want before giving her a love tap on the ass to tell her to stay there, stay still.

And then I'm on my knees behind Kate, taking her in, on all fours for me, dark, dark red hair over to one side as she looks back at me, her eyes glazed with need and want. Her back is arched, showing off her sweet round ass, and, fuck, I want to do this again, another night, a night when Cal is far away and I can hear her scream my name as I ram into her.

But this will do for now.

"Quiet, Kate," I say, palming my cock. She goes to argue with me, to tell me she will be, her stubborn streak showing, but then my mouth is on her dripping pussy, eating everything she has to give me, and she's fighting her scream. It's caught in her throat, mouth closed, eyes wide as she looks back at me.

I continue to eat her, nipping at her clit, tonguing her entrance as she rears back, riding my face the way she knows I love. One hand goes to her hip to pull her in closer, getting my face in deeper as the other continues to pull at my cock.

Until she moans. Moans loud and deep, her body tensing as it does, knowing her mistake.

I stop. She whines. "No, Dean, no!"

I smile as I straighten, eyes locked to her pussy, already swollen from my mouth and begging for my cock.

"Gotta stay quiet, Katie," I say, running a hand up her back, pushing a few strands of hair aside and then grabbing her shoulder.

"Dean," she moans, the sound quiet now, desperate.

"I know, baby. I've got you." I rub the head of my cock up and down her soaking slit, the feeling near overwhelming. "You gonna be quiet for your man?"

"Dean," she says, this one a bit louder as I slip in, just the smallest inch, but we're both so ready it feels like sweet, sweet torture.

"Answer me, Katie."

"Yes, yes!" Another inch. I glance down to see it, see my cock disappearing. It's glorious.

"Yes, what?"

"Yes, I'll be quiet, Dean." My name on her lips has me pushing in another inch just because it sounds so damn good. "God, Dean!"

"Love my name coming out of your mouth like that, baby. So fuckin' sexy. But you gotta be quiet when I'm fuckin' you, yeah?"

"God, fuck, yes! Please!" She's never going to stay quiet. I know it. She doesn't need to know the apartment is pretty well insulated though, so between Cal's noise machine still going and us being on the other side of the apartment? We should be fine. But like always with Kate, I love the game.

"If you don't be quiet, can I make you stay quiet?"

"Yes!" she says, and the whisper is also a shout. I smile, slamming in balls deep. We both moan aloud with relief because nothing feels better than this woman wrapped around me. Nothing feels more perfect, more right.

"God, baby. You feel so fuckin' good around me. Nothin' better." I pull out and she moans, low and soft, careful. So unlike my girl, and the thought of her obeying me has me pulsing inside her. "Such a good girl, being quiet because your man told you to."

I pull out again, slamming in and she squeaks, a noise to block the moan she's dying to let rip.

With that, I make it my mission to make her moan as I watch my cock glide in and out, helped by her dripping wetness. Using the hand on her shoulder, I slam her back to me with force after I retreat, my balls slapping against her with each stroke, each stroke having her clenching around me and fuck, I need to win this game.

My hand on her hip guiding her body comes back and lands hard on her round ass cheek and there we go.

"Oh, fuck! Dean!" she moans. Loud. Knew it, my baby loves when I get rough with her. I slam into her once more and stay there as she trembles around me, waiting for the next retreat.

But it doesn't come.

I stay there, planted inside, waiting.

Her head twists, looking over her shoulder, cheeks flushed, eyes glazed.

"Dean, what the fuck?"

"You got loud, baby," I say, and I'm smiling. I'm sure she'll call me a bastard later, but for a split second, I see it. I see the flash of awareness and then excitement. "Gotta keep you quiet now." Her eyes go wide as I reach over and grab the tee shirt I took off her earlier. "In your mouth."

"What?" she asks, but she reaches over and grabs it, one hand holding her up, and shit, she's never looked more fuckable.

"You've been bad." Eyes flaring, mouth opening. "Put my shirt in your mouth, Katie, so I can finish fucking you." Her eyes go impossibly wide and I wait, one second, two seconds, to see what she'll do, to see if this is too much for her. But then slowly, she brings it to her face and shoves it in her mouth before settling on both hands and tipping her ass back to get me deeper into her cunt.

I shouldn't like it.

I shouldn't.

But seeing her, on her hands and knees, my cock still planted in her, my shirt in her mouth, waiting for my next command?

Fuck. She's perfection.

Made for me.

"Good girl," I say and my hand moves back to her hip as I retreat once more. The moan that falls from her would be loud, but it's muffled now and, oh fuck, it sounds like music.

The sounds continue, raising in pitch and fever as I fuck her hard and without restraint, her hips bucking back into me, ass bouncing off my hips. My hand goes up, to her mouth, to the shirt and I press it in, leaving her nose free. I tip her head back as I lean over her so our heads are mere inches apart.

"You are the fucking hottest woman I've ever seen. So fucking perfect. You feel so fuckin' good. Such a good girl," I say, my voice gruff to my own ears, and her pussy flutters around me. She's close. I need to hold out.

I keep talking.

"You gonna come all over my cock, Katie?" Her eyes are wide, and with her mouth stuffed, my hand covering it, I've never seen something sexier.

"You like when I pound into your wet cunt? Like knowing you'll be sore tomorrow?" She nods again, a noise that I know is 'uh huh' coming through the fabric and that's it. I need this to be done.

"Come on my cock, Katie. Be a good girl and come for your man," I say and that's all it takes, all it takes for her eyes to squeeze shut, her ass to tip back and take me impossibly deeper, for her cunt to spasm all over my cock, clamping down as I come with her.

# TWENTY-FIVE

-Kate-

"Hey, Mama," I call, walking into my childhood home. "Hey, Vera," I say to the in-home help when I find her in the kitchen. A week after that night, I sat both of my parents down and had 'the talk' with them.

Dean was right—I can't do it all. I need to focus on me, and if the roles were reversed and Cal was constantly stretched too thin, I'd be mad he let it get that far without telling me he needed help. I told them they either needed to accept in-home help, someone who would come in daily and make sure the home is clean and both of my parents are in good health, or I'm looking into a nursing home.

At first, my dad objected, his stubborn roots coming out. "I can do it, Kate. It was just a rough week. I know it didn't look so great"—his hand had gone to the back of his neck, rubbing there—"but I just fell behind."

"I know you can, Papa. But I'm worried about you guys. This wouldn't even be for you, really. For me. I can't... God, it kills me, but

I can't be here every day to check on you. So much is going on between work and Cal and side jobs... If something happened and I wasn't here to check on you..." I paused, the panic creeping in. "I've been putting this off because I came home to help. So I feel a lot of guilt about it, but I just... need you to be okay with this. I'm coming to realize that I need help too."

"Jorge, let the help come," my mom had said, her voice still scratchy from her hospital visit. Her color wasn't perfect, but she looked better than that night, at least.

"Let the poor girl live her life! We got her home; we get to see our boy all the time. A girl shouldn't have to worry about her child and her parents non-stop. Look at how exhausted the poor thing is." She stared at him, and in some quiet, wordless conversation they've been sharing since I was a little girl, he nodded.

"Okay. We'll work on getting that, Kate." Three days later, I helped to interview Vera and chose her on the spot. She's been coming every morning since and all three of us are living under a much smaller cloud of exhaustion.

"Hello, Kate, how are you?" she asks, leaning over the sink in her pink flowered scrubs as she does the dishes. Every time I walk in and see her, a bit of the pressure eases, knowing they're cared for.

"I'm well, Vera, thanks. Everything good with my parents?"

"Yup, your dad just left for a poker game at the Center," she says as my mom walks in and rolls her eyes.

"Man has been horrible at poker for fifty years but keeps goin' as if that's gonna change." She sits at the kitchen table, patting the seat next to her. "Sit, Kate, darling. Sit." Like I'm a little girl, I do as she asks. "What brings you?"

"Brought you a treat," I say, taking out the small package from Rise and Grind, a slice of lemon loaf wrapped in wax paper. "Sadie sends her love."

"That Sadie is a gem," she says, grabbing the bread from me and picking at it.

"There's more for you too, Vera," I say, leaving the bag with a few slices on the table.

"Don't let your father know," my mom says. "Those are for me." I roll my eyes.

"Tell me about your life, my girl. I feel like I haven't seen you in weeks!"

"Ma, I was just here on Saturday."

"With Callum." Her words are definitive as if I should know there's a difference. I don't.

"Okay?"

"When was the last time it was just us girls?" I couldn't tell her, to be honest. The thought makes me a bit sad. "When Callum and your papa are here, you can't tell me about *boys*. And your mama wants to know about *boys*."

"Boys?!" I say, choking on the bite of dessert I snagged from her.

"Don't play dumb with me, Katherine Martina."

"Mama—"

"Callum told me all about this new Dean when we were watching him last. The football coach? Says he's taking you both on dates." I could kill my son and his big freaking mouth.

"He's just... a guy."

"A guy you're dating?" I hesitate. Of course, the answer is yes. But I don't want my mom to get the wrong idea. Fuck, I don't want *myself* to get the wrong idea.

"Yes..."

"And he's met your son."

"Well, he's his football coach, so..."

"Fine, play dumb. *And he's taken you and your son out on multiple occasions.*" I'm going to strangle Cal. "*And* he's had sleepovers with you guys?" That's it. I no longer have a son. Or at least, I won't when I see him.

"Yes..."

"And he's just a guy? When you haven't been with a man, much less let one around your son in eight years?" The cons of having a mother you're close to and love to pieces.

"Yes, Mama," I say slowly, the words holding double meaning.

"Why are you hesitating?" She puts her food down, settling in her chair with her eyes fixed on me, arms crossed on her chest. Her dark hair is short and dashed with silver, but looking at her, beauty is still there. I know I won't hate getting older.

"What?"

"You heard me. Why are you hesitating? Bask in this! This is the fun part! The exciting part!" I sigh. There's no way around this.

"It's not... It's not that easy."

"Only hard if you make it hard."

"Mama, he's not... Dean's a wanderer. He doesn't live here. He's here temporarily."

"And...?"

"And?" I stare at her, but she stays silent. "I don't want to get too attached." There. Easy.

"Why not?"

"Because if he leaves..." My words trail off and my mother's eyes get soft. It's not a softness that comes from understanding. She already knew my motivation, why I'd hesitate. The softness comes from the knowledge that I haven't quite accepted or vocalized these feelings.

"What if he doesn't?" The words come in almost a whisper, brought to me on a breeze and pinning themselves into my brain. *What if he doesn't?*

"That's not in my control."

"What is, my girl?" That makes me think. *What is in my control?* She sees this hesitation and takes advantage. "Nothing. Nothing but you and Cal, to an extent, are in your control. But you can enjoy being with him, let Cal get that enjoyment." I open my mouth to argue. "If Cal gets attached and gets hurt, that's another learning path for him, Katie. This happens. *Life* happens. That's something he needs to learn."

"There's more to it than just that. Dean has.. a lot of.. history. I think it holds him back."

"We all have history, my girl. It's about how you move on once it's recorded that makes all the difference. And who you let in to help you move forward."

This is what's running through my mind as I sit in my gloriously unbusy kitchen, waiting for the guys to come home.

*We all have history, my girl.*

We all have a history that impacts us, holds us back.

What's mine?

Leaving my hometown, loving being away, and then coming back.

Getting pregnant and doing it all alone, then making that my personality.

Refusing the help of others, others who love me and want to see me thrive.

Have those things held me back? Kept me from enjoying the now, enjoying the time I have with Dean? Have I spent years focusing on what comes next instead of enjoying where I am?

The door opens and Cal clomps in, sneakers hitting the floor as he throws his bag to the ground, running into his room.

Chaos has returned.

"Uh, excuse me, sir!" He stops, shoulders slouched forward, but doesn't turn to me. "Cal, you—"

"Listen to your mom, Cal. Get that bag and put it where it goes," Dean says before I can finish, and straight up, I think I might get a few 'down there' butterflies at that. It's strange to have another person to help with Cal. This man I'm dating throwing in on my behalf? Save me and my panties. That shouldn't be hot, right?

Even more impressive is when Cal turns around and does just what he was asked to do.

When Cal's out of earshot, I turn to Dean. "I so want to suck your dick right now." Dean bursts out laughing, the open, warm laugh he always seems to use around me, tilting his head back as he uses a strong arm around my waist to tug me into him. His lips touch mine when the laugh settles. Then his mouth is to my ear, hot breath grazing my neck.

"Save that idea for later, okay?" A chill runs down my spine.

"Only if you return the favor." My voice is breathy as he pulls back and smiles.

"Do I ever not?" I think about it, but I already know the answer, so I just smile.

"What are you doing next weekend?" he asks, changing the subject.

"Uh, working? I'm on Friday but off Saturday. On Sunday to open."

"Any way you could move that around? Close on Sunday?" His fingers come up to move a chunk of hair that fell out of my ponytail behind my ear.

"Uh, I'm not sure. Maybe? Why?"

"Tournament."

"What?"

"Just found out the boys made it into a tournament. Saturday. It's out past Easton, two games on Saturday, one game on Sunday morning."

"Okay..."

"And we need chaperones to come since it will be an overnight. All the kids got sign-up sheets, but if you're free, I can work some magic and make sure you're on my bus," he says with a wink and shit, he's handsome. So handsome, I almost forget we're not alone.

"Mom! Can you come? Please?! It will be so fun! Cody's mom is going to be there and you like her, right?" I don't mind Cody's mom—of the moms I know, she's pretty cool. But that's not what has me smiling at him. It's that he asked without hesitation, smiling from me to Dean and not even worrying about if I could make it work. That's what makes me answer how I do:

"I'll go and I'll help out, but not at night. That's my only rule. If

I'm getting a night in a hotel, I'm doing it alone," I say with a smile directed at both of them. Cal pumps his fist like he won.

"I think we can make that happen," he says.

"This is going to be awesome!" Cal says with a shout, and something about the look in Dean's eye tells me he agrees, but in a very different way.

# TWENTY-SIX

SATURDAY NIGHT I'm lying in the big, fluffy hotel bed in my pajamas, marveling at how nice it is to be alone, truly alone while Cal's having a blast with his teammates in a hotel room down the hall, chaperoned by some other parent who got the short end of the stick.

They won both games today, and if they win tomorrow, they not only get a big trophy and a check for the program, but they're going to the finals championship in November. We spent the night at some wild pizza restaurant, fifteen little boys giggling and shouting and running crazy while the grown-ups kept an eye on them but more or less let them do whatever within reason.

Watching it, I felt free.

Watching Cal laugh and shout and giggle with his friends—friends he didn't have just a few months ago when he was hating that we'd had to move here—it filled me with utter joy and comfort. Relief, even.

My phone rings from beside me as I watch some episode of trash TV with housewives arguing, a show I never get to watch when Cal's home.

Please don't be a mom needing backup...

*Dean Calling...*

An interesting change.

Hopefully, it's not some kind of emergency.

"Hello?" I answer, hesitance in my voice, fully ready to hang up if he's calling to break our deal of my being 'off-duty' tonight.

"What room are you in?"

"Excuse me?"

"Wanderin' the halls right now. I'll start knocking if you don't tell me what room number you are." I sit up in the bed, confused.

"What?"

"Kate, serious, what room are you in?"

"Why?"

"Because I'm coming over to fuck you." My entire body shivers.

"What?" My voice is lower, breathier.

"There she is," Dean says, his voice growly. "What room are you in?"

"I thought I was gonna get a room all alone?"

"Alone with me, where I can fuck you and not worry about your kid hearing." Valid. "Now tell me what room you're in before someone calls security on me.

"476."

"I'll be there in two minutes."

And one minute and forty-five seconds later (I wasn't counting, I swear), there's a knock at my door. I crack it open, leaving the chain in place. "Hello?" I'm fucking with him, of course. I don't know why, but I can't stop smiling as I do it. Something about Dean makes me feel free, giggly, and happy.

"You don't let me in right this second, you're gonna get punished." I hesitate, the idea not unwelcome. "Jesus, fuck, Katie, you want me to punish you, I will, but you gotta let me in." I close the door in his face, sliding the chain and turning the knob once more. As soon it turns, it's being pushed open, Dean walking in, pushing me back, and slamming the door behind him.

"You wanna play games tonight?" he asks, his face in mine as soon as I'm backed against a wall, his body pinning me there. My breathing is labored already, wetness pooling instantly. "Kate, answer me." I'm not even sure what he's asking anymore, but my brain tells me he's asking me if I want him to fuck me.

The answer to that is hell yes. Always yes.

I nod and his eyes go dark, pupils expanding to nearly cover the hazel.

"You wanna play games today?" I blink.

"Games?" *No, I want you to fuck me, you dumbass.* A wide, devious smile crosses his lips.

"Games, baby. Just me and you tonight, we can play all we want." Oh. *Games.* Yes. Yes, I want that. I don't know what it is, but I really want it.

I nod.

"So I'm in control tonight?" I nod again. "Fuckin' perfect." He steps back, looking me up and down. A smile stretches his lips when he sees my pajamas are just a pair of boy shorts and one of his old tees I've confiscated as my own. "Like your shirt, babe." I smile. "Take it off." I lose my smile.

"What?"

"Take off your pajamas. I want to watch." A small part of me quivers at the thought of Dean watching me strip in front of him. A much larger part panics because, despite our first time and every time since then, I'm still self-conscious about my body. But the look in his eyes, fire and heat and determination, draws something from me and I hook my thumbs in my underwear.

"Shirt first," Dean says, sitting on the edge of the comfy bed, the blankets a mess from my jumping out of it. I roll my eyes, grabbing at the hem of the shirt and pulling it up. "Slow."

"Bossy."

"Don't play games; you like me bossy." He's not wrong. With that knowledge, I obey, slowly lifting his shirt from my body, hyperaware of each inch of flesh revealed, feeling his eyes on my skin. By the time the shirt is over my head and thrown to the floor, I'm breathing heavy. "Panties, beautiful," he says, his voice a whisper, and his hand is rubbing himself over the sweats he's wearing, his cock already clearly hard.

My thumbs hook into my panties once more, slowly dragging them down my legs until they hit the floor, and I step out of them, one step closer to him. And then I'm standing in front of this perfect man who has taken off his shirt at some point, completely naked.

A part of me wants to hide, wants to put my hands over the places that are imperfect, even if they make me proud. But I don't. Instead, I straighten my shoulders, fueled by the fact that this man finds me beautiful, and stand there exposed in front of him.

"Come here," he says, and I once more obey, walking closer to him until I'm standing between his legs, his hands going to my naked hips, my center already throbbing.

It seems there's never a moment when I don't need this man.

"You wanna play tonight?" I look at him, confused. "You wanna be punished?" I can feel my eyes go wide, my breathing quickening. "Spanked" My mouth opens a bit, a necessity to keep my breathing in line. "You want that, Katie?" I lick my lips—they suddenly feel very dry. I nod, surprising myself. But... I really, really do.

"Need you to say the words."

"Yes, Dean. I want that." The words tumble from my mouth, but as soon as they do, his hand is to my neck, pulling me in and kissing me, hard and wet. Like he can't get enough of me either, like he's trying to take some unseen edge off. Then he breaks it, moving me until I'm situated with my belly over his legs.

I'm panting.

This was never on my 'list of things I thought I'd like.' I read 50 *Shades* like almost every woman at the time it came out. I read the spanking scenes and decided it wasn't for me.

And then Dean smacked my ass while he was fucking me.

And my mind has been changed ever since.

I thought Dean would be fun and easygoing in bed, the same as he is in day-to-day life, but it seems he suppresses some kind of hot Sex God vibes all day and then releases them when we're alone and naked. And I'm more than okay with that. It's why I'm already soaking when one thick finger trails up my inner thigh, swiping through my pussy.

"Already wet for me," Dean murmurs and I shiver. "You want this, baby? Want me to spank you and then fuck you?" I nod. "Use your words, Katie."

"Yes, Dean."

"Good girl. It's ever too much, you say stop and I fuck you sweet, yeah?"

I love that 'yeah.'

"Yeah, Dean." My words are shaky, my entire body on edge, ready for... more. I think for a moment he'll drag it out, or he'll mess with my head, that he'll..

But then his hand comes down, heat radiating with a sharp pain going straight to my pussy before he's rubbing the sore spot. I mewl.

And then again, a new spot, same thing—hand down hard, the sound ringing through the room, the feeling making me wetter, his hand rubbing. Again and again, a new spot each time until I'm writhing on him, moaning his name, arching into his hand to get more, to get relief from the ache he's building between my legs.

"So pretty, Katie. Your ass red from your man." I moan, loud now. "Fuck, yeah," he says, smacking again, but then he stops. "Holy shit," he says and I worry for a split second that something bad happened. "God, look how wet you are," he says, his voice filled with awe and pure sexual intensity. I feel his hand right under me, on his own leg, then moving up, through my drenched pussy, his whole hand rubbing me. My body jolts with the unexpected move.

"You're dripping onto my thigh, baby." Should I be embarrassed by that? I'm too far gone to be embarrassed.

"Okay, that's it. I need this cunt," he says before his hands are on the dip at my waist, tossing me to the bed. I'm on my hands and knees at the corner of the bed, my head facing him. "Suck your man's cock,

Katie, and then I'll reward you." My mouth drops instantly, my eyes so full of sex they can barely open, needing him, needing him to make me come. I'd do anything at this point to get it.

But as his cock slides into my mouth, as he groans and puts both hands into my short hair, grabbing tight enough it pulls at my scalp, I would do even more to hear that sound again.

"Such a pretty sight. Fucking your mouth, watching my cock disappear into you." I look up at him as he hits the back of my throat and moan at the look on his face. "Yeah, just like that. You suck your man's cock so good." We move like this, and it could be seconds, could be hours, but when my hand moves from the bed where it's bracing me down to my clit, he pulls out.

"No way, that's for me," he says. I try to move, but he stops me. "Stay there." Then he's moving around to the other side of the bed where my ass is in the air, and as I look over my shoulder, I marvel at how the bed is the perfect height. With no games, he lines himself up with me, sliding his head through my wet.

"Be loud. No one will hear you, Katie." And then he slams into me, going deep, and we both moan. The way he fits me is perfection, in a way that's almost worrisome. A part of me knows nothing will ever be this good. Ever.

Dean has his hands on my hips, guiding me, but not forcing it as I move back. "That's it, fuck yourself on my cock." And I do, moving and backing on to him, literally fucking myself, worrying about nothing more than making myself feel good. The noises coming from me as I arch my back and force the angle to change, hitting my G-spot, are near animalistic.

"Play with your clit," he orders. Shifting my weight to just one arm, I move my hand to where he's sliding into me, fingers splaying on either side to feel him moving in and out of me.

I start to wobble, the pleasure too much to balance on one arm, before his grip tightens on my hips, no longer letting me control the movements as he fucks me near savagely. I moan as he grunts, nearing that crest, clenching tight on him with each move.

"Come on, Katie," he growls, hands digging into my hips. "Make yourself come on my cock. Gonna come on your back and need you to finish first." A quiver, a step closer to the edge as I circle my clit faster, harder. "Been thinking about seeing that, my come on your back. Such a pretty sight, baby. Need you to come right fucking now."

"Dean," I whine, so close. So damn close.

"Come on your man's cock." As always, that does it. Something about being owned by him, claimed by this man, has me screaming his name as I collapse on the bed, my one arm giving out as the other continues to rub through the aftershocks which have my body jolting, the sound in my ears going blank and my body erupting.

Vaguely I hear Dean groan my name, pulling out to do as he promised, his come landing on my back. That should disgust me, but instead, a small second wind comes at the feeling, another small aftershock of pleasure.

Dean just laughs, knowing, always knowing.

Later, after Dean brought in a warm, wet washcloth and cleaned me off, after I finished getting ready for bed and after the lights were off, both of us snuggled into my big hotel bed, Dean asks, "So was it worth not sleeping alone?"

"So worth it," I say with a smile as I fall asleep, thinking I would be okay never sleeping alone again if it meant I got to keep this man in my bed.

When I wake, well rested and smiling, Dean is gone, but in his place is a cup of coffee and a note reading, 'Had to go relieve Zee— he's going to kill me. See you on the field. x D'

I have a smile on my face all the way through my shift that night.

# TWENTY-SEVEN

-Dean-

"Okay, first things first, we gotta teach you about your equipment," I say, helping Cal lace up the boots we grabbed at the rental shop when we got here. The employee discount was nice, but next year I'll make sure the kid has his own set for the season.

*Next year.*

"They're hard to walk in," he says with a laugh once they're on and laced tight. I try not to laugh as he nearly falls in the clunky snowboard boots.

"Heel toe, kid. Heel toe. Like this." I show him by kicking my heel down and following with my toe as we walk towards where our boards are. We're not doing much today, just the basics on the bunny hill, but fuck if I'm not pumped. My dad taught me how to ride when I was about his age, one of the few memories I have of the man, and I never stopped loving it. Cal doesn't have a dad to show him the ropes, but for now, I'll take over.

"At least I don't have to wear those," he says, pointing to a man in bright yellow ski boots.

"Yeah, boarding boots have a bit more give to them." I tug his board down. "First things first, we need to figure out if you're regular or goofy." I position him facing away from me.

"What's that?" With his question, I give him a push on his back and watch him jolt forward, his left leg coming forward to catch him.

"Goofy."

"What was that for?" He turns to me and his little face looks angry, and I try my hardest not to laugh at him.

"Gotta figure out which side you favor, so we know which foot goes forward. I guessed right when we picked up your board." Being his coach, watching him, dating his mom, I've spent quite a bit of time with Callum Hernandez. I'm surprised by how much I know about him, actually.

It's Sunday and Tony and Luna came home from some weekend trip late last night, so Katie offered to open the bar for her today at 11. She was bummed Cal wouldn't have a fun weekend, especially with the dump of snow we got on Friday.

I told her I wanted to take him to the mountain I'm working at this winter, now that there's a good amount of snow. It's my day off, so it's a perfect day to take Cal. I'd been contemplating it for a while, ever since he told me he's never been.

To my shock, Katie agreed.

It's the first time I've taken Cal out by myself other than for quick stops and it feels... nice. On the drive here he didn't stop jabbering, talking about how the big kids (Joey included) now say 'hi' in the halls when he passes them and how three of his teammates are in his class. (All things I've known for months, but kids are like goldfish when it comes to remembering who they told what to.) He told me his mom seems happier, and he's glad that she seems less stressed. This last one he said quieter, like he was afraid I'd think him less cool.

*Quite the opposite, kid.* The fact Katie seems less stressed, smiles more, is way less grumpy and uptight, and the fact I believe I'm a part of that thrills me.

But most of all, I just like being a part of their life. Being a part of this little family, if only in a small way. Since Jesse, I've never felt drawn to stay in one place longer than a season. Obviously Springbrook Hills was a great stop since I got to go to Camp Sunshine and stayed for the mountain, but looking ahead, I'm wondering what I can do next to stay in town longer.

Especially with the slip of paper Sadie gave me this morning burning a hole in my pocket.

This morning Cal and I stopped at Rise and Grind to grab coffee for Katie and me and hot chocolate for Cal, plus breakfast pastries to drop off at the bar before we headed out.

When I grabbed the drinks, handing the bag off to Cal who was already jumping off the walls, excited for his first day snowboarding, she also handed me a small paper cutout.

"Just something to keep in mind," she'd said as she slid it to me. I stuffed it in my pocket and we left with a wave, not looking at it until I was standing and waiting for Cal to finish getting his snow gear on.

"HIRING: Springbrook Hills Guidance Counselor"

Under that was an army of descriptions and required qualifications, all of which I met. My gut instantly sank when I saw it, churning with fear and anxiety I haven't faced in years.

My MO since Jesse's funeral, that horrid day I witnessed his mother throw herself onto the too-small casket, has been to sweep it under the rug. To put forward the happy exterior, to be the 'cool dude' who travels and wanders, making friends with everyone he meets but never a connection, never growing roots, never getting attached.

Attachment hurts.

I love what I do, being a camp counselor and helping with the ski school because I get to do what I love, what my calling is—talking to and helping kids—but I never spend enough time with them to get attached.

And then came Cal. And his mom. And this town, now full of friends, not acquaintances.

If you'd have asked me in March if I'd ever even contemplate settling into a town and trying with the job that nearly broke me seven years ago, I'd have asked you what you're smoking. But now? Could I do it? Could I try again, risk my mental health and heart and sanity?

What if it happened again, if I got attached and something horrific happened?

*What if it's time to get over that fear and live life?* a small voice asks in the back of my mind, a voice I've long forgotten and buried.

"Are we going up there?" Cal asks with fear in his voice, and it shakes me out of my deep thoughts. God, I need to focus. That can all wait. Giving this kid the best day of his life? It can't. I look up to where he's pointing and see a black diamond trail littered with moguls, boarders and skiers alike flying down. One falls, tumbling a bit and a ski popping off. Cal's eyes widen and I laugh.

"Nah, man, we're going over there." I point to a small hill with a magic carpet lift, like a grocery conveyor belt for humans. Cal visibly relaxes. "Come on, grab your board and let's go." I grab mine and show Cal how to hold his safely and we're off, trudging up to the entrance of the magic carpet, riding it until we're at the top.

There, I show him how to put on his board, tighten the bindings. We do a quick tutorial on the front and back edges, how to slow down and how to speed up before we take our first run down. It's slow going, lots of falling, and mostly just a loud scraping of the blade of his board as he tips it left and right to get down, but the look on Cal's face when he hits the bottom?

Priceless.

Pride and exuberance and accomplishment that I know I had a hand in.

We continue a few times, up and down, before I help him learn to point the nose of the board and use his toes and heels to cut down the mountain. The kid is good. Fearless. Most kids panic they'll face plant when they first start but not Cal—he just goes for it. About midway through the day, we decide to take a run down one of the beginner slopes, already upgrading from the bunny hill.

I show Cal how to get on and off the lift, and he does great down the mountain, impressing me once again. When we reach the bottom, I take off my helmet and smile.

"Awesome, kid! You killed it!" I say, putting out a hand for a high five. But he's slow to lift his hand. "What's wrong?" I look at him closer, and instantly it's clear something is wrong.

"Come, let's get you inside," Concern is overwhelming me, fogging my mind as I help him undo his board and my own, propping them up in some random spot I'll never remember and leading him into the lodge. It's warm but also loud as can be. I'm grateful when I find a spot at one of the long cafeteria style tables in a quiet corner, pulling Cal with me. I tug off his helmet, tossing it to the table, alongside my gloves. His mouth is parted, breaths shallow.

"Cal, what's wrong?"

"Asthma." The words don't come out easy, instead they come in gasps. Looking closer, I see the slightest tinge of blue on his lips. *Shit.*

"Hey, no worries. No worries." I think I'm talking to myself, not him. Trying to convince myself this is no big deal. "Okay. What do we do; what do we do? Shit." Those words are under my breath as I try to run through my first aid class like a moron. I've dealt with many kids at camp having asthma attacks, allergic reactions, diabetic reactions... all of it. I handled those fine, calm and patient with professionalism. But something about this. Being a kid I care for, a kid in my and only my care...

"Inhaler," I say, looking at Cal. "Where's your inhaler?" That's when the guilt covers his face. "Do you have your inhaler?"

His little head shakes. "Sorry... Dean... I... forgot..." Each word is punctuated with a breath. *Fuuuuuuckk.* His chest is rising and falling harshly with each attempt at breathing and my own mind is fogging with panic, seeing him struggle. *Shit, shit!*

Okay. Rational thinking. That's what I need.

I need to call Kate.

I also need to get Cal somewhere where they can help him. Because right now, I'm useless. There is nothing I can do at this moment to help and that's killing me, churning the acid in my stomach.

Which first?

Med tent.

"Come on, kid. Follow me." I leave our things there, grabbing his hand to guide him back outside. I want to run, to race there, but Cal shouldn't run. Can't run. Looking down at him, he looks so young, fear edging his eyes. So instead, I wrap my arms around him, lift him, and carry him there. "It's gonna be fine, Cal. You're gonna be fine," I say, walking with him.

But all I can think is, *will I be okay?*

————

Hours later, we're back at Kate's apartment, Cal lying on the couch playing *Madden* while I sit at the table, waiting for Kate. Normally I'd be sitting with him, playing with him, but right now I need the distance. I need to think, I need...

The front door opens, Kate walking in. Luna came in to close earlier than planned after Kate called her to tell her what happened. When we got back, she stopped in to check on Cal but had to finish out her shift.

When we got to the med tent, the doctor there told me Cal's was one of the worse asthma attacks he'd seen in a while. That made sense; his lips were nearly purple by the time I brought him there. What I never knew was the cold can exacerbate asthma, especially when paired with excitement and physical exertion. The last run was a terrible idea, that much was sure.

We spent an hour in the tent, half of which Cal had some kind of mask thing that put out a vapor to him to breathe in. The color came back to his face, and it didn't take long for Cal to start laughing with me, asking when we'd go boarding again. But all I could do was focus on the what ifs. What if I hadn't noticed? What if it had happened at the top of the mountain, what if...

When I called Kate to tell her what had happened, I expected her to act with the same level of panic I was feeling. Instead, her steady, no-nonsense personality shone again. She sighed, saying she reminded Cal to take his inhaler with him and asked to talk to him. They both seem so utterly unfazed by this experience that could have ended horribly. Do they not understand how close we were to something terrible?

Or even worse, that it was all my fault? How is Kate not freaking the fuck out on me? It's what I'm considering as I stare at the table, chipped and knocked wood that was here when Kate moved in.

"Hey," she says with a smile, walking my way.

"Hey, Mom!" Cal shouts from the couch.

"Hey, bud! How ya feeling?" she asks, sitting next to me.

"Good! Think I need to miss school tomorrow, though." Kate smiles and shakes her head.

"Good try, bud." Cal grumbles an 'aw man' as her arm goes around my shoulder before she notices how tight they are. She looks at me with confusion.

"Hey."

"Hi," I say, continuing to stare at the table.

"Everything okay?"

Not even a little.

"Yeah."

"How was Cal this afternoon?"

"Fine." I stand and quickly glimpse at her face. It's awash with confusion and... deep in there is hurt. "Are you in for the night? I have a lot to do before tomorrow. I'm working and need to make sure someone put my gloves and helmet into the break room."

Not a complete lie, but I know it was done. We never went back to the things we left behind, including our boards, but I texted a coworker while I was waiting with Cal and they sent me a photo of my stuff sitting in the employee area.

"Do you wanna stay for dinner? I was gonna order a pizza." She looks so confused and it breaks me. But I need this, this time and space to think and figure out what I'm feeling.

"I really gotta get going." I walk toward the door, shrugging on my jacket as I go.

"Hey, is everything... Is everything okay?" Kate asks quietly, eyes shifting to where Cal is because she's a good mom. A great mom. A great mom who deserves... more.

"All good, Katie. Gotta go," I say, bending down to press my lips to her forehead because I can't resist her before walking out of the door.

# TWENTY-EIGHT

-Kate-

ON MONDAY, Dean he texted to check on Cal.

> How's Cal doing?

>> Totally fine. He ran off with Cody as soon as I dropped him off this morning.

> Good.

>> Want to grab dinner after practice today?

> Can't, have plans.

After that, he didn't say anything else and I didn't push. It felt wrong, to continue the conversation he was clearly not interested in. But the words pounded in my mind all day.

Can't, have plans.

Can't, have plans.

*Can't, have plans.*

Funny how three small words can take over your mind. Three small words, not even spoken, just typed. Three small words that can absolutely destroy your mood for a day.

It's what I was thinking as I picked up coffee from Rise and Grind before I had to get my kid from school.

"Where you at, girl?" the familiar, kind voice asks, breaking me from my overthinking.

"What?"

"You were a million miles away," Sadie says with a smile. I like Sadie. She's fun and carefree, but she also has the same vibe as I do - not quite sure how we're still in this small town. I left and came back and have settled down. Since then, I've come to terms with, if not begun to love being back in Springbrook Hills. But Sadie... she left and came back, settled in, started a business... but it never seemed like she was happy to be here. Happy she settled back down where she started.

"Oh, no. Just... Well, I guess. Always have lots going on, you know?" She nods but doesn't say anything. For a talkative woman, silence means she's waiting for me to continue, to expand. Baristas can be a lot like bartenders. They see the same people day in and day out, learn their likes, their dislikes, their quirks. They also learn how to read them. And right now, Sadie is reading me.

But I'm also an expert at diverting when I want.

"Cal's got a tournament next week. Gotta take off at Luna's for a couple of days."

"Does she have anyone to help out?"

"Daisy." Sadie screws up her face when I mention the sweet yet spacey bartender at Luna's. I laugh. "And the new bartender, Micah. He's cool. I think she's training him to start helping with closing."

"Is that going to reduce your hours?" I sigh.

"Only if I want it to." Now she looks confused. "I love working at Luna's. Love how everyone has come together to help me, love living close to my job," Sadie laughs. 'Close to my job' is a bit of an under-statement. "But..." I don't know how to say it. To say I'm burning the wick at both ends and it's destroying me. Everyday I wake up more and more tired, trying to stay on top of everything. Now that things have stabilized with Cal and my parents I feel like I too need to stabilize. Need to stop doing all of the things all of the time.

It's time.

"But Cal." Sadie fills in my blank, knowing.

"But Cal. I feel like I never see him. He's getting older. He has practice and play dates now. And school full time and then most nights, I'm working. A lot of the time I get home after he's asleep and I only saw him for an hour during the chaos of getting him off to school. I know he doesn't like to ask me to do things the other kids' moms do, like volunteering or chaperoning. He doesn't want me to feel guilty, but I do still. I do." A lump has taken root in my throat and I try to swallow it and the rising, unexpected emotions down. "God, I sound ungrateful. I'm not. Not for Luna giving me a job or a place to stay, not for all of the help you all give me at night with Cal. Not even a little. I just... God. I wish I had more time."

"You don't sound selfish."

"I do."

"You sound human, Kate," Sadie says. "We've talked about it. Hannah and Luna and I. About how you're burning yourself out. We didn't want to call you out on it, you weren't in the right headspace for that. But we've talked about how we'll all help however we can when the time comes."

I stare at her in confusion. "You guys talk about me?" Sadie throws a wadded up napkin at me with a smile

"Shut up, not like that. Not gossipy. Just... you're our friend. One of us. We love you. We worry about you."

"Yeah." I sit there, stirring my drink with the straw and contemplating if it is in fact time to think about a new path.

"You know... I've been thinking." I look up at her and see she's taking me in with contemplation on her face. "I can't do this alone much longer." My eyebrows furrow, confused.

"Do what?"

"Rise and Grind."

"What? What do you mean?" She sighs and it's one I'm familiar with. It's one that comes from soul-deep exhaustion - not from lack of sleep but from lack of... life. "Sadie..." I never would have though this vibrant, exciting woman who is friends with everyone and would lay her life down for her friends... but it's here right in front of me. She looks around the shop, taking in who is around, what listening ear might record this exchange. That's another shit part about a small town - there are always ears around.

Thankfully, there's only one man sitting in one of the coworking cubicles with headphones on, completely oblivious to us.

"I love this place. Truly. I created something awesome here. Love that it's a staple for the town. But it's..." she sigh again. "Look, don't tell anyone this, okay? I haven't even talked about this to Hannah." I'm now both confused and worried. "And honestly, I'm only saying this to you because you... get it."

"Are you pregnant?" I shout, then cover my mouth, looking around again. "Holy shit, Sadie, are you pregnant?" I didn't even know she was *seeing* anyone!

"God, no. Shut up. I'm not pregnant." Her pretty blue eyes roll into her head.

"Okay, well, that's all I've got that Hannah and Sadie don't..."

"You never wanted to be stuck here." She stares at me with that look and now I know. "You never wanted to stay in Springbrook Hills. They did. Hannah and Luna? They always wanted to stay here, to raise kids here. And even Jordan - she always wanted this, to be rooted somewhere. But me and you?" She shakes her head. "You might be cool with it now, you have Cal, need to stay here and give him that stability. But you wanted out. I remember." She's not wrong. About any of it.

"I went out, saw the country. It wasn't for long. Not even two months and that's what always makes it feel even more stupid. But those months? Those two months? I felt free."

Sadie toured for a few months years ago with her then-boyfriend, the lead singer of Hometown Heroes. From what I understand, she came back after things went sour and never left, took classes online, started Rise and Grind and here we are.

"I started this place because it's what was expected of me. My mom was... disappointed with me after I came back and had no plan. So I did the good, hardworking daughter thing and created this." She waves her arm around the room. "But now it's my life. I wanted... I wanted to do other things, you know? Be creative and figure things out. But I'm so wrapped up in this that I just... can't. And Kate? It's killing me." I see it now. I see behind that fence she keeps up, keeping in the disappointment and frustration and loneliness.

"Oh, Sadie. Why don't you ever say anything?"

"I'm the fun friend. The reliable friend. Not the depressed friend," she says with a smile but it's strained. Pained.

"There's nothing wrong with being unhappy, Sadie."

"Oh, I know that. Don't get me wrong. I just... I don't know. I'm not ready for that. You know?" Her words mean more that just a statement. They're a request. *I'm not ready to share this, please keep it to yourself.*

"I know." And just like her, my words say more - this time an agreement, a promise to not say a word. "But I have to ask... why are you sharing this with me?" Then I stumble over my words. "Not that I'm not thrilled you are! Because I am. I'm so happy you're sharing, seriously. Any time you need to get something off your chest, I'm your girl." I'm rambling now, but Sadie just laughs and waves me off.

"Shut up. No, I'm telling you because... I want you to consider something." Her fingers play with already perfectly placed sugar packets. "I want you to consider coming to work for me." I pause.

"I'm sorry, what?"

"I need someone to help here. It would be mornings and after-noons. We close at five, but we could work together so you're out to get Cal, or he could come hang out here after school." I'm frozen.

"It wouldn't be full-time, not yet. And you could work with Luna to create a schedule with both of us, so you're not overwhelmed.

But... I need help. I need freedom from this place, which sounds terrible, but it's the truth. And I trust you. Luna says you're smart and good with numbers, you could manage the day-to-day stuff. I talked to Jordan really quick—she said she could help you with creating systems for the books and backend stuff I hate." I blink at her again.

"You don't have to answer now, I just... thought you might be interested." There's a long pause, a moment where we're both silent. She opens her mouth, panic and disappointment clear on her face but I speak first.

"I'd have to talk to Luna first." Sadie closes her mouth. "And figure out when she'd be able to reduce my hours. She comes first - she's helped me so much and I refuse to make things harder for her."

"Of course." There's hope in Sadie's eyes.

"And I'd need to make a plan for Cal, talk to him about it."

"Of course."

"And I'd like to keep it so I'm not working early mornings right after a late shift."

"I can do that."

"But I'd love to, Sadie." I look around and the hum of excitement runs through me. I recognize a brush of warmth and comfort I always feel when I walk in these doors, like some part of me knew this is where my next chapter would start.

And finally, finally, with Cal happy and connecting with friends, my parents finally agreeing to get some help, Dean in my life and now this? It finally feels like it's time to turn the page.

# TWENTY-NINE

-Kate-

EXCEPT, I may have thought that way too soon when Dean essentially ignores me, save for a short but sweet kiss to my forehead at practice that night. Cal was so hyped up about the playoffs happening next week, he didn't even notice the awkward moment, but I did.

I absolutely did.

And Tuesday, when I texted him my normal 'hello,' to which I typically get some kind of goofy come on, I got no response.

I sat on it for hours, overthinking everything, stressing about where I went wrong. I was slightly appeased when he finally reached out at ten that he was at the mountain working all day and left his phone at home. But still... it didn't sit well.

Things took a turn for the worse on Wednesday when he wasn't at practice. Unfortunately, I didn't find this out until Zander dropped off Cal after practice. Every Wednesday since that first time, Cal walks in with Dean and they hang out upstairs until I'm off the clock.

And truly, I was excited to see him, after the distance, after his weirdness. Excited to have a normal night for us at my place.

"Where's Dean? Everything okay?" Cal's face is unreadable but Zee's is... confused.

"He didn't call you?" I pull my phone out of my apron, checking to see if I missed something but nope. Not a call or text. I shake my head at Zee who instantly looks away.

"Zee?"

"He, uh... Dean called me this morning. He's staying at the mountain tonight, something about an early class in the morning." I blink at him, confused, frustrations building right behind it. "He asked if I could pick up Cal. Take him to practice and back here, then watch him until your shift is over." Confusion gone, frustration was front and center, *rage* right on its heels.

"And he didn't think to ask me?"

"Swear, Kate, thought you knew. No way I'd drag your kid around without you knowing." I want to yell at Zee, yell at Cal, yell at *anyone*. I really do. But... it's not his fault. Instead, I sigh.

"It's not your fault, Zee. Do you mind watching Cal tonight? I'll order you guys a pizza." He waves his hand at me.

"No worries at all; you know I love Cal," he says, looping an arm around my kid's shoulders and grating his knuckles into his hair, making Cal laugh.

"You can head out once Micah comes in, Kate," Luna says, coming up beside me. Worry is written on her face. Worry and confusion-the same emotions roiling in my own stomach.

"Thanks, Luna." Zee takes Cal upstairs and I call in a quick pizza order for them, but for the remaining hour and a half of my shift, I'm burning. *What was he thinking? And why wouldn't he have let me know?*

*Kate: Can I call you after my shift? We need to talk.*

I hate sending it, hate the words and how they sound, but they need to be said.

It takes two hours before he texts me back, the message coming as

I'm getting Cal to bed. Through those hours, the rage both increased and mellowed out. *There has to be a reason. There has to be an explanation.* He works with kids. He knows what a big deal this would be, to put the responsibility of my kid into someone else's hands without telling anyone...

*Dean: sure.*

*That sounds promising.*

The ringing of the phone in my ear as I sit on my bed sounds ominous. It's funny how mundane things can take on a new light when put in different circumstances.

"Hello?" he answers like he's not sure who this is.

"Hey, it's... me. It's Kate."

"What's up?" I blink, staring at the mirror across from my bed. Once, twice, three times.

"What happened today?" I'm giving him the benefit of the doubt. I'm giving him everything I can not to see the worst because this feels... bad. So bad. All week I've put on my rose-colored glasses and tried to see the good in this, but today was a tipping point.

Something is wrong.

"I decided to stay after my shift today. I have a class at eight tomorrow." *Eight? Usually, he's up at the mountain by seven, anyway. Why the hell is he staying there?* They have a limited number of beds in a bunk room for employees to stay in if the weather is bad, but he's never actually stayed there. Why now?

But my gut knows. My mind is just ignoring it.

And continues to.

"But I... You didn't tell me. Didn't call me." My voice is small... It's how I feel right now. Small. Insignificant. Not even worthy of a call to tell me my kid would be picked up by *someone else.*

"Yeah, I was slammed today. Figured Zee would let you know." *You figured Zee would let me know!? You chose to call your co-coach of a peewee football team instead of the mother of the kid you normally watch today? Instead of the woman you've been dating for months?*

I breathe deep, trying to pull myself together before I overreact.

Would this be an overreaction?

"I didn't know until Cal got dropped off."

"Oh, my bad." *My bad?! Is this real life?* I take a deep breath, trying to regulate my emotions before I say something I can't take back. Something like, 'You fucking idiot, what were you thinking? That was a dick move. What the actual fuck is wrong with you?'

"You can't just make plans for my kid and not tell me, Dean," I say softly. And when he pauses, I think he's sitting on it, learning from it, gearing up for some big apology, some explanation for what's been happening with him. *Anything.*

I would take anything in this moment.

"Sorry, Kate. It won't happen again." I sit there in stunned silence for minutes, waiting for more. There has to be more. There's no way he's leaving it at an apology you give your boss when you're 16 and work at the grocery store and shelve things incorrectly. Not when you 'forgot' to tell your... girlfriend her son was being cared for by another man tonight.

Nothing comes.

I wait longer, thinking surely there must be...

No.

And with how things have been this week, I don't want to push it. My gut says I should, I need to, but my heart is screaming at me to drop it, not to rock the boat, not to ruin this good thing.

So instead I say, "Thanks, Dean."

Because I'm scared.

Something in me is gnawing, a dog at a bone, telling me something is so wrong. So terribly wrong. That this beautiful glass house we built, this fragile relationship I've fallen in love with, is about to come crashing down around us. And I'll be left in shreds, shards of glass embedded so deep I'll feel them on rainy days when I move wrong.

Shards I'll never be able to dig out, forever weakening my heart.

With my words, the acceptance in them, we move on. The

conversation continues as if he can't see the cracks all around us, as if I'm hallucinating the danger.

But while the conversation moves, it's not normal. The rest of the phone call goes nearly the same, with my saying something and getting a two or three word response before, less than five minutes later, he has to go. He needs to be up early in the morning, needs his sleep. My mind flits through the dozens of times we've stayed up late into the night, fucking and chatting and laughing, trying to keep quiet while Cal slept comfortably. Through the times we've woken up after only a few hours of sleep, smiling and joking about how it was worth it.

But I don't say that. Instead, I say, "Kay. Bye, Dean. Talk to you tomorrow?"

To which he replies, "Bye, Kate."

And then I stay up late into the night, staring at my ceiling and trying to decode each of the dozen or so words he said to me today. I never quite manage it. The rock in my stomach grows that night, settling and growing limbs to attach to the walls.

———

Thursday, I finally talk to Luna about Sadie's offer and she's over the moon.

"Kate, you *have* to do it!" She's... excited. I'm not sure why this surprises me after my talk with Sadie.

"I don't know, Lune. I don't want to leave you in a lurch."

"We'll make the move slow, once Micah starts. And then you'll still be here, of course. Just not all the time. Not all the nights." She stares at me, and I stare back before she places her hands on my shoulders. "Kate. You've got a kid. You need to spend time with him. You also need a life. This?" She waves an arm around the bar. "This is my life. My baby. I'm lucky because Tony works nights, so our schedules work together. But also, babe, I'm the owner. This ever got to be too much, I could hire someone. But you—this is your job so you're stuck doing nights. You gotta keep Cal in football cleats and Doritos." I smile. "You need to do this. You need to take the job." I nod, accepting the truth she's giving me.

"You're right. But I... I still want to work here, okay? And... live upstairs. For now. If that's okay?"

"Oh my god, stop. Don't be stupid, of course! Not even a *question*. Stay as long as you need. Forever! And you know we'll all still be your sitter when you need. But you need to say yes to Sadie, Kate. For you. For Cal. For... whatever's going on with you and Dean." She squeezes her hands on my shoulders, her encouraging smile turning wicked. I wince before her face goes from fun to concerned. "What?"

"I don't know. Things have been weird for a couple of days. I'm sure it's nothing but... He took Cal to the mountain last weekend and he had an asthma attack. It freaked him out." I don't tell Luna about Jesse or Dean's clearly unaddressed trauma from his death because it's not my place, but I'm not stupid enough not to see the connection.

I just don't know how I can fix it if he's avoiding me.

"Oh, poor Cal! Is he okay? Zee didn't mention anything about him being weird at practice."

"No, Cal's fine. It happens. Not a ton anymore, but he forgot his inhaler, and it was just a perfect storm."

"Oh, well, I'm sure it just freaked him out. Men are weird. Let him have his space and then talk when he's over it." Once more, she waits a beat before talking. "He likes you, Luna. A lot. Zee says he's great with Cal." I smile back and nod.

"He is." We giggle together before we're interrupted.

"You ladies done yet? I could use a refill," Sheena, a Luna's regular, says, lifting her gin and tonic glass in the air.

"Yes, Sheena," I say, lighter than I have felt in days.

———

That night I text Dean again, snuggled in bed and waiting for his text goodnight. He texted me once this afternoon, telling me he couldn't call me because he'd be driving home from the mountain late. Another brush off I'm attempting not to read into.

*Kate: I'm taking the job at Sadie's. My first day is tomorrow!*

I send off the text and sit there, still so confused. Is my gut right? That this is weird and off? I really haven't ever dated—I was so young when I got with Cal's dad, and since he was born, I've really been too busy for anything serious. Maybe Luna's right and men are just... strange.

My phone rings in my hand.

*Dean Calling.*

The rock currently growing in my stomach gains another ounce.

"Hey," I say. There's the sound of a car quietly driving in the background—I must be on Bluetooth.

"Hey, Katie." The name. It's warm and familiar, melting the rock, warm water running through my veins in what I recognize as sweet relief. He's back. I know it somehow.

"Hey," I say again, but it's different from my initial greeting. The same as his—familiar, warm. Happy to be talking to him.

"I figured out how to set my phone up to my car, so I thought you could keep me company."

"Okay," I say, quietly.

"You start at Sadie's tomorrow?"

"Yup," I say, excitement in my voice. "I go in right after I drop off Cal. I'll be able to pick him up after school and he can hang there until I'm out at five.'

"Sweet gig, babe. Proud of you. Luna cool with it?"

"Yeah, she actually told me I need to do it."

"She's not wrong. You're running yourself ragged. You need to take care of yourself." I snuggle into my blankets at his caring tone, a hint of strictness I love as I balance my cell on my ear

"Yeah, well. This is a good start."

"It's a great start." We're silent for a minute, a quiet, comfortable silence. "I missed you, Katie." And there it is. What I needed to feel better about this, to melt what remained of that rock, to kick out the anxiousness I've been feeling all week.

"I miss you too, Dean." And that feels right too, a confession I've never made to anyone other than my son. Admitting to him and myself I can miss someone, I can need someone other than friends or family in my life. This man has become such a vital part of my day, of my life, not having those simple gestures, those simple reminders he's *mine* threw my entire week off.

The thought should scare me, but I knock it aside and for once bask in the now.

———

"Okay, so first you fill this part with the espresso and use this to press it down," Sadie says, showing me a weird stick with a flat end. "You have to make sure it's even or it doesn't work the right way." She tamps the espresso grounds into the little cup. "Then you put it in here and twist, put a cup under and..." The bell above the door dings, interrupting her lesson. We both look up and Dean is walking in, a small smile on his face, hands in his pockets. *God, this man.*

"Hey, Sadie. Hey, Kate," he says as he walks up to the dark, reclaimed wood counter, popping up onto a stool and leaning into his forearms. "How's it going?"

I feel like 16-year-old me when I worked at Rita's and Zander Davidson came to get an Italian ice in the summer and my teenage heart fluttered way harder than it should. Stuttering and blushing and sweaty palms and all. Did I have a crush on the way-too-old for me Davidson boy? Yes. Does Luna know this and make fun of me regularly? Also, yes.

"Hey, Coach Fulton, how's it goin'?" Sadie asks, hip checking me. Dean rolls his eyes but his smile grows as I blush.

"Not much. Just came to say hi to my girl on her first day." Cue blush turning into a third-degree sunburn.

"Oh my god, you guys are way too cute. Love. Love this." Dean just smiles, all sunshine and flirting and too-handsome good looks. Normal Dean. *My* Dean. *Thank god.*

"You wanna make me a coffee, babe?" I keep staring at him. "Katie?"

"Oh my god, *Katie.* I love it," Sadie says in a coo, holding clasped hands to her face like a cartoon character.

"Sadie, shut *up!*" I say, turning towards the normal coffee maker, knocking a tower of coffee sleeves over to spill on the counter. "Shit!" Dean laughs, deep and happy and carefree. Relief continues to pour through me with each reassurance he's back.

I make his coffee the way he takes it when we come here on the weekends with Cal, when he sleeps over my house, when he makes it for himself, sliding it across the counter to him.

I'm dying to hop the counter, attack him and kiss him and hug him and reassure myself the weird blip is gone and that while we need to talk about it like adults, it's in the past and we're moving on. But it's my first day, so I just lean on my elbows, feigning profession- alism, staring at Dean as he winks at me and takes the cup.

"Lord, Kate, go around and give your man a kiss!" I roll my eyes but don't argue, walking around the barista bar and straight toward Dean, who wraps me into a hug, pulling me in and kissing me soft and sweet on the lips.

"Hey," I say, lips brushing on his with my words, a smile on them.

"Hey," he whispers back, mirroring my look.

"Adorable," Sadie says, and I look up to her, holding her cell in her hand, snapping a shot.

"Sadie!" I say, but secretly, I'm dying to see the photo. Dean pulls us apart, his wide carefree smile on display, and he puts his arm around my waist, pulling me in close.

"Shut up, trust me, you want this photo. I'll send it to you." I roll my eyes but also smile internally.

"How's it going, Deanie?" Sadie says.

"Deanie?"

"Testing out nicknames. I give them to everyone. Deanie doesn't fit, though. Give me some time. I have a feeling you'll be stopping in more in the next couple of months," she says with a wink. Cue another roll of my eyes. "So how's it going? How's the mountain?"

"Good. A storm's coming in, which is good news for us." I groan at the idea of more snow so early in the season. "You free tonight?" Dean says, looking at me with that same warm smile.

"Uh, kind of. Not working the bar tonight but I've got Cal," I say, and for a moment guilt suffuses my system. That's because for the entire time I've ever been a mom, I've never felt that—bummed I had my kid around. Bummed I had mom duties.

"I can watch him," Sadie says. "He's coming here after school, anyway. I'll go back to the bar with him after. It can be a Cal and Aunt Sadie night. Junk food and candy and stupid movies." I love that. *Aunt Sadie.* I love knowing I've given that to my kid.

Makes moving here all the more worth it.

"You don't have to—"

"Girl, I love being the cool aunt. I live for that shit. You guys have fun, have a fun grown-up sleepover at Dean's and I'll have a fun kid one at your place." I look from Sadie to Dean to gauge his interest and I can see this plays right into his plans.

"Cool by me if it's good by you," he says, putting it in my hands like he always does when it comes to Cal. Another thing I love about this man. The list is getting longer by the day, making me wonder if I love things about this man or if maybe, I just plain... well...

"Okay. Yeah, that works if you're good with it."

"Totally, I'll pop out before you go get him, grab stuff from my apartment for sleep and some sleepover essentials for Cal, and then I'll just take it straight to your place."

"Awesome, thanks so much, Sadie," Dean says, and it's sincere.

"No problem. So, uh, you ever get a chance to look at that thing I gave you?" And with her words, Dean freezes, his entire body going stiff, the light running from his eyes. My face scrunches in confusion.

When I look at Sadie, she's staring right at Dean, avoiding my eyes. Adamantly refusing to look at me.

"No, not yet," he says then shakes me off, grabbing his coffee. "Alright, I gotta head out. Just wanted to check in with you guys, see how your first day is going." I'm confused, staring at him with his distant look back in place, then back to Sadie who looks... guilty. His hand goes to his pocket. "What do I owe you for the coffee?"

"Uh... nothing. It's on me, Dean," Sadie says. "I'm sorry, I didn't mean to—"

"No worries, thanks a lot, Sade." He pulls me in, pressing a kiss to my forehead once. It should help, should make me feel better, but it just doesn't. "My place at six?" he asks me, stepping back.

"Uh. Yeah. Sure. Six." He nods once, leaving the coffee shop. I turn to Sadie whose eyes are still on the door.

"Uh, what the hell was that?" I demand, walking around the barista bar back to her. "What just happened?" I'm not mad at her but I sure as hell am confused.

"I... I don't know... I mean... I do but... shit." She sighs, finally moving her gaze from the door to me. "Last time he was here, I gave him a clipping from the paper. They're looking for a new guidance counselor at the elementary school. I know he used to... From Hannah. I told him to look into it. He fits here, and thought maybe it was time... I was out of line, I know. But you're so happy, and Cal, and he seems..."

"Oh, Sadie." I don't blame her, but her nosiness just made everything going wrong that much clearer. That much more poignant. "Sadie."

"I know. It was wrong. Especially... okay, I'm a fucking terrible person, but I googled him. So... I know. About the kid." My gut drops, face blanching. "No, no. I didn't tell anyone, I promise. I just mean... I get why he'd be hesitant. But he seems happy here. He's great with the kids on the team and with the kids at the camp—both Hannah and Mags can't stop talking about it. It's clearly his calling. I just thought maybe..." I sigh and rub my eyes with my hands, knowing she meant well. "Here. Here's the listing," she says, swiping through her phone and then handing it to me.

It's a photo of a newspaper listing reading, "Now Hiring: Springbrook Hills Guidance Counselor." The listing is short and sweet, mostly telling them the requirements, the school (the elementary school) and when they'd be starting (ASAP). My gut clenches because, shit, it would be perfect for Dean.

"It would be perfect," Sadie says, speaking my thoughts aloud. It would. And he could still work the camp in the summer if he wanted. He'd be around for the team, could work weekends at the mountain if he wanted. *It would be perfect.*

"Sadie, Dean... he..."

"I know. Well, I don't *know,* but I can assume." She looks at me with soft eyes, a mix of hope and regret and apology in them. "I meant well, Kate. I promise. I shouldn't have brought it up, or at least not caught you off guard, but... He belongs here, Kate. He fits. I know you know, but so do all of us." It's interesting to me she feels it too, that the crew feels how easily he slipped into our ranks.

"Yeah," is all I can say before I sigh and get back to work.

———

I pick up Cal, bringing him back to Rise and Grind before he heads back to my place with Sadie and I meet Dean at his place. The night goes well—it seems he's back to happy Dean, attentive and kind and touchy. The conversation runs through my mind through the entirety of my night with Dean though. Sadie's words about how it might be time, how he fits...

We make love sweet after eating takeout and lie on the couch together, watching some dumb movie, naked, neither of us talking, but it's a comfortable silence.

And then I do it.

I'm not sure why—maybe because of what Sadie said, maybe

because I already know this is a facade. I know underneath this, something is so wrong between us. I've felt it for a week now.

"So, what was Sadie talking about today?" Before the words even leave my mouth I regret them in so many ways. I hate playing this game right now, acting like Sadie didn't tell me about the guidance counselor position, and I hate that I'm bringing it up when things are so *good*.

His body tenses instantly. "What?" I know he heard me. His body tells me as much. But still, I keep my eyes on my hand, watching my finger draw shapes on his bare chest like I'm not on red alert.

"About a position?" Nothing. No answer. "She asked if you'd looked at a position or something." Silence. "Was that... for a job? Or...?" He doesn't respond, but I stay quiet still, not giving in to my need and desire to back down. He moves to sit up, jarring me from my position on his chest and forcing me to sit up beside him. The look on his face is one I've never seen.

Guarded. Shuttered. My happy, carefree man burdened, bruised, and scarred.

*No, no, no.*

I open my mouth to say something, say *anything*. But before I can tell him to forget it or change the subject or jump on top of him and *make* him forget it, he's answering, the words clipped and curt.

"Guidance counselor. At Springbrook Hills Elementary." They sound like poison on his tongue, like he needs them out of his mouth before the mere thought kills him.

"Oh, that would be... good, right? I mean it sounds like—" He's standing, reaching down to grab a pair of boxers and pulling a shirt on over his head. My eyebrows gather with confusion.

"You wanna get ready for bed? I'm gonna go brush my teeth." He's already heading towards the bathroom and I'm lost. He never wears anything to sleep if it's just us. And when Cal's around, just boxers. I've never seen him wear a shirt to bed.

And he's walking off like he could care less if I follow, if I go to bed at the same time.

Shit, if I even stay.

"Dean—" I start, confusion and worry clear in my voice. The sound makes him pause, freeze in the doorway to his room, his back to me still. A small relief as the worry manifests into tears that well in my lower lids. "Dean, are... are we okay? I'm sorry if I—"

He keeps his back to me when he says, "We're fine, Katie. Let's get ready for bed." And despite the soft tone, despite the fact he holds me close all night, I know we are not, in fact, fine.

Something is very, very wrong, and it terrifies me.

# THIRTY

-Dean-

THE NEXT MORNING, Kate's face is mashed against my chest, her soft sleeping breaths caressing my skin, and I can't get over the rock in my gut.

I thought I could.

I thought we were good, thought I'd handled it.

I thought a week to myself would fix it.

And then I was reminded why this won't work.

That *fucking* guidance counselor position.

It reminded me why I don't make connections. The stress of the memory of Cal gasping for breath in a med tent cemented the thought that's been brewing in the back of my mind all week.

It's time to leave.

It's time for this to end.

I can't lead her on any more, can't do that to Cal either.

This is not what I want: this stress of getting too attached, the risk of things going badly and destroying me. So it needs to end. I need to save myself before it goes too far.

For a split moment, a voice inside tells me to stay. To hold on and be brave and risk it. A voice I've heard muffled and muted for seven years but ignored for just as long.

A voice that's gotten louder since I came here.

But then the image of Jesse's mother falling to the grass, destroyed after her eight-year-old son was lowered into the ground flashes behind my eyelids, reaffirming my decision. My body jolts at the reminder and I open my eyes but the movement wakes Kate as well.

Her face creased with sleep moves up to mine, smiling sweet and sleepy and something in me breaks.

"Morning," she says.

There will be no more of this. No more sleepy smiles, no more happy to see me, no more 'morning's' I feel in my gut and my dick... No more video game nights with Cal, no more trips to the boardwalk. No more taking him to school. I won't have the right to the pride I feel when I watch him on the field.

But I have to do this.

She sees it on my face.

"What's wrong?" she asks, voice dripping in concern.

"I can't do this." The words come from my chest, I know because of the rumble they make, but I didn't tell my mouth to release the thoughts from my mind.

But here we are.

Unveiling the truth.

The truth I've sat on for a week now.

Sunday was the reality check I never wanted to have—a reminder of why I don't want kids of my own. A reminder of why I don't stay in one place, why I refuse to make a lasting connection wherever I am.

Things happen. Things happen in the blink of an eye, turning your world on its axis, and sometimes there's not a single fucking thing you can do about it.

Sitting in that med tent, watching Cal gasp for air with fear in his eyes, lips blue from the cold and the lack of oxygen, I knew I was already in too deep. So fucking deep, if anything happened to this kid it would obliterate me.

Jesse getting sick was horrible. He was a good kid. Kind and funny and a blast to talk to. He was young—so fucking young—and towards the end he was *scared*. I'll never forget the last conversation we had in my office before he died.

*"Mr. Fulton, do you believe in heaven?" The question had socked me in the gut, taking the air from my lungs as I worked on writing a letter to a parent about aggressive behavior. My fingers had stopped moving, my eyes on the screen, never shifting to him, but I knew he wasn't looking at me. He was looking up at where I had these little glittery stars stuck to the ceiling, a good way for the kids to distract themselves and open up when we were talking.*

*"I... uh... I mean, yeah. I do. I think there's a heaven." I took a deep breath, each molecule shredding the skin in my throat as it went into my lungs because although I had to ask my question, I knew the answer. I knew the answer and I didn't want it. "Why do you ask?"*

*"I hope there's a heaven," he'd said, not answering my question but also answering it all the same. "I hope there's a heaven for me to go to." It felt like an eternity until I could get words together.*

*"Why do you say that, kid?" And then he looked at me, face stark, pale and thin, a ball cap covering the head that had lost all of his hair months ago, acceptance in those bright blue eyes that were too deep set to be healthy. He knew. He knew what no adults around him wanted to know, wanted to accept.*

*"I'm going to die." The words cut me, killed me, a flash of fear in his eyes at the words, then shock that he'd actually said them out loud. I'd had training—training for tough moments like this, moments that no child should ever experience, moments where I was supposed to act professional, supposed to act within the guidelines, supposed to act like the adult in the room. But as I saw a single tear drop down his cheek, all of those went away.*

*They all went away.*

*I froze, not knowing what to say, not allowed to get close, to hug him and pull him to me. I froze, the words drying in my mouth as I selfishly thought about what I would do when he was gone.*

*And I never made him feel better, never comforted him and told him it would all be fine. He changed the subject before I could try to argue his statement, tell him it would be okay. I never did what he needed, and every day for seven years, I've wondered if that was what made him finally let go. Three days later, I was being called into the hospital at two am. Three days later, they were declaring an eight-year-old boy dead of leukemia.*

*And I did nothing.*

When I finally look up, Kate is sitting across from me on the bed, at some point having sat up and pulled the sheet to her chest. Her eyes are wide and scared, lips parted.

"What?" *The sound of it.* The sound is soft and hurt and... fuck.

I need to remind myself that this will hurt one hundred times more if I keep it up, if we don't stop.

"I can't do this anymore." I add words for emphasis, but I don't think it matters. She doesn't move. "Us." Her shoulders drop.

"Us?"

"God, Kate, yes. Us. I can't do this. I can't... I can't."

"What?" The word cracks, and along with it, a piece of my heart —what is left of the shriveled mess, what she and Cal had fixed and mended over the last month or two—falls and crumbles to ash.

"We need to stop. I'm... I'm moving up north for the winter, once the football season is over. And then I'm headed to my next stop."

"You're... leaving?"

"My lease is month to month. I'm not re-signing. I'm gonna stay at the mountain. I stayed there this week to... finalize things."

"Finalize things." I wait, staring at her.

"I can't do this." She's quiet and I'm internally begging her to speak. Begging her to say she understands, that this has been fun. She'll miss me but she understands, that, that, that...

"Why?" The word kills me.

Why.

Why?

*Why?*

"Why, Dean? Why?" In any other situation, I'd be proud. Proud of her voice for strengthening, proud of her back for straightening. Proud of my girl.

*Not your girl anymore.*

"We want different things."

"We want different things?"

"I'm not a settle down kind of guy. I don't want to be stuck here." The flash of hurt in her eyes sears through me, knowing she didn't want to get stuck here.

"We could... in the summer, we could—" She'd mentioned this a week ago, and I remember smiling into her hair as she lay on my chest, talking about things we could do, fun we could have, adventures we could take.

"I don't want that," I lie.

"Dean, we don't have to—"

"We do. You need to understand."

"Dean, I—"

"I don't want kids." The silence is oppressive, my words thick in the air between us. I almost reach out, try to wipe them away with my hand like it's a foggy mirror.

"You don't want kids?" I stare at her, not answering, which is the answer in and of itself. "And I have a kid." The words slice me.

If I could choose a kid, the perfect kid, the kid I'd want to raise and call mine, it would be Callum Hernandez. Hands down.

"I can't care for him. This is... this is more than I signed up for." A sound breaks from her, a wounded sound like my words are causing true, physical pain to her. "This is too much responsibility. I travel. I wander because I don't want the responsibility. I like my life the way it is." She stares at me, taking in the words, and I pray she understands.

When she speaks, it's clear she does.

"This isn't what you signed up for? *This isn't what you signed up for?*" She stares at me incredulously and I don't blame her. I want this, in a way. Want her to hate me. Want her to make the break easy. If she hates me, she won't wonder. If she hates me, I won't be tempted to go back.

"You know what? Fuck you, Dean. Not what you signed up for. Too much responsibility. You know what? This isn't what *I* signed up for. I wanted easy. I wanted to live my life with Cal and give him everything he needs and that's it. That's all I wanted." Her voice wavers. Something in me follows suit, and it takes everything not to backtrack.

But this has to be done.

"But then you fucking came, and you told me to give it a chance, that it would be fine. And you tricked me into thinking it would, tricked me into letting you get under my skin, letting you *change* me. Change my mind on—fuck, everything." Another deep breath, another shred of my soul.

"But all of that? All of that I could take. All of that, I could handle. You want to come in, sell me daydreams, and make me think that we have a future? Fine. You want to show me how fucking beautiful it is to let myself fall, let myself give into the exhaustion and ask for help, accept help? To have someone in my corner, helping me with the weight? You want to give me all of that and take it away from me? *Fine.*" The word is a near yell. "I can handle that blow. I can handle that disappointment. I can let it break me and wake up in the morning with a smile on my face so no one knows."

I know what's coming.

I know.

It burns deep in me, the knowledge of what she's going to say next.

"But no, that's not what you did. You dragged my son into this. You gave him you. Gave him hope, hope of having someone in his life, someone who he can talk to and confide in. A man in his life to fill in the gaps that, it fucking *kills* me to admit, but I cannot fill on my own. You made Cal fall for you too. And that? That's unacceptable. Because I can't explain to an eight-year-old that the man he looks up to 'can't do this anymore.' That he's given up on me. On him. On *us*... I'm not going to be able to explain to him why he has to start spending the night at his grandparents again, why there won't be guys' nights or video game days. I can't explain to him that it's not him, because I'm telling you right now, Dean, he's going to think it's him. You think he doesn't know? He's smart, Dean. Gonna put together the last good day we had was Sunday and that it all ended after that. He's *going to know*. You're going to *crush him*. After everything I did—we did—to make him feel good, you're going to—"

"Do you think I don't know that, Kate? Think I don't know what it's going to do? Fuck, I've been trying to figure out all week how to handle it, how to get around hurting him."

"How fucking gallant of you, thinking of how to make yourself feel better about dipping out on an 8-year-old while keeping your hero status. Great, Dean."

"Kate, I can't do it. I don't want kids. I don't want that pressure. You knew that. You're not dumb, Kate. Knew I didn't want strings, that I haven't stayed in one spot for long."

"But you did. You stayed here, stayed with the team. Stayed here and didn't leave."

"It was convenient."

"Convenient? Jesus, Dean, stop lying to yourself. You stayed here because you *belong* here. You fit here, and you know it. You feel it." *She knows.* I need to end this.

"Stop this. Stop trying to convince yourself of these things. Stop trying to twist it. You knew we weren't forever. You forced me into your life, forced me into Cal's life. You let that happen. That's on you." The lie falls off my tongue with malice, and I regret it the instant the pain flashes in her eyes. God, so much pain. I'm fucking this up so bad. Beyond repair.

But that's what I need, right? I need to leave not a scrap of hope so she can break it off, move on to something good and stable and undamaged. "I don't want a family. Don't want kids. I don't want that to..." I almost tell her the truth.

Tell her I don't want it because I'm scared, because if I have a kid and something happens like it happened to Jesse, it will *destroy* me. Instead, I say the worse thing I can think, what some sick part of my mind clung to when she told me about Cal's dad. "I don't want a family to hold me down." That's what does it. I know it. Those words snap it for her, the tether she'd built between us, the invisible string, the thin wire that transmitted her feelings from her to me.

It snaps.

"Well..." She laughs, a vicious, hurt sound. "I'm so sorry I held you down. Go. Be free, Dean. We'll be fine without you. We were before; we will be after." And then she walks around my apartment, grabbing her sweats and a tee, putting them on. She's throwing things in her bag, stuffing them in haphazardly and heading for the door.

"Kate, that came out wrong—"

"Stop. No need, Dean, You made yourself perfectly clear." Her hand is on the doorknob, but she turns to me before she opens it.

"I hope one day you see. See you fucked up. You almost had something beautiful, but you were too damn scared to go after it. Fuck, you didn't even have to, you already had it, nothing to go after. It was yours."

Her voice cracks.

"We were yours. I hope one day you look back at your sad, lonely life that you lived with smiles and sunshine and a good time and see it was hollow and empty, that all this time spent trying to protect your-self really ate away at any potential happiness, any joy you could have had. And I hope that feels just as horrible as I feel right now." She turns back to the door, a hand to it, turning the knob before I stop her.

"Kate." She turns, and the sliver of hope there nearly kills me. "You don't have a car here." Her face falls, that first tear falling with it, and all I want to do is change my mind, run to her, pull her into my arms and hold her and let her tell me it will be okay, we'll be okay, that my fear is normal and we'll work through it together. "I can drive you home," I say instead.

"I'm not going anywhere with you."

"Don't be like this, Kate. Let me drive you home."

"I'll be fine, Dean. I'll figure it out by myself. I always do." And then she's slamming the door behind her and I'm wondering why the fuck I just let her go.

# THIRTY-ONE

-Dean-

ONE WEEK after the break up we're in late November, two weeks from Thanksgiving. We're one town over in Bridgeville for the final game of the season—the championship the kids were so pumped to have qualified for.

The feeling is... conflicted, at best.

On one hand, I have no reason to stay in Springbrook Hills now. Practices and games will be over and I can officially end my lease, move to the employee quarters on the mountain until I find my next temporary home. I should start packing my shit, the little things I travel with from location to location.

But on the other hand...

I'm going to miss these kids. They're all good kids, awesome and kind and hardworking. They love the game, reminding me of how it felt to be their age, joining a team, working hard to win together,

And I'll be leaving this town.

The town where I've become way more connected than with any other I've stayed in over the past seven years. I have friends here—

people I can call up nearly any day of the week and grab a drink with, shoot the shit with. Friends who I can vent with, make plans with.

And then there's Kate and Cal, of course. Not that it matters since I fucked that all up so royally.

Part of me thinks I must be living in some sick nightmare where I let my own anxieties and stress and fears take over and win again. But the other half knows I haven't had Kate in my bed, Cal in my ear for weeks.

Kate hasn't come to a single practice since that day, Sadie or Hannah or Luna dropping Cal off each time. And while Cal comes to practice and hangs out with his friends, chats with Zander, it's as if I don't exist.

He knows.

And every time he looks at me, it's filled with anger and disappointment, and betrayal. The little bulldog with the 'C' initial on his collar burns on my skin. Here we are at the last game of the season against the apparent town rival and he's still ignoring me.

To be honest, I'm kind of over it. Should I be the adult in this exchange and be understanding, let it go? Yes. Will the familiar voice that's been yelling at me for weeks let me? No.

"Cal, you need to follow the plays Zee gives," I say as he takes a sip of water on the bench during a timeout. My breath creates clouds in the cold air and it's the only way I know I actually said anything. His body doesn't even flinch at acknowledging me. "Cal." Nothing. "CAL!" I say, my voice getting louder. Kids next to him are mumbling, Cody to his left elbowing him to get his attention as if Cal doesn't know what he's doing.

He does.

He's being a little jerk, but I'm proud all the same.

Annoyed, but proud.

I would have done the same when I was his age.

I deserve this.

But the other half of me? The other half needs him to listen to me.

"Cal, look at me." Nothing.

"Cal, you need to talk to Coach Dean," Zee says, voice firm. We haven't talked about what happened, but between Cal's cold shoulder, Kate skipping practices, and now this, I'm sure he can figure it out.

"Why?" Cal asks and fuck, he's not just annoyed—he's furious.

"Why what?" Zee asks.

"Why do I need to talk to him?" He sounds ten years older. It's a sound I know well. When the world around you is unfair to you and those you love, the jadedness creeps in.

"Well, I—"

"He doesn't care about me. Or my mom. Doesn't care she's a mess and everything has been shitty again. He doesn't care about anything but himself. He wants to go have fun and be free or whatever, and that's fine. But he didn't have to drag us into it."

"Cal, I don't—" I try to step in. I have no idea how he knows this. I know there's no way Kate would talk this openly about us to Cal.

"Kids talk, Dean. I know you're off to go to a new place and have fun with new people. New kids who are cooler than me and new girls without kids to hold you down." His voice cracks and it cuts. I know what he's thinking.

"That's not true, Cal," I say, my voice softer. All of the kids' eyes are on us. Shit. This is the absolute worst time for this.

"Whatever, Dean. You said you were here to help; you were helping Mom and you were helping me. Helping doesn't mean making her cry." My eyes drift to the stand where Kate was standing with Luna and Sadie, a big homemade 'Go Bulldogs!' sign hung between them, decked out in red and black.

Her eyes are locked on us, face pale and not just from the shock of watching Cal stand his ground. The few times I've seen her since that morning, she's been pale, tired. Not eating, maybe. Definitely not sleeping. But now she's looking at us, unsure of what to do, mouth wide open as Sadie turns to her and says something in her ear.

"Fuck this, Dean," Cal says, taking off his helmet and throwing it to the ground. Then he reaches under the bench to grab his bag.

"Callum!" Zee says, though any other time we'd just laugh off an F-bomb, even from an eight-year-old.

"Sorry, Coach Davidson. I'm leaving," he says, bag over his shoulder as he stands and heads for the fence surrounding the field.

"Cal, don't you dare leave—" I start, grabbing his arm. I shouldn't, it crosses so many fucking lines, but what's one more. But when he turns back to me, I stop. He's not just angry, he's hurt, tears in his eyes.

"Why? Everyone else does." And fuck it guts me. His shoulder move, jerking my grip which has already loosened, and I watch his hand go to the fence as he jumps over it, the move smoother than any 8-year-old has a right to be. Then he's gone, walking up to where Kate's already standing, sign rolled up, arm out to bring her boy into her.

I watch them walk away, Kate's head dipped low to Cal's as they walk, the girls trailing behind. Luna waves halfheartedly, but the movement is to Zee, definitely not me.

Sadie's eyes are the only ones to meet mine. I half expect her to flip me the bird, but instead, she just shakes her head like she's disappointed in me.

We win the game, but the win feels hollow.

# THIRTY-TWO

-Dean-

I SHOULD BE SHOCKED when Tony Garrison takes the seat across from me at Hannigan's, the pub in Springbrook Hills, but I'm not. It's been a week since the shit show that was the championship where Cal walked off the field.

A week since I last saw Cal and Kate.

Two weeks since I broke it off with them.

And he's right—he had every reason to be angry with me. I broke it off with both of them because Kate is a packaged deal any man would be blessed to have. I'm just not the right guy.

"Tony," I say, tipping my beer at him.

He doesn't speak when he sits down, but the face speaks volumes. Shit. With his stern, disappointed face, it's like a dad coming in to give you a talk about something you won't want to hear.

"Is there something wrong with Cal? With Kate?" The words fall from my mouth before I can stop them, stress and concern and panic flooding me. He looks me over, not saying a word, taking me in. Detective mode activated.

"Strange reaction for a man who doesn't care."

"Never said I didn't care about them," I say, defensiveness taking over.

"Didn't you?"

"Are they okay?" Once again, his assertive eyes look me over, taking me in.

"They're fine." Relief floods me. "Physically, at least." My body tenses. "Cal's been acting up in school again. Standoffish. Kate's working crazy hours, nonstop. Stayin' busy."

"She always does that."

"Not like this. Workin' at Sadie's then comin' in to work the bar. Even when she's not on the schedule." My eyes close. "Avoiding the world." I stay silent. "You know anything about why?" I try not to roll my eyes at his leading questions. Being Zander's best friend and Luna's man, there's no way he doesn't know.

"What are you, some controlling big brother?"

"Pretty much, yeah," he says, quick, not a moment of hesitation. "Don't have a sister, but I grew up with Lune and her brothers. The way they defended her? That's how I feel about Kate. She's family."

"Glad she has that, man," I say into my beer, moving a fry around, dragging it through ketchup. I refuse to make eye contact with him.

"Fine, I'm just gonna talk. You can listen. Or not, whatever. Choice is yours, but I'll tell you, you'll want to hear my story." I fight rolling my eyes. This guy is a self-righteous prick. I like Zee, like Luna, but this guy... There's no way he's as cool as everyone makes him out to be.

"Luna was kidnapped. Two years ago now. Kate had just started working at Luna's. Lune had an admirer. Guy was a fucking creep, and it just got worse until he took her." I can feel my eyes widen. People in town have mentioned Luna's 'drama' and 'experience' but I never knew...

"In my line of work, I see a lot of things. Terrible things. Kidnappings and stalkers, domestic violence, child abuse. We're lucky it's not too common here in town, but we still see it, all of it. It happens. And every time it does, every person in my office will tell you they put a loved one in that place. For a split second, you don't see a victim. You see a sister, or your son, or your mother. You see your best friend or your girlfriend. It doesn't last long, but the feeling stays with you. Sometimes it's suffocating, so hard to live through, you want to leave it all behind. But you keep going. You talk to people, move on with your life. Best way to honor those we've lost is to enjoy those we haven't." He pauses, staring right at me. You have to appreciate Tony Garrison and the way he doesn't pull punches, doesn't beat around the bush.

"I don't think—"

"Know your story." I figured as much, but didn't expect it all the same. "Luna and the girls, they're all nosy as fuck. You get used to it. It's kind of cute, most of the time." Maybe for him. "You get your head out of your ass, you'll see Kate's the same way too." Pause.

"I know your story. Can't imagine what that was like. I've seen some things though. Things I'm sure you've been better trained to deal with than I was. Kids reporting things no kid should experience. Neglect, Abuse. Worse. Seen it. Had to go home with that on my mind, had to go on with my day knowing that evil is in the world. A few times I've let it get to me. It makes you wonder sometimes. Wonder if you should add any more kids to this world. If you should make a kid suffer through this life. If you could handle it if, god forbid, something happened to them. I know you know that feeling."

The image of Jesse's parents breaking down comes to mind, his mother screaming his name at his funeral. I checked, later. Years later. It only took two years for them to divorce. They were so in love, and I thought nothing could break that.

Jesse did.

His cancer broke them.

And in the past two weeks, I've come to realize it broke me too.

"Then Luna comes home, smiling and goofy and telling me stories from the bar or lugging in some piece of shit she found on the side of the road she thinks would go well in our guest room, and I remember. I remember I want a little girl with my hair and her eyes, and that I want to show a little boy with her hair and my dad's eyes how to throw a ball. I remember how we went through hell and back and held on to each other through it. I remember the look on Steve's face when he came into the bar to tell us Aut's expecting again, the look on Cal's face when he's smiling at his mom."

A knife to my gut at the reminder of something I love to see.

"And that fear washes away. I can't guarantee my life won't be shit, or shit things won't happen that will scare the fuck out of me. But knowing the beauty my life will be if I suck it up and give it a shot? Worth that risk. I bet you ask that kid's parents, they'll tell you they wouldn't take those years away to avoid the crush of losing him." His words settle in me because I know they're true. I know they loved him, wouldn't change having him for anything.

"I'll leave you with this—something happened to Cal, to Kate. Something happened to them and they were gone from you forever. Would you wish they'd never walked into your life? Would you wish you'd walked away sooner? Or would you regret wasting these fuckin' weeks staying away from them because you're too scared?" Final blow dealt. He stares at me for one long moment before nodding, standing, and walking away.

And although I have no fucking clue what just happened, I do know that I fucked up and need to win them back.

Somehow.

# THIRTY-THREE

-Dean-

THE PROBLEM with fucking up this big is unfucking it up.

It's not as simple as going into Luna's, running up the stairs and saying, "Oh shit, I'm a dick and your boss's boyfriend helped me see that, 'kay thanks, we good?"

Feelings have been hurt.

Promises broken.

Trust demolished.

It's my job to figure out how to fix that, how to win Kate and Cal back. Because they're a package deal and I want them both.

Forever, if they'll have me.

Knowing this, I know I have a lot of work to do.

But I also know of the two people whose trust I broke, of the two people who right now probably hate me, one needs to be dealt with first.

I also know I'm going to have to do some groveling in order to get there.

So when I'm in the back room of Vinnie's Pizza for the team's end of the year party, I'm reminded of the groveling and bribing and million and seven promises I made to Zander and his sister in order to make this happen. This is because Cal walks in, shuffling his feet and glaring like he has no desire to be here.

Zee walks up to him, hand out, and does a hilarious interpretation of a man hug but with a kid half his size. They talk for a few minutes before he's swept away by teammates, looking around the room, searching. When he doesn't see what—or who—he's looking for, his body relaxes.

Me. He was looking to see if I had come, if he'd have to avoid me. *Shit.*

Zee comes back to the corner I'm in and sits down.

"Kid's pissed."

"Got that."

"Doesn't think you're here."

"Got that too."

"Told me Kate forced him to come, but I know Luna forced Kate to force Cal to come. They're having some kind of girl's night tonight at Hannah's."

Makes sense—it's a Monday, so the bar is closed.

I stay silent longer, eyes still locked on my little dude. Because he is. Regardless of my fuck up, regardless of the fact I need to win them back, he's mine. And I'll make that true in all aspects when I get the chance. A chill runs through me at the thought, a thrill of excitement for a future I didn't think I could handle.

"You gotta plan? For how to handle him?" I keep staring. "You got nothin', huh?" I keep staring.

I have a plan.

I just don't know if it will work.

"Kid loves his mom. More than anything, wants her happy. He's mad at me for fucking that up. He trusted me to take the pressure and stress off of her, thought he could be a kid again. He's spent his whole life not being a kid because he's gotta support his mom. It's fair he's mad." I keep staring at Cal, now chatting animatedly with Cody and

Joey, probably about some video game or a birthday party or who knows what.

"So, what are you going to do?" Zee asks.

When I said I need to win Cal back first, I actually lied—Zee was the first I had to win back. Thankfully, it took little; the man is as trusting and understanding as any I've ever met. But soon after my chat with Tony, I called up Zee, who pled my case to his little sister.

I also promised him I had a plan.

Which, wasn't a complete lie, but...

"You'll see," I say, and I pray to God that at the end of the day, I don't make this all worse.

After pizza is eaten and kids have screwed around and chatted until my ears felt like bleeding, we move on to awards. Most improved, most team spirit, best sportsmanship. That kind of thing.

Until all but one has been given out.

"And finally, our last award." I pick up the little trophy from the table. The kids are getting restless, parents coming to stand in the back, ready to get the kids and take them home. There's school tomorrow, after all.

"This award goes to the Team Hero. A hero is someone who is always looking out for others, always working to make things better. This player didn't stop when things got hard, kept working to keep the team strong. He never backs down when he sees something isn't right. This player even put me in my place when I deserved it."

Kids around me whisper and Cal's eyes meet mine. He knows.

"He works hard every day. He came to the team not knowing as much as some, not great friends with you all, but he won you all over in a day. That's all it took. Who here considers Cal Hernandez a friend?" Every little hand in the room goes up and Cal looks around, eyes wide. My hand is up too, and I see in the corner of my eye Zee's is raised. But my eyes are locked on my boy. "But I'm gonna take the claim that he's my *best* friend."

Cody lets out a "hey!" and I can't help but laugh.

"Cal is kind to everyone he meets, works hard to make our team better, and gives his everything to make sure those around him are treated fair and kind. He deserves this award most of all. Come on up, Cal." I'm not sure what will happen as he sits there. Will he come up? Will he leave the room? Will he spit in my face? I'd deserve it all.

But as always, Cal does what I least expect, standing with a small smile and walking over to me.

"Thanks, Coach," he says, voice small and quiet.

"Need to talk to you after everyone leaves, okay?" He looks at me and, again, I wonder if maybe he'll hit me or yell or run out. But nope. He just nods, taking the little plastic trophy with a gold football player on top back to his seat between Ethan and Cody.

# THIRTY-FOUR

-Cal-

Everyone is gone and Zee is sitting in a corner, messing around on his phone. while Dean and I sit, face to face. I kind of wish I were Zee right now. That sounds a lot more fun than this conversation.

The truth is, I'm really mad at Dean. Like, really mad. I think that's clear by how I acted at the championship, though it wasn't my best moment. Mom got so mad at me, even though I think in a weird way she was a little proud.

But also, I miss how it used to be, when Dean and I would hang out and play video games and Mom was happy. She smiled a lot. Now she... doesn't. I don't know what happened with them, not really, but I'm pretty sure it's all my fault and that makes me even madder. Because I know it was so dumb not to bring my inhaler, but like, I can't control that stuff. I'm a kid. And it's not fair Mom had to be sad because of some dumb mistake I made. Plus, I was fine, I was—

"I want to talk you, man to man, okay? You're old enough to hear this story and hopefully, once you do, you'll understand what happened with me and your mom." I try not to look impressed, but I totally am. Everyone treats me like a kid and like I can't handle things, but I can. I can totally handle things.

So I nod, preparing to hear his story, whatever it is. I know some of the big kids have looked up Coach Dean on the internet. I've heard some of them talking at camp and even school, but I never listened. My mom taught me other people's business is not mine.

"Before I became a camp counselor, I was a guidance counselor in the elementary school where I grew up. Kind of like your mom. I left, went to school, and then came back to my town and settled down, worked there. It was fun. You know I like hanging out with kids and talking with them and helping them with their problems." He pauses and I nod before he takes a deep breath.

"My first year, I met a kid. He was in second grade, like you. He came to me a few times and we were friends. Kind of like us. We'd joke around and laugh. But then he started getting really tired all the time, not feeling great. We found out in the winter he had cancer, and he just kept getting more and more sick. We were friends, really good friends. I loved him. His name was Jesse. I loved him like I love you, Cal."

My tummy does a weird flip and I have to scrunch up my nose. "He'd hang out in my office and take naps when he was at school. He trusted me. He talked to me about anything and everything. We had a connection, just like you and I do."

Dean breathes in deep, looking around the room before looking at me again. "He was really sick, so sick, Cal. It sucks to tell you this because I don't want you to ever have this on your mind, but he died. And it made me... really, really sad."

He stops again, breathes again.

"I'm telling you this because you're a big kid and I think it might help you to know where my head is at. After Jesse died, I left my town, and never went back. I still wanted to hang out with kids, help kids like you. But I couldn't... get attached. So I'd go work at summer camps like Camp Sunshine and do ski school in the winter. That's how I ended up here. You know that. But I never stayed anywhere longer than a season."

"But you've been here since the summer. That's more than a season, right?" He stares at me and nods, a small smile on his face he gets when I say something smart.

"Yeah, bud. I stayed. I was only supposed to help with the team, live up at the mountain come fall."

"But you didn't."

"But I met you. And your mom. And... without realizing it, I stayed. For you guys." My belly does that flip thing again. "Sometimes grown-ups do things they want to do without realizing they're doing them. I stayed in town to get to know you guys better. Get to know you and your mom better. And I got attached."

I nod. That makes sense.

"But I was still scared, whether or not I'd admit it. I..." He stops and looks at the wall behind me. "I never wanted to have kids of my own." Belly flip. "Not after Jesse. I saw how that could go and I didn't want that kind of pain, you know?"

"Then why would you bother with my mom?" I can hear how annoyed I sound, sticking up for my mom and, I guess, myself. "You know, you'd be stuck with me too."

He laughs. Dean *laughs*. What a jerk. Maybe it's best mom stays far away from him.

"Not gonna lie, it wasn't my intention. But... things happen. And I fell in love with you too—playin' football and eating pizza and playing video games with you. Goofin' around and picking on your mom. And I fell in love with your mom. Shit, I really fell for her." I want to tell him that's a dime for the swear jar, a habit I started to push on him, too, when he was around all the time, but I resist.

"So what happened? If you fell in love with Mom and with... me. Why haven't we seen you? Why is Mom so sad?" His face flashes with the same sad Mom's has had.

"Snowboarding." He leaves it at that and my belly goes from flipping to sinking. I look at the floor to see if it's there, but it's still sitting in me, nice and safe, I guess.

"I'm really sorry, Dean. I didn't mean to forget my inhaler, I swear, I haven't needed it in—"

"Cal, stop. That's not your fault. I'm an adult. You're a kid. Kids do dumb shit and grown-ups are supposed to keep it together long enough not to have a meltdown. I... didn't. I had a meltdown."

I look away, not wanting to meet his eyes. "Cal, look at me." I do as he asks. "I'm sorry. Cal. That wasn't cool. But I... I panicked. I saw you there, sick and scared and nothing I could do. And every part of me hurt, thinking something was wrong, something I couldn't fix, and that I was there when it happened. And... I got scared. I got in my head. I tried to stay away, to get my mind right, but all I could think about was Jesse and how sad I was after what happened to him. How sad his parents were. And how, if I was this attached to you already, it was only going to get worse." I stare at him, unsure of what to say, waiting for him to continue on.

"But I talked to some friends here, and they helped me see where I went wrong. I can't live my life scared something would happen to you or your mom or... any future kids we might have." A part of me lights up at that.

"Future kids?"

"Oh yeah. You think it would be cool to have a little brother?"

"I think Mom would like a little sister," I say, trying to play it cool. "You know, so she's not outnumbered." Dean laughs and part of me feels better already, like we're back in his apartment and eating pizza and not the gross salad Mom made us get.

"But I need your help with getting your mom to see I mean business. That I love her and I love you and I want to be a... family." My eyes burn and I scrunch my nose again to fight it.

"Well, how do I know you won't go off and get scared again? Run away this time?" I cross my arms over my chest, and in the corner, I hear Zander laugh. Dean glares at him. I keep my mean face on, but I really want to laugh too.

"I got a job here."

"Well, duh. I know that."

"Not the mountain, Cal."

"Camp Sunshine?"

"Springbrook Hills Elementary," My eyebrows come together. "What?"

"Sadie told me there was a job there. A guidance counselor. It's... it's what kind of made my brain go crazy. Between you getting sick and this job being open, it felt... scary. But I fought through that, Cal. You said some things at the tournament that really hit home. You were right—I was being stupid and selfish. I love you and I love your mom. And I want to give you a chance to be a kid, not to be a grown-up version of a kid that has to help your mom. And you know what? You're right that I act too much like a kid too. I do. I need to face my fears like a grown-up and work with the people who love me to get over them. So... I took the job. And I'm kind of stuck here."

I wait for a while, thinking before I speak again. "But like, if you're a real grown-up now, does that mean we can't play video games and eat pizza anymore? Because I liked that part." Dean laughs and it sounds less nervous. That makes me happy, knowing it's in part because of me not yelling at him and running out like I did at the game.

"Not that much of a grown-up, kid. Your mom's enough of a grown-up in that way for both of us." I nod. That makes sense. "But I need your help."

"With what?"

"With your mom. I need help to convince her I mean it and I love her and want to stay with you guys." He stops and I just stare. "If I promise to make your mom happy, to make you happy, will you help me win her back?"

"Will you make her cry ever again?"

"Gotta be honest with you, and one day, you'll see what I mean. But I can't promise that. Men are stupid. We say dumb shit and we do dumb shit, but it's all about learning from our mistakes. I'm gonna make lots. But I can promise when I make your mom cry, I'll make it up to her tenfold. Deal?"

I stare at Dean for a few minutes, just to keep him on his toes. Tony told me that makes guys shake in their boots. I look at his feet. No boots. Will it still work then?

I scrunch my nose, but I already know my answer. Mom was happy and now she's not. Dean is sorry and really loves Mom. Like Tony and Luna, and Hannah and Hunter, and Autumn and Steve, and Tanner and Jordan. People think kids don't notice these kinds of things, but we do. We totally do.

"Deal," I say, putting out my hand and giving him a firm shake, just like Rosie's uncle Hunter taught me. "But you owe me."

"Oh yeah? What do I owe you?"

"What are you thinking?"

"Don't know what you mean, kid."

"Like, what is my help worth to you?" Dean stares at me for a long time and it's the same way Steve looks at Rosie and Sara when they're being goofs. I wonder for a split second if it would be weird to call Dean 'Dad.'

One day.

Maybe.

"I'm thinkin' tickets to an Eagles game."

"Are you trying to bribe me into getting you something to help me win back your mom?"

"Is it working?"

Dean just laughs, putting an arm around my shoulder and rubbing his knuckles into my hair. I laugh, slapping at his hand before he stops. Then he pulls back, looking me in my eyes, no longer a laugh on his face.

"You're a good kid, Cal. Thanks for forgiving me."

For some reason, my throat starts to close like it does when I have an asthma attack and my eyes feel all prickly. I can't talk, so I just nod.

Then he pulls me in, pressing his lips to my hair the same way Mom and Grandma do, giving me a big hug.

It's not until Zee is driving me home, after Dean and I stayed later than all the other kids trying to plan how to win Mom back, that I realize he never agreed to my bribe.

# THIRTY-FIVE

-Kate-

IT's a tradition to go to my parents' house on Thanksgiving morning, eat my mom's homemade cinnamon rolls, and watch the parade. It was the tradition even when I was back in Seattle, braving the holiday traffic to fly back even if for just a weekend. I'm sitting in the loveseat at my parents', sipping coffee and licking my fingers free of the cream cheese frosting I helped to whip up while Cal and my dad watch the parade.

"You look... tired, Katie," my mom says, looking at me in the way only a mother can. I never understood it until I had kids of my own. The way a mom can look disappointed and intrigued and worried and sad all at once. It's because it's what's going through our mind at any given time.

"I'm always tired, Mama. I work nights at a bar."

"You have that new job though, no?" I sigh, not wanting to have this conversation.

Since Dean ended things with us, I've been utilizing the help of friends to watch Cal while I work nights again. This job was supposed to be the perfect opportunity to relax more, sleep more, be on a better schedule with Cal, but down time, free time? It just gives me freedom to dwell on what went wrong, on what could have been.

On what ended.

And everywhere I looked in that apartment, I saw him.

The couch where he teased Cal about losing to him at some dumb game.

The kitchen table where he left me bagels and coffee and a note.

The mirror in my room I smiled into that first week when we'd spend hours on the phone together, him convincing me slowly, minute by minute, word by word to give him a chance. That worked well, obviously.

It's funny how the most mundane things, the things you've spent years looking at, being around, have a new painful meaning after a breakup.

"I'm trying to save up. For Christmas, you know?" Cal's head swivels to me, joy and child-like excitement on his face. It's good to see. The weeks after the breakup hit him hard as well: fighting at school, talking back to me and any adult who tried to get close, going right to his room after school, barely speaking.

Most of the time I have to remind myself he's going through a breakup too, in a way.

"Katie, you can't just work to death," she says, a sad look on her face.

"I'm not, Mama. I promise," I say, a fake smile on my face. She doesn't buy it, but she nods. She's a good mom, if not a little over-bearing and stubborn. I like to think I inherited some of it from her.

"Look, Julia. They've filled that position down at the school," my dad says to my mom from behind the paper. "Springbrook Hills Elementary finds new guidance counselor." My stomach drops and I fight a reaction, but Cal's eyes move to mine. All I can think is the look in Dean's eyes when I asked him about that stupid listing Sadie told me about. How I should have let it be. How looking back, that was the final thread that broke us.

"Thank god. Kids need a good person in their life to talk to," my mom says before the conversation shifts again to something else. But as always, my mind is stuck in the past.

———

"Mooooom, let's gooo!" Cal whines, standing at the door with some kind of Giant's hat with a big puffy pompom on top. I have no idea where he got it, but he's already in his jacket with his shoes on.

"God, Cal, stop being a little jerk. It's Thanksgiving. Family day."

"Oh, Katherine, your mother and I are well past tired. We need our nap!" My dad laughs, tipping his head towards Cal. "Let the boy go play with people half our age and other kids!"

"I don't want to miss the football game!" he says from the door, stomping his foot in a way so reminiscent of when he was a toddler, I almost laugh

"Calm down, I'm sure Zee and Tony won't start until you're there," I say.

"Bye, Papa. Bye, Mama," I say, kissing my mom on the cheek. She looks better. So much better and the house looks so much more livable. They look happier, healthier. I can't help but feel just a fragment of guilt knowing I put so much pride in being the one to help them out, I held them back from having Vera.

"No, no, my girl. Don't you do that. You meant well, my girl. You're stubborn, like your father. Won't let anyone in, won't let anyone help you. I pray to God every night one day a good man will come and make you see the light." My mind drifts to a man who did just that, but then took it all away, before I shake my head.

"How do you know what I was thinking?"

"A mother knows, Katie." Another twinge. "Go. Let that boy play some football. Let him be a *kid* instead of hanging around his old as dirt grandparents." My mom smiles at me.

"Speaks for yourself, woman!"

"Oh, hush you. You're older than I am."

"I'll prove to you just how young I am later, my love." I gag a little.

"Alright, that's it, we're out of here," I say, standing and walking towards the door. My dad just laughs.

"Happy Thanksgiving, guys!" I shout, walking out the door and heading to The Davidson's house for a big mess of a Thanksgiving filled with a different kind of family and lots of love.

When we pull up to Tony and Luna's house, cars line the road. We actually have to park three blocks away and walk in the biting cold to get to the house, but Cal is *skipping*. Quite literally skipping to Luna's home.

Last night, the bar was packed with SHHS alumni all catching up and drinking, bemoaning the impending family dinner. I had more than a few repeats of the conversation I had with Becca and gritted my teeth the whole way through. Thankfully, the girls and most of the guys were there to entertain and distract.

During the minimal down time, Luna explained her family, Tony's family, and the Hutchins/Sutter crew would all be at her place. Essentially, one giant house party. They actually had to erect a tent in the backyard, set up by Luna's former construction working father. It's equipped with space heaters to keep everyone warm but make sure they have a seat.

What Cal is most excited about, though, is the football game, which apparently happens every year. Last year we were invited, but Mom was still sick and Cal was still standoffish, so we stayed at my parents'. But this year there is no way I could have begged Cal not to go, regardless of the fact that I am physically and emotionally exhausted.

These last few weeks, working, starting the new job, watching Cal drift again, fight at school, the emotional turmoil of the breakup... It's been a lot. Sadie and Luna both insisted I take off the entire weekend, so while I plan on doing a bit of Black Friday shopping from my couch tomorrow, that's the extent of my plans. All I want is to veg out and sleep. I need it.

But first, I must people, if only to show those in my life who love and worry about me I am, in fact, totally fine.

Totally and completely fine.

Except I am so totally far from fine when I walk in the front door, greeted by 'hellos' and 'heys' and other greetings I don't even hear.

That's because when my eyes sweep the room, my smile falls when they hit the huge comfy couch in front of the TV blaring the big game. I freeze on a head of short, dirty blond hair on tan skin, blue eyes locking on mine as he looks over his shoulder at the front door.

Dean.

Dean is here.

Why is Dean here? Shouldn't he be at the mountain? Or back home? Or at the very least, far, far away from me?

And that, in an of itself, when combined with the small, knowing smile on Dean's face directed straight at me, should be enough. Should be enough to make me confused and frustrated and turn around and grab my son, who was also broken by this man, and just *leave*. Send a text to Luna saying I'm sorry, we had to leave, but also I hate you for not warning me.

But then another shock hits me.

Because Cal, my sweet Cal who spent three weeks clearly sad and upset his newfound idol was no longer a part of our day-to-day life, getting into fights at school and talking back, sleeping like shit and having a terrible attitude, smiles and then *skip*s to the couch, sitting his tiny bony ass between Dean and Tony and smiling at me. If I didn't know any better, I'd think maybe he was Dean's kid, the learned smirk having the same tilt and holding the same taunt as Dean's.

"What the fuck is going on?" I murmur under my breath, and before anyone can answer, Luna comes over, wraps an arm around my shoulder with a laugh.

"Let's get you a drink, babe. Yeah?" I nod in a daze and walk toward the busy kitchen. The next half hour runs past me like when you drive home with your mind on something. You know you got from point a to point b, but you have no idea if you stopped at stop signs or saw Bigfoot.

I have half-assed conversations as I listen to Cal giggle, cheer on whatever team is playing, get picked on in a friendly way by Tony and Dean and Zee in the other room.

"Hey, Mom?" Cal asks, popping his head in the kitchen.

"Yeah, bud?"

"Can I go outside with the guys? Play football?" Standing behind him is Dean, his fleece jacket and hat already on, leaning against a wall with his hands in his pockets, eyes locked on me. Locked in a way I can see he's trying to read me, decode me, and not just to see what my answer will be to Cal's question.

"I uh..." Because I'm a bitch, I throw it out there. "Do you have your inhaler? Just in case?" I hear Cal huff a 'Moooom' and can almost feel his eye roll, but I keep my eyes on Dean. I need to see his reaction to my dig. Because if I can't figure out what he's doing here, I'll just mess with him.

Nice? No.

Does it feel good after he broke my heart?

I mean, kind of.

His eyes flare, not with anxiety or stress or disappointment or even guilt like I'd expect.

But with challenge, an eyebrow lifting.

"No worries, kid, I've got one in my truck."

*Excuse me, what?*

"I'm sorry, what?" I say the first words to Dean I have in weeks.

"I have an inhaler for Cal in my truck."

"Why?"

"From the mountain. Med tent gave me one. I figured it would be good to have on hand." I stare at him longer. And then because I'm nosy and I can't help it...

"You have a truck?" Last I checked, Deal has a small 4 door that he leased while in town.

"Bought it last week."

"You bought a truck?"

"Yes." He's smiling at me. *Smiling!*

"Why?"

"Winter's coming. Not safe to be driving around in the little car." What the... I want to ask more questions, but Cal tugs Dean's hand.

"Let's go, Dean!"

"Is he cool to play with us?" Dean asks, waiting for my response instead of just going, and dammit, I want to be mad but I just can't. I can't be mad when he's being considerate about making sure I'm cool with whatever my kid's doing.

"Yeah. Sure." He smiles at me and I recognize it as the one he gives me when he likes my answer, and it sends a warm rush down my spine I try hard to ignore as I watch the two of them walk out the front door, Cal near dragging Dean.

When I turn back to the table of my friends and people I've grown to love with my whole being, every eye is on me, most with knowing smiles, like they know something I don't yet.

"What is going *on?*" I say, not just to them, but also the universe at large.

"All in due time, my girl. Let the boys be boys," Luna's Aunt Maggie says from the stove next to Luna as she takes out the turkey. Instead of questioning the always vague woman, I stand to help get dinner out faster, because the sooner we eat, the sooner I can go back into the hiding place of my apartment and overthink this entire interaction.

———

"No, no, Zander Davidson. Don't you dare try to eat a single bite," Luna's mom says, leaning over to smack her son on the hand, the fork clattering onto the plate.

The table is laden with dishes and plates and people, at least three tables lined end to end in the back yard to fit everyone. Cal is sitting somewhere far from me with Rosie and Sara, Autumn and

Steve's two little girls. Maggie is sitting to my left and, to my horror, Dean Fulton is sitting across from me.

Fuck me.

"Ma, I'm starving. You've been starving me all damn day."

"Stuff it, Zander. Let your mom have her fun and then we can all fuckin' eat. You don't stop your bitchin', she'll use it as a learning opportunity and then we'll all suffer," Mr. Davidson says with a grumble.

"Michael! Language!"

"Everyone is an adult here."

"There are literal children here."

"You don't think they've heard a curse word before? Shit, you ever met Steve Sutter?" He's not exactly wrong. Autumn's husband Steve has a mouth on him just about as bad as Luna's dad.

"He's not wrong, Mrs. Davidson," Autumn days. "My girls know not to repeat the bad words."

"And what about poor Cal?"

"He's a boy. Boys need to be taught how to speak like a man." Everyone at the table groans, knowing the battle that's brewing.

"Michael Davidson, I know you did not just say that sexist shit."

"Ah fuck, Ma just said shit... It's bad," Zander says under his breath.

"Zander Michael Davidson! Mouth!" Mrs. Davidson says, looking with wide eyes at her son who points his face to the top of the tent, mouth moving in silent prayer.

I love the Davidson family.

It's always like this with them and something about it is so unbelievably comforting.

"Can we get on with the meal? Give thanks and all that?" Tony says, a safe distance from both his own mother, who would smack him upside his head for getting in someone else's business, and his one day mother-in-law.

"Yes, yes, let's do that! Let me go!" Mags says, clapping her hands, the loose duster jacket she's wearing moving wildly. The table is filled with grumbles and nods, most just looking to get whatever chaos is bound to ensure over with so we can all eat.

"This year we are all so very thankful for so very much. Our Hannah is finally going to get married and get her happily ever after." All eyes go to Hannah, who blushes but still smiles, Hunter pressing a kiss into her hair.

"Moonbeam and her Tony finally are together, after pussy footing around each other for years. Autumn's ready to pop and Steve's finally gettin' his boy." A round of gasps and cheers. Seems the news Autumn's baby is going to be a boy wasn't widespread. A round of congratulations is exchanged before Maggie continues. "We gained a new family member and a new friend in Jordan."

Jordan's eyes tear up, and without my realizing it, mine do too. Jordan went through so much, felt so untethered for so long, it must feel amazing to be sitting here with this big family supporting her. "We have our growing family, good food, and health in our favor!" Everyone cheers and Zander's eyes look around, searching, searching for someone... but who?

"And, of course, I'd be remiss not to mention our newest addition! They finally found a replacement for Mr. Jenkins down at the Springbrook Hill Elementary." I remember my dad reading the paper but just like then, I don't let my mind dwell.

Big mistake.

Huge.

"We're all so happy we'll now have a permanent summer counselor in Dean now that he's decided to settle here and take the job!"

And then my world crashes around me as my eyes lock to Dean, the room getting silent, and he smiles that beautiful, cocky smile.

———

The rest of the dinner goes quickly but also slow as molasses as I move food around my plate, passing dishes back and forth but not eating a bite despite the fact I know it's all delicious.

How can I when my stomach is full of anxious butterflies?

I keep my eyes down, never looking up again after that last smile from Dean. Occasionally someone will ask me something and I give the best answer I can without it even registering in my brain what was asked. I could have agreed to join the circus or to sell Callum in exchange for a pair of socks and I wouldn't even know.

But when the dishes start to get taken away and I'm forced to look up, to stand and offer help, I finally meet his eyes again.

Dean is staring at me in a way telling me he's been looking this way for a while. Maybe the whole time, waiting for me to glimpse up. Waiting to catch me, to not give me the chance to escape the conversation I'm sure we're bound to have.

Before I can open my mouth to help Maggie and Luna, who are already gathering dishes, Cal's voice breaks through my mental fog.

"Mom, you need to go talk to Dean, okay?" Cal orders from beside me. I look over my shoulder, unsure where he came from.

"What?"

"You need to talk to him. You have things to talk about."

"What?"

"You. Need. To. Talk. To. Dean." With each word, Cal's little head bobs, hair sticking up on top of his head, reminding me he needs it cut badly.

"What are you talking about, Cal?" I look from him to Dean, who's smiling and staring at Cal, then back to my son. He sighs and rolls his eyes like I'm a moron.

"Mom, did you think I just wanted to come here to *play football?* Jeeze, you're so easy." He rolls his eyes, and before I even get the chance to chastise him or threaten to ground him for eternity for that attitude, he's running off to go play with Rosie.

"What the..."

"We do." My head turns to Dean.

"What?" A smile from him. The big one, the goofy carefree one I never thought I'd see again. My belly flops.

"We need to talk. He's right. A bit of a jerk, and I'll talk to him about that later, but he's not wrong."

"You'll... talk to him about that later?"

"Yeah. Come on. Let's go." He stands and walks around the table to my side, putting a hand out to me. I take it, the warmth of his big hand around mine familiar and crawling up my wrist, my arm, settling in my soul.

"But I have to help..." I look around at the mess that is the post-Thanksgiving feast, but before I can say any more, Maggie's head pop up.

"You two don't run off and figure this out right now, I'm throwin' you in a cabin at the camp and locking you in there until Monday."

"Aunt Maggie!" Luna shouts from across the table.

"I doubt she'd mind after about twenty minutes," Sadie mumbles under her breath.

"Sadie!" Hannah shouts at her longtime best friend.

"I mean, she's not wrong," Dean says from beside me.

"Dean!" I shout and it's too much—I can't help but laugh, the sound free and open and joined by the rest of my friends and... family.

"Go. Now," Maggies says once we all wind down.

"You sure?"

"Lord, girl, never had to push so hard. Go!" And the Dean takes my hand and leads me back into the house, up the stairs of Luna's home, and into a guest room. I have to wonder how much of this was planned, who knew what, and if I was the only one in the dark.

And also, what the fuck is Dean Fulton going to tell me?

# THIRTY-SIX

-Dean-

"WHY DON'T YOU... SIT," I say, pointing to the bed. There's a bed and nightstand and a small desk with a single chair in the room that's decorated in a mish-mosh of colors, styles, and textures. Luna's doing, undoubtedly. This isn't Tony's style, that much I know. I try not to laugh at the mental image it evokes. Kate does as I ask and I take the chair, turning it so I can face her before sitting. Not too close to make her uncomfortable, but close enough to see the expressions she hides in her eyes.

And then I stare, taking her in.

She's tired.

Overworking, overthinking,

Because of me.

The time I spent helping her out, helping her so she could rest and relax and enjoy life, undone in three weeks.

Shit.

"What's going on, Dean?" Her words are curt, cut and frustrated.

"We have to talk."

"I think we talked enough weeks ago. You said all you needed to say."

"Maybe then."

"What does that mean?"

"It means two weeks ago, I said all I needed to say based on what I *knew* two weeks ago. On what I was able and ready to talk about two weeks ago."

"Stop talking in riddles, Dean. I don't have the energy for it." I sigh. She's not wrong. I just... don't know where to start.

And part of me is scared that when I start, when I open up and explain, when I let my wall down, she won't accept it. That it will all have been for nothing, what we had is fucked beyond repair.

But then I look at the circles under her eyes that had faded just weeks ago, remember her laugh, her fingers playing on my chest at night. I remember Cal's disappointment and his acceptance of my apology. I remember there is essentially an entire town downstairs cheering us on, hoping for the best. The least I can do is try.

"I was scared."

That's all I say. That's the basis of everything either way, right? I know it's not enough, but the pause I make after speaking it out into the world has Kate opening her mouth. "I was scared, and that's not your fault, but I was fucking terrified, Kate. And I still am, but do you know what scares me more? The idea of living my life without you." Another deep breath.

"Losing Jesse took everything from me. I was young, and I should have sought some kind of therapy, but it broke me. It wasn't even that, not really. It wasn't losing Jesse. It was going to his funeral and seeing his parents. They were... Fuck, they were broken. The pain they felt hung in the air and we all breathed it into our souls and it never left mine. I couldn't... I couldn't let that happen to me. So I lived a life that allowed for distance. I still wanted to work with kids, still needed that connection, to make that impact, but... Allowing myself to get close? Never again.

"I spent seven years avoiding that connection. That fear was so deep. And then I came here, and I started working at the camp. It's like the world knew my time was up. Knew it was long enough, I'd held that hand up for too long. For the first time in seven years I agreed to stay longer, to help Zee with the football team. I thought it would be safe. Thought I'd stay for the fall and leave like I always do."

"And then Cal got into a fight," she says, and I smile.

"And then Cal got into a fight. And you walked into the counselor's cabin and winked at him to let him know he wasn't in trouble, and I think a part of me knew then. I needed to get to know you more. Then you cried and opened up and, fuck, Katie, you were so overworked. So stretched thin and so fucking worried for your kid. I think that day you worked some magic and part of my wall started to crumble. Like it knew then time was up and here was a woman and a kid who could fix me.

"And that's not your job. Your job isn't to fix me, never will be. But you showed me I need to fix myself, need to forgive myself to move on. And I fell for Cal. Fell for him before I fell for you even." Her voice hitches. "You've done well with him. He's awesome. Fun and kind and always wanting to help. So fucking loyal, he knew I fucked you over and he stood his ground. I thought that was best, Katie. You gotta believe that. I thought a clean break was best for all of us.

"But I talked to Tony, and he reminded me that life is not guaranteed. Nothing is. And living life to avoid the things that can hurt, that can be sad, any of it... it's not honoring Jesse. It's just suffering, not living." I pause here. I don't know what else to say, but Kate is still looking at me, shell-shocked and confused.

"Did I tell you I wasn't even supposed to come here? I had a camp in Colorado lined up and it fell through. It wasn't going to be open in time. So I was transferred to this location. And... here I am. I'm here, in front of you, begging you to give me the chance to live. To live with you and Cal and enjoy life and, in a way, honor Jesse. Honor what he should have had. To make up for the years I threw away, searching for you. I think that's what I was doing all that time. Searching." She starts to cry, big silent tears running down her already pale face.

"No, Katie, no." I put my arms out to pull her to me, but stop. It's not my place. Not yet, not until she tells me it is. But my arms ache with the emptiness. "Don't cry, baby. Please. I can't... I fucked up. So bad. Knowing I hurt you and broke your trust kills me. But seeing Cal sick like that, when I was so helpless to do anything... All I could think about was the months Jesse was being treated, the helpless look on his parents' faces. The cries his mother made at his funeral. It was like a sick video loop in my mind I couldn't shake. I... I got scared. And then Sadie gave me that position and it was a sign, but I couldn't see it. It was too much, too much for me right then. I wanted to escape, to run."

"You did. Run, that is."

"No, I didn't. I haven't left Springbrook Hills. And I quit the mountain last week. I start at the elementary school next week so... I'm stuck here."

"You quit the mountain?"

"Mostly. They said I could work weekends but... I wanted to... talk to you first. If this... goes bad I'll work weekends there. Nothing else to do." Her face softens and I know in that moment she's mine. The realization that I never truly lost her brings tears, my own tears, a washing of my soul.

When she sees them, she moves, and it shatters the remaining brick of my barrier, never to grow again. Because when she moves, she moves herself into my lap, burying her face in my chest as I hold her tight.

"I'm so sorry, Kate." God, I feel like an idiot. "I didn't mean to hurt you. To hurt Cal."

"You did though."

"I'll spend a lifetime making it up to both of you." She sniffles. "Though, don't kill me, I bought Cal Eagles tickets." Her head moves back.

"What?"

"That was his condition."

"His condition?"

"He accepted my apology and agreed to help me win you back, but he had a bribe request."

She leans back, no longer against me, but my arms around her stop her from moving away. "And you gave in?"

"I really needed him on my side."

"Are you kidding me?" I'm about to answer, but a knock at the door sounds before it opens.

"Have you guys made up yet, because—" Cal walks in, Maggie on his heels. "Oh. Seems you did." Maggie laughs and, to my surprise, so does Kate, the happy sound moving through me, into my gut and my bones, into my blood and filling every part of me that went dark and cold without her warmth. "I want pie. Hannah says I can't have any until you guys are done. Are you done?" I laugh.

"Get your ass downstairs. We'll be down in a minute," I say to him, and he smiles.

"That's a nickel," he says, and when Kate laughs, I know we'll be okay.

"Come on, Cal, let's go convince Hannah to let us have some whipped cream before dessert," Maggie says with a wink, ushering him back down the stairs.

Kate's still laughing when I pull her into me, kissing her, the kiss setting my entire world straight.

Because all I need to keep me grounded is Kate and Cal Hernandez.

And through the kiss, all I can think about is how I can't wait to change their last name. Both of them.

Dear Reader,

Thank you for getting this far! Before you continue, I just want to give a secondary warning—the epilogue contains content about pregnancy. If you're struggling with infertility or loss and not in the head-space to read that, know you are seen and that Kate, Dean, and Cal get their HEA.

Love always,
Morgan

# EPILOGUE

-Kate-

WHEN DEAN WALKS IN, I'm putting the last of the bags at the front door of the apartment we moved into three months ago. He just got back from dropping Cal off at Cody's where he's staying for two whole, glorious nights. It's Memorial Day weekend and the joint Bachelor/Bachelorette party for Hannah and Hunter.

"Babe, how much shit do you need for two days?" Dean asks, staring at the pile.

"It's not that much," I say, rolling my eyes and eyeing the large purse I way overfilled sitting on the couch. I haven't added it to the pile yet.

Okay, maybe it is *that* much.

"Okay, well, it's my *and* your stuff."

"I need a pair of board shorts and two outfits."

"What? No. We're all going out! You need to bring clothes. Daytime *and* nighttime clothes."

"Katie, I don't need different clothes for day and night."

"Yes, you do." *God. Men.*

"I'm gonna wear board shorts all day and then I'll throw on a tee and shorts to go to the bar. It's a bachelor party, not a weekend in Vegas."

"A weekend in Vegas sounds fun." He eyes me, head to toe like he thinks I'm insane before he shakes his head.

"Maybe a while from now. We'll go with Jordan and Tanner. She can show us around."

"Ooh, that'd be fun!"

"But tellin' you now, babe, I don't check luggage. You bring one bag to Vegas if we go." His eyes drift to the pile of bags. "What's even in those?"

"I need options."

"Bikinis don't take up much space." I roll my eyes at him.

"I can't just wear bikinis all weekend, Dean."

"Says who."

"Uh, says everyone?" He comes to me, putting his hands on my hips as he takes another step with me until the back of my legs hit the back of the couch. I wrap my arms around his neck.

"You overpacked, babe." His lips brush against mine, and the way his body is pressed to me, I almost forget our conversation.

"You afraid you can't carry it down the stairs?" His lips twitch up, something I feel rather than see.

"Babe, I think I've more than proved I can lift things. Remember last night in the shower?" A chill runs down my spine remembering how he lifted me in the shower, pressed me against the wall, and continued to ram into me until I bit his neck so hard, it left a mark. My eye glaze over the spot, noting he didn't even bother to wear a shirt that covered it.

"I have no idea what you're talking about," I say, returning the smile.

"No?" I shake my head. "I guess I'll have to remind you, huh?" I just smile as I push my hips into his, where he's already growing. The hands on my hips grab me, lifting until my ass is sitting on the back of the couch, the perfect height for his now hard cock to press into the soft center of my leggings. He steps forward until there's no room between us and those hands pull me forward harshly, a clear indicator fun, goofy time is over.

When he speaks again, I'm already panting against his lips that haven't even kissed mine yet. "We're all alone here, Katie. Expect you to be as loud as you can, yeah?" A chill down my spine. "Think I'm gonna start on this couch—been thinking about it since that first night, you ridin' my leg until you came." Another chill, my mouth drops open as my center clenches, eyes going hooded. "Fuck yeah, my girl likes that idea." And then finally, his lips are on mine, devouring, tasting, nipping. My body is on fire, hands scrambling to find the bottom of his shirt. We break only for a moment while I remove him of the obstacle, hands splaying across naked skin, running up and down.

His hands begin to creep under the front of my shirt, mouths still connected as he undoes the clip of my bra. My over-sensitized breasts tingle at the sensation of being released, drawing a deep moan from me. "Yeah, Katie, you tell me what feels good," he says, a growl in my ear, before moving to take my shirt off so both of us are bare on top. His chest hair grazes my nipples and I moan again before his hands are there, lifting their weight with each hand. His thumbs graze the sensitive peaks, and my back arches, neck tipping back as another deep, satisfied moan falls from me.

Then Dean's lips are gone, moving down to my neck, until his body disappears from mine as his lips circle my nipple, pulling deep. I *scream* at the sensation running through me, like a cord is connected from my nipple to my clit.

"Jesus, Katie." And then hands are pulling me down from my perch until my feet are back on solid ground, those hands going down my thighs and pulling my leggings down with them as the thumbs hook in the waistband, taking my tiny thong with it.

And then I'm naked, legs spread, leaning against our couch for support as Dean kneels before me, eyes on my pussy. "So fucking pretty, Katie." That name always takes on a different meaning when we're like this, carnal and hot.

His thumbs go to either side of me, pulling at the skin until my clit is exposed to the air. "Dripping," he says, eyes fixed and nearly glazed as he stares at what he's revealed. A single finger moves to circle my already swollen clit, once, twice, three times before moving down to my entrance.

Then it goes in, my head snapping back as he instantly crooks a finger, rubbing against my G-spot. This *man*. He knows my body like an expert, knows the places to touch, the speed to stroke, and the way to move to have me moaning his name. In no time at all, I'm already nearing the edge, just one finger inside of me.

Long ago, I'd have been embarrassed. But this is what he likes, what he craves. Dean lives to make me crazy. And he does just that when he removes his hand and puts both to my hips, moving me. "Turn," he says. Once I do, he instructs me again. "Bend over." Then his warm hand is pressing the small of my back until I'm at a 90-degree angle over the back of the couch. I can't see anything anymore and can't feel his body on mine. The anticipation is killing me. Right when I'm about to beg him to fuck me, to slide in and make me come, I feel him moving up and down my slit, tentative, teasing.

But it's not his cock.

It's his tongue, the very tip dipping into my entrance and sliding down to my clit as I arch my back more to give him better access.

"Oh my god, Dean."

"This fucking pussy is so sweet. Could do this all day, baby, eat this cunt." And then his hands are on either side of me, using his thumbs to hold me open, his tongue delving deep and eating me like his life depends on it.

"Fuck, Dean, fuck." I'm no longer able to form coherent sentences or even words as I moan and grind on to his face. I don't know if I've ever been this wet, a mix of my own wetness and his spit sliding down my leg as I creep closer to the edge, so fucking close, I just need...

And then, as Dean loves to do, he's gone.

My head pops up, looking over my shoulder to yell, but fuck, this man. He's standing there, surveying what is his, body on display for my eyes alone as he strokes his cock in his hands, a drop of pre-cum shining from the tip.

If I could spend all day watching this, this alone, I would die a really fucking happy woman.

And he's all mine.

"Dean," I whine. I don't care if I sound pathetic.

"What do you want, Katie?" This game. I love it; I hate it. The 'love it' aspect comes in the form of my pussy clenching, a movement his ever attentive eyes don't miss.

"I want you."

"You have me."

"I want your cock."

"It's all yours, baby. Only yours."

"I want you to fuck me, Dean."

"How?" *This fucking man.* I know what he's looking for. Happy go-lucky, playful Dean still exists in the bedroom, it's just in a different way. A way that looks like challenges and games. "How do you want me to fuck you, Katie?" He takes a step closer to me, relief washing over me. But not close enough. "Do you want me here?" A single finger, thick, but not thick enough, slips into my drenched pussy. Out it goes, then it strokes back in with a second. I moan, rearing back. "Uh, uh, stay still, baby." I moan again, this time aggravated. "Or do you want me here?" His wet finger presses into my ass, slowly, torturously. This isn't the first time his finger or his cock has been there, but it's not often. But every time he gets the idea in his head to...

My body bucks, rearing back as his other hand comes around me to gently touch my clit. It's so swollen, dying for release. "Where do you want me to fuck you?" *Oh god, oh god!* The finger slides out, and a second drenched finger slides in alongside, moving to stretch me.

"My ass!" I shout, the words not passing my brain before they leave my mouth.

"Dirty girl," he says with a growl, fingers going deep. "Here's how this is going to work." His chest is over my back, my hands braced on the couch as he continues to pump his fingers in, stretching me. "I'm gonna get my cock nice and wet in this dripping fucking cunt of yours, and you will not *come, Katie.*" His words strike me hard.

"Dean, no—"

"You're not gonna come, Kate. And then once you're so fucking close you want to cry, I'm gonna slip into your ass and then you can come, but not until I'm all the way inside you. Then I'm going to pump your ass full of my come, yeah?" Why is this so fucking sexy? I swear there's a switch that flips as soon as his cock gets hard where he becomes some hard assed sex fiend and I'm a maiden he needs to terrorize. "Answer me."

And I fucking *love* it.

"Yes, Dean, god, yes. Just fuck me already."

"So impatient," he says, a smile in his voice as his hand not in my ass guides his cock to where I need him most—for now. He slides in with not an ounce of resistance and we both groan aloud, the feeling so perfect, so right. "Fuck Katie, this pussy is so damn perfect." I can't do much more than moan as he slowly pumps into me, filling me, grazing every over sensitized nerve ending. I moan loud when he bottoms out, ramming right into my G-spot and pushing me closer to coming.

"Fuck, Dean!"

"Don't you dare fucking come," he says, adding a third finger to my ass now, stretching me, preparing me for him. His back is pressed to mine, his mouth and heavy breathing against my ear as my sensitive breasts press into the rough fabric of the couch cushions.

"God, Dean, I—"

And then he's out of me. Body off me, leaving me cold as I look over my shoulder.

"Don't fucking move, Katie," he orders, a hard smack to my ass, the feeling going straight to my clit so swollen with need, it has an aching pulse.

He walks a few feet behind me, footsteps heard, but I dare not move, dare not do anything that could stop him from helping me finish.

And then he's back, cool liquid dripping onto my ass, making me moan.

"You ready, Katie?" he asks, voice in my ear again.

"Yes, Dean."

"Tell me what you want." Any other time, I'd relent, be shy, mince words. But right now, the state my mind is in...

"Fill my ass, Dean," I say, a plea and a moan all at once.

"That's my fucking girl."

And all things considered, all the roughness and harsh words, he should slam into me, fill me, tear me in half. But not Dean. Not my Dean.

Instead, he notches the head of his thick cock in my ass and slowly presses in, retreating a millimeter, pushing in, slowly letting me get used to his size until he's past the point of resistance and all the way in, hips to my ass, completely filling me. I breathe out, now exquisitely full, pulsing, needing. Dean's voice in my ear is strained, like it's taking everything in him not to go chaotic.

"Such a good girl, taking me. So fucking good, Katie," he says, the words a coo in my ear. "You good?"

"Yeah, honey," I say, and it's a single spot of sweetness and cottony soft in between what's happened and what's coming next.

"You ready?" I push my ass back, arching my back and taking him just a millimeter deeper. We both groan at the sensation. "You're ready," he says, moving so his back is no longer against mine, hands to my hips. I look over my shoulder to see his eyes locked on where his cock sits in my ass and I'm done. I need this.

"Dean, fuck me," I beg.

"Anything for you, Katie," he says and pulls out before slamming in. "Fuuucccck, this fuckin' ass," I moan, a sound coming from deep in my chest that's more animalistic than human, and with each deep thrust, the sound gets deeper until it's just a grunt into the pillows. The hands I was using to hold me in place have gone limp as pleasure over takes my body, a pleasure so different from normal sex.

"God, fuck, Katie, wish you could see this. You take my cock so fucking well, such a good girl. You like this?" A grunt from me. "You like when my cock is buried in your ass?" Another grunt and he just laughs.

"You need more, don't you, baby? You ready to explode around me?" he asks, and it's his teasing voice, but underneath that is strain, like he's holding back, ready to go too. I just nod into the pillows, hoping he won't require words because I have none.

When one hand slips from my hip down, down to my entrance, I know he got the hint, his finger grabbing my wet that's dripping down my leg and dragging it to my needy clit. I jolt as soon as he touches me, the feeling almost too much, and he chuckles. A strained chuckle, but one all the same.

"Is this what you need, Katie?" he asks, chest to my back once again, bucking into me repeatedly, the only thing preventing me from bruised hips in the morning being his arm between me and the couch, gently playing with my clit, teasing.

When I buck back, fucking him as he fucks me, I can tell play-time is over. His finger goes from gently, teasingly, circling my clit to three fingers, rubbing the needy spot vigorously.

It takes all of two circles before my vision goes blank, my heart skipping a beat, an inhuman scream leaving my chest.

"Fuck yeah, Katie, come for me. God, you're so fucking beautiful when you come, taking my cock and coming like this." His own words are coming as a crazed train of thought, lost in our moment as he pounds into me one, twice, three more times before he growls his own release, pumping into my ass. He collapses on top of me, arms braced into the pillows to keep his weight from me.

Long moments pass before either of us speaks as we catch our breath.

"That was so much better than I ever imagined," he says, and all I can do is laugh.

————

The sun is pounding as the girls and I sit on the beach, facing the water, surrounded by other beach visitors on this perfectly warm Memorial Day weekend.

You never know what you'll get in Jersey this time of year, but a hot weekend is welcomed. Though you won't catch me dead in that ocean, which won't warm up for months still.

"Kate, I have to say, your boobs... Holy shit, they look amazing today," Sadie says, tipping her eyes to my bikini top. I groan.

"Yeah, well, they're killing me." I cup one, wincing.

"They hurt?"

"Yeah, I think my period's coming," I say, taking a sip of the lemony ice water I've been living off of for a week now.

"Does that normally happen to you?" Autumn asks from a chair under the umbrella. We're all in black bathing suits except for Hannah, who is wearing a bright bridal white version.

"Uh, I mean, not really. But sometimes?" I say, but the truth is, now that I think of it... it doesn't. Autumn's eyes narrow.

"I only ask because that only happens to me when..." The blood drains from my face. "*No fucking way.*" No, no no no!

"What?" Hannahs asks, sitting up, eyes wide with alarm, ever the mother hen, even at her own party.

"It can't be..." I say, thinking back. When... when was my last period? *When!* Come on brain, think, think, think...

"What is going on?" Sadie says, both confused and amused.

"Is what I think is happening, happening?" Luna says, sounding concerned as she wears her giant floppy hat to block the sun from her fair skin. A small smile can still be seen from under it, though. Reaching for my phone, I start scrolling to find the app I use to track and...

"Oh my fucking god," I say, the words barely coming out, but it's enough to clue them in.

"*Oh my fucking GOD!*" Autumn screams and then stands.

"Yup, it's happening," Luna says, setting her drink aside and sitting up.

"Okay, you've lost me," Sadie says, taking a slug of her drink as if she's given up on the game and is just going to wait.

"She's pregnant," Jordan says, a smile on her face, looking from her half sister to me. "Aut's tits hurt every day for three months when she was pregnant with Colin."

"OH MY GOD!" Sadie says with a shriek, standing and jumping up and down. "OH MY GOD!" Now people around us are turning heads, mumbling, and trying to figure out what's happening.

"Sadie, calm down. You're freaking the girl out," Luna says.

"When!?" Autumn says, and my phone tumbles onto the beach blanket as I stare at the ocean.

"*Fucking antibiotics,*" I say under my breath, remembering the killer sinus infection I had six weeks ago. I should know better—it's how I got pregnant with Cal.

"You didn't know, did you?" Hannah asks, seeing the panic on my face.

"I need a test," I say, still in a daze. "I drank last night, I—"

"You had one drink. You said you didn't feel well," Jordan reminds me. I didn't. I've been off for a week or so now, and I thought I needed a probiotic after the antibiotics. I thought... oh my god. *Oh, my god.*

Hannah's already packing up the chairs, stuffing towels into beach bags. "Oh, Hannah, we don't have to... It's your—"

"Shut up. We're going to CVS right now," she says, mother hen mode activated.

"I can't believe this!" Autumn says in an excited squeal and shit.

Neither can I.

———

An hour later we're all huddled into the thankfully large bathroom, Jordan, Luna and Sadie sitting on the lip of the tub and Autumn and Hannah carefully watching the four—yes, four—tests of various brands. I'm sitting on the toilet, my head in my hands.

It's a good thing I love all these women, since they all just watched me take a piss into a plastic cup.

"It's going to be fine, Kate," Sadie says, a hand rubbing my back.

"What if it's positive?" I say, my voice small. All eyes go to me.

"Would that be bad?" Autumn asks. It's not judgmental, just wondering.

"I... I don't know."

"Cal would make an *amazing* big brother, Kate."

"But..."

"But Dean," Sadie says. Working with her so often means she knows a lot about Dean's past, his history, and most importantly, the reason we broke up all those months ago.

"Dean loves kids," Hannah says, clearly confused.

"Kids scare the shit out of Dean," Sadie informs her. Or reminds her, because chances are, Hannah knows the story as well.

"But he's great with Cal," Jordan says.

"And the inhaler thing was like, years ago," Luna says. I glare at Sadie, who has the world's biggest mouth. She just stares at her nails.

"Look. I get it," Autumn starts. "Steve was an only child, and he lost his dad when he was young. When I was pregnant with Sara, I panicked. But babe, something happens when it all clicks. They just... get it. It's going to be fine."

"Plus, we don't even know if she's—" Hannah starts, but stops. All eyes go to Autumn, whose eyes are locked on one of the tests before she meets my eyes.

"Congrats, babe. Cal's getting a sibling." And with that, I give into the hormones I've been denying were there for weeks and hysterically cry in a bathroom with all of my best friends.

————

Hours later, I'm breathing deep, sitting in the hotel room and waiting for Dean to come back. After my cry fest, it only took a few minutes to get over myself and realize how fucking awesome this was. I love Cal. Love being his mom. Another kid to love up on? Perfection. Bonus if he or she looks like Dean.

And... if Dean isn't up for it, it's kind of a blessing in disguise, right? I want more kids, period. We haven't had the talk yet, my being too nervous to bring it up, but I always got the sense he'd be open to it. But if it turns out he doesn't want this kid, that he's not looking for... this... no reason to stay together, right?

Right.

It's no big deal.

I almost have myself convinced of this when the door clicks and opens, Dean walking in, hair that needs a cut tousled and a tank top over board shorts.

He wasn't wrong. He isn't wearing more than shorts and his bathing suit here.

"Hey, you," he says, a smile on his face as he drops a backpack to the floor before walking to me. When he's between my legs on the couch, his hand reaches for the back of my head, tipping it up and pressing a soft kiss to my lips. When he pulls back, his huge, goofy smile that seems goofier as of late is directed straight at me.

I don't want to lose this.

I love this man.

"I love you," I say, my voice cracking with the words. His brows furrow, confused.

"What?"

"I love you."

"Love you too, Katie. Everything okay?" I sigh, looking to the side and trying to remember my perfectly crafted speech. Hannah even practiced it with me while we opened up presents and the girls drank champagne in her suite.

"Katie, what's wrong?" His face is washed in worry, and he kneels before me, holding my hands.

"I... I just love you. And I... have something to talk to you about."

"Okay..."

"It's important. Really important."

"Katie..."

"And I want you to know before I say anything, that whatever you say, I accept. I don't... expect anything from you." A mix of frustration and that worry are on his face now.

"Kate, you're freaking me out." I know I am. I'm freaking myself out too, to be fair,

"I... Do you remember when I had that sinus infection?"

"Yeah, you were miserable for a week."

"Yeah. So the thing is... Okay..." And then I spill. "I'm an idiot, right? And like, I should know these things by now; I should remember. And really, it's not my fault, not completely, because I'm on an IUD now and like, that's pretty effective, right? I didn't think... Anyway, I should know. I should get, like, some kind of mental warning pop up when I pick up the pills! But I didn't. And I took them, and it was, like, 4 weeks ago and now..."—my hands are playing with the edge of Dean's collar, trying to stop my mind from going to far down a rabbit hole—"I'm pregnant," I say, the words a shock even though I've said them more times this afternoon than ever before. I suck it up and force my eyes to meet Dean's. He's staring at me intently, but no emotions are there.

"Oh. That." He looks at me seriously, and he must see the confusion on my face. "I knew about that two weeks ago when you missed your period."

I don't breathe.

"I'm sorry, what?"

"Babe, I plan my entire life around when I can fuck you. You don't let me fuck you when you're on your period."

"Okay?"

"Plus, your tits have been fucking glorious, but you're a wimp when I look at them sideways."

"I'm sorry. Are you telling me you knew I was pregnant?"

"Yup."

"And you... didn't tell me?"

"I don't know; you're Katie. I thought you might have some kind of master plan. I didn't want to mess it up."

"You... didn't want to mess it up."

"You didn't know?"

"No! I just figured it out! I spent all day panicking and taking tests in Hannah's bathroom!"

"Oh, babe," he says, arms going around me with a laugh in his voice. "I swear I thought you knew."

"I didn't!" And then I start to cry, tears falling onto his grey shirt, turning the fabric a dark grey. A few minutes later when the tears subside, Dean still holding me in his arms as he's done every time I have what he calls a 'Katie Moment,' he speaks.

"How do you feel about it?" My body stiffens. Here's the moment of truth. I think because he knew, and he didn't instantly run off, that's probably a good sign, right?

"I feel... good? A little scared. Happy, I think," I say into his shirt.

"Good, Katie." That's it.

"How do... I mean, what are you thinking?" No response. My stomach drops. That's *not* good, right? "Dean?"

"Look at me." It's a command. I do, tipping my head up. "I will love Cal until the day I die, love him like he's my own kid. He's the best thing that ever happened to me. You're the second best."

Some people would be crushed by that, knowing they don't come first in the eyes of their man. But for me? I couldn't ask for anything more. I hiccup, trying to choke back a new cry. "No, Katie, no. None of that. This?" His hand goes to my belly that's still flat for now, the warmth seeping through my shirt. "This is going to be the most amazing thing that's ever happened to me. Ever. To us. To me and you and Cal. We're just adding to the fun, Katie. That's it." And with that, I lose it, crying hysterical pregnant woman tears into Dean's shirt.

———

"Hey, buddy. Can you sit with us for a bit?" I say, tapping the cushion next to us. It's the following Monday and Dean and I both took the day off to go to the obstetrician's office. He held my hand the entire time as the doctor brought us into the room with the ultrasound, showed me the tiny beating heart. I promptly cried, just like I did when I was pregnant with Cal, but this time I wasn't alone. This time, Dean leaned over, kissed my forehead, and looked at me with tears in his own eyes.

"You're amazing," he'd said.

"What's up?" Cal says, looking from where I sit to Dean, who is in the love seat. "Are you guys getting married?"

*Oh my god,* as if this couldn't get any more embarrassing than telling my 8-year-old that once again I'm pregnant out of wedlock.

Apparently, it's a specialty of mine.

"Oh, god, no Cal." He sits next to me and Dean looks at me with humor on his face.

"That adamant, huh, babe?"

"Shit, I didn't... I didn't mean it like that. I—"

"Not yet, Cal," Dean says and they smile to each other, some unspoken conversation and a warm rush runs through me. Another topic we haven't covered. Technically, we've not even been together a year yet.

"What's up then? Because Joey said when his mom married that guy, they had a big sit down like this and Mom looks like she's going to puke,"

"I do not."

"You kind of do, babe," Dean says and there's a mix of teasing in there. I never got morning sickness, not really with Cal, but each day I've been getting increasingly more and more nauseous.

"I'm fine."

"You sure?"

"Jesus, Dean, can we get this over with?"

"Go on," he smiles with a wave of his hand, and I try not to flip him off.

"So. You know I love you, right Cal?" He nods. "And you know I freaking love being your mom. The coolest job ever." Another nod. "And you know... you know Dean's here.. for us. To stay. We're... a family." The words come harder, both a mix of anxiety and emotion.

"We're a family, Cal," Dean says, no hesitation, all assurance.

"Yeah, I know."

"So, sometimes, when people love each other—"

"Ew, Mom, I don't need that talk."

"What?"

"I don't need that talk."

"I'm sorry, what?"

"Dean and I already had that talk. The boys and girls talk?" My mouth drops open as I stare at Dean.

"I'm sorry, *what?!*"

"Kids on the team were talking about things. He had questions."

"He's *eight!*"

"Rather him get the correct information from me than some shit heads on the team." I hate that he's right.

"We should have talked about it!"

"He needs to know he can come to me about shit without me running to his mom to rat on him." *Again,* right. Jesus Christ. My eyes move to Cal who's watching us like a volleyball tournament, a smile on his face.

"Fine." It's a huff and Dean laughs. "When two people are in love, sometimes they decide—" Dean scoffs and I flip him off. Can't he let me have this small bit of artistic freedom? "To grow their family. Sometimes this means adding another baby to the mix."

"What your mom is saying, kid, is she's pregnant, and in a few months, you'll have a baby brother or sister." We both stare at him as he takes in our words. Anxiety fills me.

"Cal, you need to know I'll always love you. That won't change. Moms have an infinite capacity to love, I promise. This won't change anything between us, between you and Dean. It's just going to be adding a bit more fun to our lives." More silence.

And then he talks.

"Oh. That." My eyes go wide and Dean laughs out loud.

"I'm sorry, *what?!*"

"I knew that."

"What?!"

"Dean said when a girl doesn't have her period, that's how you know she's probably pregnant." Silent, confused, blinking. "And you didn't have you period. So I figured..." Dean is now in full on hysterical laughing as I stare at my eight-and-a-half-year-old son, who has always been an old soul and way too fucking smart for his own good.

"How do you know about my period?"

"You buy Oreos and Phish Food. I always get some. We didn't have any in, like, a month."

"Are you telling me you rely on my period to get your junk food fix?"

"Well, it's not the only time, but... yeah."

"Ah fuck, you're going to make a great man one day, kid," Dean says, wiping tears from his face.

"But I'm happy for you, Mom. You're happy, then I'm happy," he says with a smile.

And all I can think is that Dean is right—he is going to be a great man one day.

And it's all thanks to Dean.

Eight months later, Jesse Daniella Fulton is born, ten fingers, ten toes, and perfect in every way.

# ABOUT THE AUTHOR

Morgan is a born and raised Jersey girl, living there with her two boys, toddler daughter, and mechanic husband. She's addicted to iced espresso, barbecue chips, and Starburst jellybeans. She usually has headphones on, listening to some spicy audiobook or Taylor Swift. There is rarely an in between.

Writing has been her calling for as long as she can remember. There's a framed 'page one' of a book she wrote at seven hanging in her childhood home to prove the point. Her entire life she's crafted stories in her mind, begging to be released but it wasn't until recently she finally gave them the reigns.

I'm so grateful you've agreed to take this journey with me.

Stay up to date via TikTok and Instagram

Stay up to date with future stories, get sneak peeks and bonus chapters by joining the Reader Group on Facebook!

# NEW TO SPRINGBROOK HILLS?

If you're looking for spicy small town romance, Morgan Elizabeth has you covered! Check out these releases:

Get book one, The Distraction, on Kindle Unlimited here!

### *The last thing he needs is a distraction.*

Hunter Hutchin's success is due to one thing, and one thing only: his unerring focus on Beaten Path, the outdoor recreation company he built from the ground up after his first business was an utter failure.

When his dad gets sick, Hunter is forced to go back to his hometown and prove once and for all that his father's belief in him wasn't for nothing. With illness looming, distractions are unacceptable.

Staying with his sister, he meets Hannah, the sexy nanny who has had his head in a frenzy since they met.

When Hunter's dad gets sick, he's forced to leave the city and move back into the small town he grew up in at his sister's house. Ever since he watched Hannah dance into his life, he's finding himself drifting from his goals and purpose - or is he drifting closer to them?

**_She refuses to make the same mistakes as her mother._**

Hannah Keller grew up watching what happens when a family falls apart and lived through those consequences. When it's time, she won't make the same mistake by settling for anyone.

But when the uncle of the kids she nannies comes to stay for the summer, she can't help but find herself drawn to the handsome, standoffish man who is definitely not for her.

Can she get through the summer while protecting her heart? Or will he breakthrough and leave her broken?

Out now in the Kindle Store and on Kindle Unlimited

*He was her first love.*

Luna Davidson has been in love with Tony since she was ten years old. As her older brother's best friend, he was always off-limits, but that doesn't mean she didn't try. But years after he turned her down, she's found herself needing his help, whether she wants it or not.

***She's his best friend's little sister.***

When he learns that Luna has had someone stalking her for months, he's furious that she didn't tell anyone. As a detective on the Springbrook Hills PD, it's his job to serve and protect. But can he use this as an excuse to find out what really happened all those years ago?

Can Luna overcome her own insecurities to see what's right in front of her? Can Tony figure out who is stalking her before it goes too far?

Out now in the Kindle Store and on Kindle Unlimited

**She was always the fill-in.**

Jordan Daniels always knew she had a brother and sister her mom left behind. Heck, her mom never let her forget she didn't live up to their standards. But when she disappears from the limelight after her country star boyfriend proposes, the only place she knows to go to is to the town her mother fled and the family who doesn't know she exists.

**He won't fall for another wild child.**

Tanner Coleman was left in the dust once before when his high school sweetheart ran off to follow a rockstar around the world. He loves his roots, runs the family business, and will never leave Springbrook Hills. But when Jordan, with her lifetime spent traveling the world and mysterious history comes to work for him, he can't help but feel drawn to her.

Can Jordan open up to him about her past and stay in one place? Can Tanner trust his heart with her, or will she just hurt him like his ex?

# ALSO BY MORGAN ELIZABETH

**The Springbrook Hills Series**

The Distraction

The Protector

The Substitution

The Connection

The Playlist

**Holiday Standalone, interconnected with SBH:**

Tis the Season for Revenge

**The Ocean View Series**

The Ex Files

Walking Red Flag

Bittersweet

**The Mastermind Duet**

Ivory Tower

Diamond Fortress

# WANT THE CHANCE TO WIN KINDLE STICKERS AND SIGNED COPIES?

Leave an honest review on Amazon or Goodreads and send the link to reviewteam@authormorganelizabeth.com and you'll be entered to win a signed copy of one of Morgan Elizabeth's books and a pack of bookish stickers!

Each email is an entry (you can send one email with your Goodreads review and another with your Kindle review for two entries per book) and two winners will be chosen at the beginning of each month!

Milton Keynes UK
Ingram Content Group UK Ltd.
UKHW021317121023
430469UK00022B/627

9 781088 102794